BLIND DECEPTION

KINGS OF RETRIBUTION MC MONTANA

SANDY ALVAREZ

CRYSTAL DANIELS

TWO PENS-

CRYSTAL *Daniels*

Sandy ALVAREZ

-ONE STORY

PROLOGUE
LELANI

The flower garden at my uncle's estate is my favorite place to be alone. I can spend hours a day sitting out here on the bench with the sun shining down on my face while listening to one of my favorite audiobooks. As a child, I loved to read. I remember the day my mom introduced me to Harry Potter. I was eight years old. For the past three years, though, my taste in literature has changed. I joined an online book club when I was nineteen, not knowing it was a romance book club. The recommended title didn't sound like what I would consider romance. Imagine my surprise when by chapter five Trevor had his cock in his hand, stroking it while telling Lexi how much he'd like to see her lips wrapped around it. I blushed with embarrassment at what I was hearing and pressed pause on the audio.

A few minutes later, curiosity got the best of me. Needless to say, I stayed up all night listening to the book. When it was over, I quickly bought the next book in the series.

That's when my love for romance novels started. BDSM,

enemies to lovers, cowboys, second chance, small-town romance, you name it, I listened.

My current audiobook is a historical highlander novel and is the current topic of discussion in my book club tonight.

With my personal life being nonexistent, all I have are fictional stories filled with passion and romance. Books keep me company. The characters in the stories are like old friends, and in a way, they give me hope that one day I too will experience a love like the words spoken in my ear every day. They give me a yearning to one day be free of this prison I call home.

Sighing, I close my eyes and concentrate on the words coming through my headphones. Just as I'm coming up on the last chapter, someone lightly taps my right shoulder. Removing my headphones, I tilt my head back.

"Hey, Lelani," Carla grabs my attention. "Sorry to interrupt. Your uncle wishes to see you." I adore Carla. For years she has worked for my uncle. Besides cooking and cleaning, Carla helps take care of my needs. She has since I was fourteen and came to live with my uncle. Carla is my only friend.

I smile. "No problem. Is he in his office?" I stand.

"Yes. He is waiting for you. Would you like me to take you?"

"I'll be okay. Thank you, Carla."

"Would you like me to place your Kindle in your room?"

"Yes, please. Thank you." I hold the Kindle out in front of me for her to take.

After making my way from the garden to the house, I slip through the back door, where the kitchen is, then down the hall to my uncle's office, where I knock on the closed door and wait for him to answer.

"Come in."

I slowly push open the door and step into his office. The strong scent of cologne, not belonging to my uncle, is the first thing to alert me to another presence in the room.

Nervousness settles in my belly. Usually, the only time my uncle summons me is to inform me when he is leaving town. Other than that, he treats me as an afterthought. "You wanted to see me?"

"Yes. I'd like you to meet Cillian De Burca."

Suddenly all the oxygen is sucked out of the room. I've heard stories of that name. My mother was a Fitzpatrick and was meant to marry a De Burca until she chose to go against her family's wishes and married my father instead. The Mancinis and De Burcas spent years at war because of the fallen union between my mother and De Burca. I heard whispers here and there a few years back that the De Burca family had dropped off the face of the earth and the De Burca empire had fallen when Ronan De Burca crossed the wrong people.

I hear someone to my right move. Knowing rudeness is not tolerated in my uncle's presence, I hold out my hand. "Hello," I greet our guest, but I receive no reply in return. I drop my hand.

"You are lucky she is beautiful, Mancini. For that, I will look past her unfortunate defect."

A shocked gasp leaves my mouth at Cillian's harsh words. "I am not defective, Mr. De Burca." I sneer, disgusted with his insolence.

I quickly learn my action is a grave error on my part and find myself being backhanded across my face. The blow is a force so hard, I stumble backward, tripping over the table behind me, and fall to the floor. I cry out from the pain and bring my hand to my face, feeling wetness on my skin where Cillian's ring sliced open the flesh across my cheek.

"I'll have my work cut out for me with this one," Cillian spits. "Her lack of respect disgusts me."

Shocked and confused with what just happened, I climb to my feet and wait for my uncle to do or say something, only he doesn't

SANDY ALVAREZ & CRYSTAL DANIELS

step to my defense. No one has ever laid a hand on me before. I don't know how to react.

Finally, my uncle speaks. "I'm sure Lelani's attitude is something you can groom in time."

"Indeed," Cillian replies and continues, "our engagement will be short. I have some business to attend out of the States before the wedding."

"Of course. I'll make sure the details are taken care of by the time you return."

Engagement?

Wedding?

I snap out of my confusion the moment a fingertip brushes across my swelling cheek. "I'm going to enjoy owning you." Cillian's declaration sends a chill down my spine.

"What are you talking about?" I turn, searching for my uncle. "Uncle Arturo, what is he talking about? What's happening here?"

"You will marry Cillian. You are going to fulfill your duty to this family, Lelani. It is time to make right the wrongs of the past. Cillian marrying you is part of our agreement."

"What about me? I've agreed to nothing!" I raise my voice in rebellion to being married to a man I don't know—don't love.

"Know your place, Lelani," he warns. "It's time you contribute to this family for once in your existence. You will marry Cillian. Our two families will become one. This is how alliances form. You know this."

"My parents would not want this for me!" I cry.

"Your parents are dead!" Uncle Arturo slams his fist down on his desk, causing me to flinch. "I'm the head of this family, Lelani, and you will do as I say."

My heart hammers against my ribcage, and my soul fills with despair at the cold realization that my life is in the hands of Cillian De Burca, a man whom I have only just met but already fear.

"Tony," my uncle calls one of his men. "Take Lelani to her room while Mr. De Burca and I finalize our futures."

"Let's go." Tony places his meaty palm around my upper arm and wordlessly escorts me out of the office. Once back in my room, I crumple to the bed and release the tears I held at bay.

All my hopes and dreams shattered. My life was stolen from me in the blink of an eye. I cry until my eyes burn from the tears falling down my cheeks. I drift to sleep out of mental exhaustion, knowing my life is nothing more than a bargaining chip for power and status.

1

LELANI

A chill surges down my spine at the sound of the floorboards creaking. I hold my breath in anticipation of a looming presence just outside my bedroom door. "You ready?" Derrick asks.

Taking a deep breath, I nod at my brother's question. "I'm ready."

"Come on. We don't have much time." I get a whiff of cigarette smoke as Derrick snatches the suitcase clutched in my hands.

"Where's Tony?" I ask before silently counting the steps I know it takes to get from my room to the staircase's first step. Tony is one of my uncle's men and is usually the person assigned to babysit me.

"He's out by the pool house getting his dick sucked by Carmen."

I don't balk at the unsavory information spewing from Derrick's mouth.

"We don't have much time. I want to be back before morning. My ass is grass if anyone finds out I'm helping you."

The alarm panel beeps when Derrick enters the code, and a rush of warm Las Vegas air hits my face as the door opens. My heart begins wildly beating as I walk behind my brother toward his car. He grabs hold of my bicep at the exact moment I hear the car door open. Without saying a word, I climb into the passenger seat. My palms start sweating when the engine turns over, and the car lurches forward. I keep waiting for someone to stop us or for my brother to change his mind. He wasn't lying when he mentioned the trouble he would have if the family caught him helping me escape.

A couple of months ago, I asked my brother to help me leave Las Vegas, and escape a life my uncle was choosing for me. One I don't want. My uncle dictates every aspect of my life. His decision to marry me off without my consent ultimately led me to my current situation.

I've been sheltered my whole life and don't know much about the world's ways, but I'm willing to learn if it means freedom to live my life the way I choose. I have no clue what I want to do, but I'm determined to remain strong enough to figure it out. "Thank you again for helping me. It means a lot." I wait for a response, but all I hear is the sound of him taking a drag from his cigarette. "I'm going to miss you. Do you still promise to call in a few days to let me know how things are? I want to make sure nobody finds out you helped me and that you're okay." Derrick told me about some friends of his in Arizona who have agreed to let me stay with them until the dust settles. The plan is to meet his friends an hour outside the city, so when the car stops not long into our journey, I ask, "Why are we stopping?" Before he gets a chance to answer my question, the passenger door opens, and I startle. My first thought is Tony or one of my uncle's men, caught us, but it's not Tony's voice I hear.

"You're late, Derrick."

"Shut the fuck up, Bobby. I'm here, aren't I? Now let's get this over with."

"Derrick?" I'm confused. "Derrick, who is Bobby? You told me your friend's name was Scott and that he and his wife Melinda were picking me up."

"Just get out of the damn car, Lelani." My brother's gruff voice throws me off, and an uneasy feeling settles in the pit of my stomach. I feel someone looming inside the opened car door. I've learned to trust my gut. I'm blind, but my instincts are telling me something is not right.

"I've changed my mind, Derrick. Take me home." I stay planted in the passenger seat, unwilling to move.

"Too late." A hand clamps down around my arm and drags me from my brother's car. With no time to gain my balance, I fall to the ground, landing on my knees. The gravel assaults my palms and tears at my flesh, and I cry out. "Let me go! What are you doing?" I attempt to break free and crawl away, but my feet get caught on the material of my ankle-length skirt.

"Jesus fucking, Christ," my brother spits, getting in my face. "You've always been a pain in my ass. I'm glad to be getting rid of you finally."

"Rid of me? What?" Tears stream down my face as fear and panic starts to consume me. "What's happening?"

"You fuck everything up, Lelani. You think I'm going to let you take what's rightfully mine?"

"I don't want anything, Derrick."

"Shut up, Lelani. I'm so fucking sick of this innocent act. If it weren't for you, our parents would still be alive, and I'd have everything owed to me."

I cringe at my brother's words. He's never spoken to me like this before. "You don't mean that. Where is all of this coming from?"

"Blind and stupid is what you are, dear sister. A goddamn waste of fucking space and a drain on the family," my brother spits as if I'm the dirt beneath his shoes.

"Derrick, please," I beg. "I don't know what's happening, but let me go. I promise to leave and never come back." I reach out in front of me and fist his shirt as uncontrollable tears stream down my face.

"Oh, you're going to leave alright." He knocks my hand away, and the rocks crunch beneath his feet. "And I'm going to make sure no one ever finds you."

Those are the last words I hear my brother speak before something sharp pricks the side of my neck.

I wake sometime later disoriented, nauseous, and the moment I sit up my stomach rebels. I double over and begin to dry heave. Once I get my queasy stomach under control by taking a few deep breaths, the recollection of how I got here starts to flood my body with dread, causing me to panic. Standing, I place my hands out in front of me and take a hesitant step, all while trying not to hyperventilate. "Hello?" I call out, taking another move on shaky legs. Nausea starts coming in waves, and my body doesn't feel like my own. Just as I take another step, my hands come in contact with a cool metal wall. I feel around to try to figure out my surroundings, but all I can feel are steel walls surrounding me, keeping me prisoner. Soon my panic state overtakes me, and my breathing becomes erratic. I do my best to control myself while swallowing the bile that threatens to rise in my throat. "Help!" I ball my fist and pound on the wall. "Is somebody there? Help me please!" My pleas go unanswered. The only sound I hear is my heavy breathing and cries for help echoing off my prison walls.

Twisting, I slump down to my butt, pull my legs up to my chest and hug my body. As time passes, I get my anxiety under control. My ears pick up on what sounds like music playing. Not wanting to give up, I climb to my feet and try again to figure out where or what I'm in.

Over the next several minutes, I count eight paces from wall to wall. I'm not in a house. It's too small. Maybe it's a storage unit of sorts?

Next, I pick up on two men's muffled voices, followed by the sound of metal scraping against metal, then a sudden burst of air. I stand frozen in place when a man speaks. "Look who's up."

"Where am I?" I ask.

"Asking questions won't get you anywhere, girly. Neither will all that fucking banging you're doing."

"Please, you can't do this. Let me go." I rush forward in the direction of the man's voice. I don't make it far before a hand presses against my chest, pushing me backward, causing me to fall on my butt.

"You're not going anywhere, bitch." A different man is now in my personal space. His rancid breath washes across my face as he grabs a handful of my hair and wrenches my head back. "Being stupid will get you killed." His warning sends a chill down my spine. I swallow past the lump in my throat and remain silent. Happy with my lack of response, the guy lets go. I breathe a sigh of relief at his retreating footsteps.

"Load them up."

I listen closely to shuffling feet, followed by the slamming of a door. Silence falls around me. "Hello? Is someone there?" I get no response but know I'm no longer alone. I feel a presence. On my hands and knees, I crawl to the left, jerking when my hand comes in contact with a shoe. Reaching out again, I feel my way up a leg and the person's back until I reach a mass of long hair. I suck in a sharp breath and shake the woman. "Hey. Can you hear me?" The woman doesn't answer, but a groan comes from the space beside her. When I reach across the woman, I discover another body. After inspection, I find it is another woman. Both are alive. "Oh, god. What do I do?" I choke out a sob, feeling helpless. I feel like screaming, desperate to plead for my freedom, but as quickly remember the man's warning from earlier. My only choice is to sit here and wait for these two women to wake up.

I can't believe I'm here. How could my brother do this to me?

Sure, we are not as close as a brother and sister should be, but he has always been there for me. Not once has he spewed the kind of hatred toward me like he did tonight. Never in my wildest dreams did I think he hated me. I can't fathom why my brother would put me here. What's worse, I have no clue what these men have in store for me.

Heavy breathing pulls me from my thoughts. One of the women is waking up. She starts panicking. "Hey," I whisper in a calm tone. "You need to calm down before you pass out."

"Who are you? Where am I? Where is Jia?" she cries, and I assume Jia is the other woman.

"My name is Lelani, and if your friend is the other woman brought in with you, she is right beside you. Those men probably gave her something."

"Jia," the woman calls out her friend's name several times, trying to wake her.

"Piper," the other woman moans. "Piper, I don't feel so good. Where are we? I can't see you."

I listen as Jia's voice raises in alarm, and the other woman, Piper, tries to calm her down. A moment later, one of the women heaves then proceeds to vomit.

"Your friend will probably start to feel better now that she has thrown up whatever was in her system," I tell her.

"Do you know where we are, Lelani?" Piper asks me.

"No, but the walls and the floor are metal, so I'm almost certain we are not in a house. And you said it was dark and that you couldn't see anything. Also, when you were brought with your friend, the door sounded heavy. My guess is we are in a metal shed or some sort of storage container."

Just as I finish telling my theory to Piper, the door opens again, and a woman screeches, "Let me go!" Followed by the unmistakable sound of flesh hitting flesh.

"Shut the fuck up, bitch," a man barks, and I recognize him as the guy who shoved me earlier. Shortly after, several sobbing women now join us.

"Time to roll out," a man comments. "What are we going to do about the blind bitch?" My stomach drops at his question.

"That asshole Derrick said he was going to bring us a prize."

They are talking about my brother.

"He failed to mention the girl is blind. We'll let the boss decide what he wants to do with her. In the meantime, I want you to find Derrick. If that fucker thinks this makes us square, he better think again. One body doesn't wipe out his debt."

It takes all I have to keep my mouth shut as these men talk about me. Their casual conversation leads me to believe kidnapping women is all in a day's work for them.

Out of nowhere, Piper speaks. "You have no idea what you've done." Her stern voice carries a warning.

"Oh, yeah," a man says in a condescending tone. "And what are you going to do about it?"

"I won't have to do anything, asshole," Piper continues.

"What the fuck does that mean, bitch?"

I start to get worried for Piper when she continues to square off with these men.

"You'll find out soon enough."

The air around me intensifies. I hold my breath waiting to find out what happens next.

"Leave it alone, Boz. The bitch is just running her trap. We need to get on the road."

Several seconds pass before the door slams shut once more.

"Piper?" Jia rasps.

"Yeah?"

"What do you think is going to happen to us?"

Jia's question causes a knot to form in the pit of my stomach, and the other women whimper.

"My family will come for me," Piper states with conviction. The way she says it has me wondering who her family is and how they could find us. Just as those thoughts enter my brain, a truck engine roars to life, and the steel floor beneath me begins to vibrate. We lurch forward. It's then I realize we are on the move.

I don't know how long we have been on the road, but it feels like hours. My bladder is screaming in protest, and it's so hot and humid inside our prison my clothes are drenched in sweat. Just as the silence starts to wear on me, Piper's voice rings out. "Lelani?"

"Yeah?" I croak.

"The guy those men were talking about, Derrick. Who is he?"

"Derrick is my brother."

"Your brother did this to you?" Piper asks, and I can feel the sadness in her voice.

"Yes," I croak. I want to believe this is all a mistake and my brother wouldn't do this to me. But no matter how much I wish, the truth is, he did.

"Well, don't worry, Lelani. We'll be getting out of here soon."

"What makes you so sure?" one of the other women asks.

Jia, Pipers' friend, is the one to answer. "Because Piper's badass biker family will find us. Won't they, Piper?"

"They will. I know they will," Piper reassures her friend.

"How will they know where to find you?" I cut in.

"They just will. Trust me."

"I pray you're right," I say, my voice sounding small. If what Piper says is true, that her family will somehow find her, that might be our only hope of getting out of here. I'm also curious about who these bikers are.

I'm not sure when I managed to doze off, but the next thing I know is the truck comes to a screeching halt, startling us. A minute later, the door swings open. I welcome the fresh air seeping in.

"You have five minutes," a man says, followed by something

crashing near my feet. I scoot back further against the wall, unsure of what's happening.

"For what?" Piper seethes.

"To piss," the asshole counters.

What is he talking about?

"We're not peeing in a bucket," Piper growls.

Did this man toss a bucket at us to relieve ourselves in it?

"Suit yourself," he replies. "What about you?" A second later, I feel a hand on my thigh. "Since you can't see, I'd be willing to make an exception for you and lend a hand." I cringe at the creep's words and slap his hand away. In a flash, there is a movement to my left.

"Keep your disgusting hands off her." Piper comes to my defense.

"Listen here, you little whore!"

"I'm not a whore!" Piper shouts.

"You will be. In fact, maybe I should be the one to break you in."

I gasp at the crude threat coming out of the man's mouth.

"Over my dead body, asshole," Piper says with conviction, and suddenly the man who was taunting her roars. "Ahh! You fucking bitch!" The man sounds like he is in pain, and I have a hard time keeping up with all the commotion until a body lands in my lap. I immediately know it's Piper. I wrap my arms around her and do my best to protect her.

"The next time you pull a stunt like that, I'm going to kill your friend." Piper, who I'm still holding onto, stiffens in my arms at the menacing threat made by one of our captures. With his parting words, the door slams shut on us once again.

"What just happened?"

"I just Maced the hell out of that son of a bitch who put his hands on you," Piper answers.

· · ·

A LONG TIME LATER, the truck stops. I wait with bated breath for the door to open again, but it doesn't. All of us women are quiet as we listen to doors slamming and men talking. "Do you still think your family will come for us?" I ask Piper, my hope fading with each passing second.

"I know they are." Piper grabs my hand and squeezes. "You don't fuck with the Kings of Retribution. These assholes are in for a rude awakening. I'm willing to bet they are already here. I can feel it." Just then, all hell breaks loose, and the sound of gunfire erupts beyond the steel walls that hold us captive.

"Told you so," Piper declares.

2

AUSTIN

Night has fallen as eight of us head south, toward our destination. Cowboy, Riggs' Ops partner from Texas, reported more than an hour ago. The men who have Piper are roughly three hours out, giving us a small window of opportunity to hopefully get hidden to ambush the compound before their arrival. My bike rumbles as I increase my speed. Before long, Riggs and his men steer us to back roads to avoid drawing attention to several MC members racing like hell. Adrenaline courses through my veins. It's been a while since we Montana men have seen action. As we travel into more rural areas, the street lights space out further apart.

Judging by the number of houses we've passed by, not many people live out this way. Eventually, darkness swallows us completely. The air is humid, sticking to my skin, and a heavy, haunting feeling settles in my bones like death himself is at my back.

There will be bloodshed here tonight. Men who took one of our own will meet their day of judgment at the hands of the Kings of Retribution. A few days ago, my club made the trek from

Montana to Louisiana to help our New Orleans Chapter celebrate the opening of a second Kings Custom. On the day we were scheduled to head back home, we got word that Nova's daughter Piper and her friend had been kidnapped while on a trip to Vegas, which brings us here.

UP AHEAD, Riggs and Jake slow, making a right onto a dirt road, overgrown with tall grass on both sides. We roll to a stop less than ten miles down. The smell of decaying vegetation and cow shit gets stuck in my nostrils, along with the distinct aroma of tainted fish water. Riggs turns off his bike and walks down the row of Harleys. "We leave the bikes here," he orders. Behind us, Cowboy arrives in the passenger van. He climbs out, joining the rest of us. "Target site is situated at the end of the next road over, nestled along the inlet. We travel on foot from here."

In unison, every man checks his weapon. I tuck my handgun back in the holster, then retrieve the sawed-off shotgun strapped to the side of my bike. Always bring backup. That's what my grandad, who is ex-military, always told me. He's the one who taught me how to use a weapon. Before tumbling down a rabbit hole of memories, I push my thoughts aside and fall in behind Gabriel and Logan. We begin trekking our way through the tall grass, trudging through muck that coats our boots.

Ahead of us, dimly lit lights come into view as we crest a small hill. Riggs throws a fist in the air, stopping our movement. From this vantage point, I can make out shipping containers, situated on the far end of the property, along with a few armed men milling around the yard.

The rumble of an approaching vehicle causes most of our heads to turn. The air brakes of the semi-truck hiss as it slows to a complete stop. Men climb from the cab and stroll toward two guys walking in their direction. They pause for a beat, holding a brief conversation, then they head for the back end of the trailer.

I listen to my heartbeat thudding in my ears while we stay hidden amongst the tall grass. With guns aimed, they order the women to exit. To my right, Kiwi tenses as his eyes zero in on Piper, who is the last to jump to the ground. One guy shoves her hard, causing Piper to lose her footing. Kiwi makes a move, but Logan grabs hold of his arm, pulling him back. Once on her feet, Piper clutches two other women, but there is so little light, I'm unable to make out any physical features.

Facing us, Riggs fires off his command. "Logan, you and Reid keep low and head for the north end of the camp. It gives you the highest vantage point to use your sniper rifles." Shifting, Riggs looks to his left and orders Nova and Fender to make their way around the south perimeter. After giving his commands to a few other brothers, Riggs turns to me. "Stick with Jake and me." He looks around before everyone parts ways. "They outnumber us. Timing is everything. When you hear my signal, move in. This ambush needs to be quick. We don't stop until every man is dead, and Piper is safe."

Jake, Riggs, and I make our way up the center of the compound, in the direction of a single-wide trailer sitting off to the property's east side, isolated from the containers. The murmurs of other men talking close to our location cause a pause in our movement.

The grass coverage in this area is sparse. We lower our bodies to the wet ground and belly-crawl another several feet, getting as close to the perimeter of the open yard as we can. Jake, Riggs, and I watch men move about the compound. The same men who delivered the women stroll across the compound toward the trailer. The door opens, and a suited man steps outside. He lights a cigar, then blows out a puff of smoke as he speaks. "Get the boats ready to transfer the women." A few feet away, with rifles slung low at their sides, two men take off toward the south side of the property near the water. The man in the suit strolls to a dark gray sedan with blacked-out windows parked close by. Soon after, the trailer door swings open again and out files a second man. Dressed in all black and heavily armed, the guy makes his way toward the car. He opens the back door for the suit. Activity increases around the yard with the man's presence.

Keeping his eyes forward, Riggs whispers, "Jake, two o'clock." Prez lifts his long-range handgun and aims at a man standing near the trunk of the car. "Austin, take out the bodyguard," Riggs then orders me, and I lay the shotgun down at my side and pull my pistol in the holster inside my cut.

A rush of adrenaline courses through my veins as I get the big son of a bitch in my crosshairs. A few yards away stands an armed man taking a piss. Riggs aims at him, then pulls the trigger. The bullet rips through the fucker's head, and his limp body falls to the ground. Simultaneously, Prez and I fire at our targets. Jake's bullet hits the man in the suit. Gripping his neck, the man struggles to get in the back seat of the car. My shot hits the bodyguard in the chest. The man goes down behind the sedan. Our gunshots set off a chain reaction, and a hell storm of gunfire erupts all around us.

Grabbing my shotgun, the three of us emerge from the grass and rush the compound. Bullets whiz by my head as I run toward the gunfire. Aiming, I take down another man rushing us.

"Sweep the trailer!" Jake shouts above the chaos.

My back hits the side of the trailer as I avoid getting hit by bullets. I make my way up the rickety wooden steps. Men shouting and gunfire fade into the background as I kick in the trailer door, praying like hell I'm not met with the end of another man's gun. The smell of weed and booze hits me the moment I step inside and scan the room. The living room resembles a crack house. Used needles lay in the open on the coffee table nearby. I move through the trailer. Empty whiskey bottles clutter the kitchen counters as I make my way toward the back. A bullet pierces the window above the kitchen sink, and shards of glass pepper my pant leg. My heart thunders against my ribcage as I enter the dark hallway heading for the back bedroom. I kick open the door. "Shit." Lying on a dirty mattress in the center of the small room is an unconscious woman. With my gun raised, I scan the room, clearing the scene before kneeling. With the low lighting, I can't decipher if she's breathing or not. So, I press my fingers against her neck and feel for a pulse. It's faint, but she's alive. The sorry son of bitches left her for dead. Knowing I risk her life and my own if I carry her out in the middle of a gunfight, I leave the young woman behind. She is safer where she is until this is all over. Before I exit the trailer, the gunfire outside ceases.

The silence only increases my alertness. I cautiously step outside and round the corner of the trailer. Out of nowhere, a force slams me to the ground. I lose my grip on the shotgun as it's knocked from my hand. I'm face down in the dirt, and my handgun is also pinned beneath me. A blow to the back of my head causes my vision to blur. A few jabs follow the impact to my kidney region, and pain radiates across my lower back.

I struggle to gain control beneath the weight of the guy who has me pinned but finally, I can maneuver my body enough to reach the hunting knife sheathed at my waist. I thrust backward, feeling the initial resistance before my blade sinks into his flesh, and the man grunts out in pain. Rolling onto my back, I look up at the man hovering over me. It's the big motherfucking bodyguard.

"Didn't anyone tell you to make sure the dead stay dead?" His massive hands wrap around my throat, my blade still stuck in his side. "Now, you will be the one to die." He squeezes, cutting off my air supply. Blinded by his urge to kill me, he never sees me reach for my gun tucked away inside my cut. I press the end of the barrel under his chin and pull the trigger. The man slumps against me, and his hands go lax. Oxygen floods my lungs as I take a ragged breath. A rush of his warm blood drips onto my face. I shove his dead weight off to the side.

Getting to my feet, I find my bearings and look down at his lifeless eyes fixated on the night sky. "Who's dead now, motherfucker?" I'm still breathing heavily from the fight between us. Lifting the hem of my shirt, I wipe his blood off my face. Reaching down, I pull my knife from his side, wiping the blood on my jeans. I spot my shotgun two yards away and lift it from the mud it lies in.

I head to where the other Kings are converging on the two shipping containers holding the women. Logan glances my way, taking in my battle-worn appearance. "That your blood?"

"No," I tell him. "There's a young woman, barely alive back in the trailer," I make sure to mention as we wait for Kiwi to break the lock on the container.

The moment the heavy metal doors swing open, my brothers and I rush inside. The air is hot, musky with the smells of sweat. No time to think or to take in each set of eyes staring wildly at us, wondering what might happen to them next, I kneel, reaching for a victim to help.

"Who are you? Don't touch me!" the young woman screams, pulling from my touch hard enough the back of her head smacks against the metal wall behind her.

"I'm not here to hurt you." My words come out a little harsher than intended, and it causes the woman to flinch. There isn't much light shining inside the container, but enough I can make out her dress's blue color and curly fiery red hair covering her downcast face.

Piper appears at my left and lowers herself to the side of the frightened woman. "Shh. It's okay. These men are my family, and they are here to help." Piper comforts her, then looks at me.

"Her name is Lelani. She's blind."

Fuck. It makes sense why she responds differently from the other women the men are escorting out in the fresh night air. I give Piper a look, assuring her I have it from here. "Lelani, my name is Austin," I say, hoping a brief introduction will make her experience easier. Her head lifts, turning toward my voice, catching a flicker of light that reflects off her face. A large bruise marks the side of her cheek, and tear streaks stain her porcelain skin. My eyes lock with hers. For a split second, I forget she can't see me. I shake the fog from my head. Now is not the time to be taken by how beautiful she is. "I'm going to touch you now," I warn her before slipping my hands beneath her. Weighing no more than a small child would, she is light in my arms as I lift her and stand, then tuck her petite frame close to my chest. Lelani's body trembles as her fingers grip my cut. "You're safe with me," I tell her, feeling an overwhelming need to protect her. Her breath is warm on my neck as she rests her head on my shoulder.

Lelani is the last woman to emerge from the container as I carry her out. No one stops me as I pass by them. I continue to hold Lelani until Cowboy arrives with transportation a short time later. Logan approaches after retrieving the young woman from inside the trailer and carries her onto the passenger van. The rest of the brothers rush to load the remaining women. "She's going back with us, along with Piper's friend, Jia," Logan informs me before I carry Lelani onto the van along with the others as he makes a final headcount.

The club hustles, helping Piper, Lelani, and Jia onto another vehicle to carry us back to our bikes. We have less than twenty minutes to get our asses down the road before the explosives Cowboy left inside several structures go off. "Let's get the hell out of dodge," Jake barks, beating on the side door of the flatbed truck before climbing into the cab. While the women huddle together, the vehicle lurches forward as we leave the compound and the dead behind.

A moment later, we're transferring from the truck to our bikes. Jake instructs Jia to get on behind him and hold on tight, which she does. Without hesitating, I reach for Lelani, leading her toward my Harley. Being protective, Piper assists, quickly helping her settle in behind me. I touch her hand that rests on my side. "I need you to hold on tighter," I command, my voice firm. Bringing her body closer to mine, I feel her breasts press against my back. Both her hands slide along my abs, and her hold on me tightens. I'm not going to lie. I fucking like the heat of her skin against mine.

Our bike tires kick up dirt and gravel as we take off. The rumble of our Harleys awakens the night as we haul ass down the road.

A heavy silence falls as the tires turn against the asphalt. I twist the throttle, increasing speed, putting distance between us and the destruction we are leaving behind. In my side mirror, I watch the night sky turn bright orange. Thunder breaks the silence. It cracks like a whip at our backs as a bomb detonates. Another loud boom follows it. Plumes of white, grey smoke billow in the air. Lelani's fingers clutch my waist for dear life as she seeks comfort from the only person she can at the moment—me.

THE RIDE BACK TO THE KINGS' compound wasn't a short one, but I found myself wishing it could have been longer. I didn't want to lose the touch of a woman I knew nothing about except for her name.

THE GATE OPENS, and our bikes roll into the yard. I park alongside Jake. Lelani still has a death grip on my cut as I turn off the engine. I touch her hand. "You're safe," I assure her, and she slowly lets go. Climbing off my ride, I slip my hands around Lelani's slim waist, lifting her off the backseat, and attempt to carry her inside.

"You can put me down now." Her voice is soft and sweet. Reluctantly, I lower her bare feet to the ground. Lelani rests her hand in mine, and allows me to lead her into the clubhouse, where the old ladies are anxiously waiting. Kiwi releases Piper, who walks toward me. "Thank you, Austin," she says, her eyes falling to where my hand still clutches Lelani's. "Lelani, come with me, and we'll get you in a room and get cleaned up."

Turning, I face Lelani. "I'll check on you later," I tell her, then let her hand slip from mine. Rooted in place, I watch the women lead Lelani up the stairs.

A hand clamps down on my shoulder. "You okay, brother?" Reid asks.

"Yeah," I tell him, crossing my arms over my chest. He follows my line of sight, looking up the stairs where the women have already disappeared. "I'm gonna grab a beer and unwind." Reid takes his leave.

"Church in the mornin', men. It's been one hell of a day. Piper and those women are safe. We'll deal with the aftermath tomorrow. Mission accomplished. Get some sleep," Riggs announces.

While the others down a beer, waiting for their women, I walk behind the bar, grab a half-empty bottle of whiskey, and then head out to find some solitude.

The muggy New Orleans air smacks me in the face the moment I step outside the clubhouse door. I noticed a roof access ladder attached to the side of the building a couple of days ago. In search of it, I round the corner. It's rusted and missing some rungs, but I decide to climb it anyway.

Once on the clubhouse's flat-top roof, the loose gravel crunches beneath my feet as I stroll across to the side facing the water. Sitting on the ledge, I swing my legs over the side. I pull in a lung full of Louisiana air, breathing its heavy smell deep into my lungs. There isn't another place like the Big Easy. Putting my lips to the bottle in my hand, I tilt back my head and down a shot of whiskey.

My thoughts shift to Lelani as I stare out over the Mississippi River. I take another drink, then set the bottle down beside me. I pull a cigarette from my pocket. I retrieve a book of matches tucked inside the cigarette pack and drag the match tip along the black stripe. On the ground below, about twenty yards away, I notice Kiwi and Fender sitting near the water's edge, passing a smoke between the two of them. I take a drag, then blow it out.

I'm not sure how long I sit on the roof of the clubhouse, but it is long enough for me to feel the effects of the liquor taking hold. Standing, I cross the rooftop and climb back down to the ground.

Once inside, I find my way to my room. Bella steps out of the room two doors down, softly closing the door. She looks at me. "Are you okay?"

I run my hand down my face. "Yeah." My mind wanders back to Lelani again.

As if she reads my thoughts, Bella says, "Lelani is sleeping. Teagan gave her something to help her rest." Always one to worry about others, Bella adds, "You should clean up and get some sleep too." I reply with a nod, and she smiles. "Goodnight, Austin." Bella walks across the hall into her and Logan's room. I only move when she closes the door.

Instead of entering my room, I pause outside the door of the room where Lelani sleeps. My hand hovers over the handle, debating if I should go inside. The need to put eyes on her wins out, and I quietly enter her bedroom. Spotting the chair beside her, I cross the floor and stare at her as she sleeps. Her red hair is pulled back in a loose braid. A few loose curls are falling across her bruised cheek, but I don't dare to brush them away. Not wanting to wake her, I sit for a short time just watching her. I find myself falling into a calm state, and my eyes begin to grow heavy as I listen to her softly breathing.

Fuck. What am I thinking? I stand abruptly. The last thing Lelani needs after what she just went through is to wake up to the presence of a man in her room. I don't want to frighten her. I want Lelani to feel safe.

I gaze upon her one last time, then leave her room.

Too tired to wash, I remove my cut, place my weapon on the nightstand, along with my keys and phone, then kick off my boots. I stretch out across the bed.

Before closing my eyes, I reach over and set the alarm on my phone. With only a few hours to rest, I finally allow my body to relax into the mattress, letting the past several hours fade away. It's not long before I feel myself drifting off to sleep.

I WAKE to the sound of music playing from my phone and open my eyes to the dim light of the sun barely cracking through my bedroom window. Knowing church will take priority before our day begins, I drag my ass out of bed. I stretch, feeling soreness in my muscles. "Fuck," I say as I roll my neck, trying to work the kinks out. I pick up my phone and look at the time while turning off the alarm. A few hours of sleep is better than none. I stand and head to the bathroom. Avoiding anything brighter than the sunshine already filtering in, I forgo flipping on the light switch, turn the shower on, and strip from yesterday's clothes.

When I step beneath the spray of hot water pelting my skin, my achy muscles relax as the heat helps release the tension throughout my body. I splay my hands on the tile wall in front of me and hang my head, letting the scorching water penetrate as it rolls down my back.

I stay in the shower until the water runs cold before turning it off and stepping out. Having wasted enough time, I quickly brush my teeth and run a brush through my damp hair and beard before

SANDY ALVAREZ & CRYSTAL DANIELS

tossing on some clean clothes. After lacing up my boots, securing my weapon, and shrugging on my cut, I walk out of the room.

The smell of strong-brewed coffee leads me downstairs toward the kitchen. Several of the men are already assembled in the common room as I pass through. Quinn and Emerson are in the kitchen when I enter, and Quinn is busy shoving a pastry into his mouth.

"Hey, Austin." Emerson greets me with a lazy smile. She looks as tired as me.

"Mornin'," I say, yawning, then grabbing a disposable cup from the stack near the freshly brewed pot of coffee.

"Damn, these beignets are good," Quinn says, plucking another from the brown paper bag. I stroll across the kitchen with my coffee in hand and flip open the lid to one of the four doughnut boxes on the table. I can't help but notice the shirt, with an image of a rooster on the front of it, Quinn is wearing beneath his cut. "You starin' at my cock?" Quinn says, and I damn near spit out the sip of coffee I just took. He grins, and I shake my head. Quinn is the only brother who can pull off wearing shit like that.

"Ignore him. He's an adolescent trapped in a grown man's body." Emerson rolls her eyes.

Quinn marches up to his woman, grabbing a handful of her ass, and pulls her to him. "You love me, woman." He kisses her.

I watch their PDA for a beat. The men showing love for their women isn't anything new to me, but for some reason, I find myself wishing I had someone who looks at me the way Emerson looks at Quinn. Like myself, my brothers aren't perfect, but they found women who accept that about them and love them regardless of those flaws.

Just as quickly, I find myself thinking of Lelani and the way she put her trust in me when we rescued her and the other women hours ago. She melded into my body as I held her in my arms and carried her out of that container. Her touch burned my skin like fire but awakened something in me I hadn't felt before, and I'm not sure what to make of the feeling and thoughts raging through my mind and body because of her presence.

Wanting some fresh air, I leave the kitchen and find my way outside. I stroll across the yard and take a seat on the picnic table situated a few yards away from the edge of the water. Setting my coffee down, I reach inside my cut and retrieve a cigarette and lighter from the pocket. I watch the flame flicker as I light my smoke and pull the nicotine into my lung. I watch a large barge off in the distance drifting down the river and listen to the choppy water slosh against the grassy bank a few feet in front of where I sit. Beads of sweat slide down my temples from the humidity, and I long to be back home in Montana. New Orleans is a beautiful city, but they can keep the heat.

SOMETIME LATER, laughter and talking turn my head. I look behind me and watch the women filing out of the clubhouse. With them is Lelani.

"Austin," I hear my name called from the entrance of the clubhouse to see Logan standing there in the opened doorway. "Church."

For the next couple of hours, all of us men remain behind closed doors, getting a run-down of the early morning events. Riggs got word from his sources that the compound was destroyed in the blast, and several of the bodies left behind burned beyond recognition. So far, no witnesses have come forward to what happened out there in the bayou, and Riggs is confident it will remain as such. Cowboy safely reached his rendezvous point with the other women rescued. The team he is working with are working hard to get those with families back to their loved ones, and those without will be going to a secure location to start a new life.

"What is the plan with Lelani?" Wick asks.

Jake runs his fingers through his beard. "We need to know more about her if the club plans on helpin' in any capacity."

Riggs sighs. "Let's break for a beer. Pop should be by with some grub any moment now. We'll sort it all later before the end of the day," Riggs says. "That's it, for now, men." Riggs slams the gavel, and we file out of the room.

Cold beer is waiting for us at the bar. I down mine, immediately seeking out Lelani, and find her still outside with the other women.

It's not long before Jake and Riggs walk up, wanting to speak with Lelani. Her posture changes, and she becomes nervous. "It's okay, Lelani. You can trust us. My uncle only wants to help. I promise," Piper reassures her. Lelani wrings her hands together.

"Is it true that your brother is to blame for you ending up in the back of that storage pod?" Riggs addresses Lelani.

My gut twists with anger. I've done some awful shit in my lifetime, killed men, broken laws, but who the fuck can sell their flesh and blood? My baby sister is everything to me. I will move mountains for her and do whatever it takes to keep her safe. You have to be a special kind of fucked up to commit an act as her brother did.

"Yes," Lelani says, and we all hear the pain in her voice. I raise my eyes to look around the room and find the rest of the family share the same look of disgust.

"Alright, sweetheart," Riggs says, then drags a chair from a table nearby across the floor. He sits directly in front of Lelani. "The club is willin' to help. Just know that whatever you choose, my club is willing to help. Option one is we help you get back home.

Lelani sinks into the back of the sofa. "Go back to Vegas?" I focus all my attention on Lelani, blocking out everyone else. The mere thought of going back frightens her. I don't hear anything else until she says, "I don't have anyone—no family. I don't think I can go back." I grip the back of the sofa, my knuckles turning white as she states that she always depended on her piece of shit brother.

"What are your feelings about Montana?" Bella mentions, and her question brings me out of a rage-filled fog. I listen to her and Alba convincing her to come back with us. I feel myself leaning over the edge, looming over Lelani, waiting to hear her answer.

Lelani draws in a deep breath and lifts her chin. With a confident voice, she says, "I think Montana sounds lovely. That's if you're sure about your offer." She then straightens her back. "I refuse to be anyone's burden ever again."

"You're not a burden," I growl, causing Lelani to jump. I feel everyone's eyes on me.

Jake clears his throat. "It's settled then. You'll be coming back to Polson with us." He turns to Blake. "You cool with Lelani ridin' with you tomorrow?" As he asks my brother the question, he eyeballs me.

"Lelani will be on the back of my bike," I quickly cut in, squashing any plans of Lelani being that close to another man other than me.

Jake studies me for a beat. Satisfied with my statement, Jake states, with a sharp nod, "Alright, brother."

3

LELANI

After spending a few days on the back of a motorcycle, I've come to realize I love it. At first, I was terrified. I held onto Austin as if my life depended on it. It didn't take long to let the fear go and embrace the wind on my face and the overwhelming sense of freedom that comes with the ride. It helps that with Austin I feel safer than I've ever felt in my entire life. It's a crazy notion, considering Austin is a stranger. The same goes for the rest of the men I hear him refer to as his brothers. To tell you the truth, I don't know what an MC is, but in the short amount of time I have spent with this group of men and women, I feel their kindness, passion, welcoming nature, and loyalty. All those attributes don't sugarcoat that I am very aware that I'm putting my life in the hands of men who are also ruthless and seek vengeance on anyone who dares to threaten or harm the people they love or consider family. I understand why Piper had so much faith and conviction in her family when we were being held captive. Without a shadow of a doubt, she knew they would come for her and help the rest of us in return. I'm both happy and jealous that Piper can live life with that kind of security.

What I wouldn't give to spend every waking moment of my life knowing there are people out there willing to go to the ends of the earth to keep me safe. If anyone found themselves stupid enough to try and take that away from me, they would see themselves coming face to face with the devil himself.

Just as my thoughts turn to anger, Austin squeezes my right calf twice. I picked up on his little signals for me by the end of our first day on the road. His squeezing my right calf a couple of times lets me know we are making a right turn and stopping. A few moments later, Austin parks the motorcycle and cuts the engine. Bracing my hands on his shoulders, I swing my leg around and cumbersomely climb off while Austin keeps his large hand wrapped securely around my forearm for support.

"Here," he says in his gravelly tone. His palm then slides down my arm, causing my skin to prickle at the heated contact. Gripping my hand in his, he tugs me a step closer to him. My breathing picks up when his breath fans across my face. "Let me get that for you." Austin's fingers work at unbuckling the helmet from under my chin, and I don't miss the way his thumb brushes just below my bottom lip. "Thank you," I whisper.

Austin doesn't reply, but he does retake my hand, and I fall in step beside him. "We're going to grab a bite to eat. Prez doesn't want to spend another night in a hotel, so we'll probably be rollin' into Montana and the clubhouse pretty late."

"Clubhouse?"

"Yeah, babe. Our clubhouse is like a home away from home for the club members and their families. It's also where we conduct business. A few of us brothers live there too," Austin answers. "Just like the one we left in New Orleans."

I nod.

When we walk through the door of the restaurant, the smell of smoked BBQ assaults my nostrils. Over the next few minutes, we go through the task of being shown to a table, and the waitress takes everyone's order.

Murmurs fall among the men and their women, and Austin, who is seated beside me, is in deep conversation with Logan. The two are discussing something about an order for the garage being late.

My bladder decides it needs relief, but I continue to ignore its protest, not wanting to interrupt anyone to ask for help locating the restroom. Alba speaks up from across the table. "Lelani, are you okay?"

"Umm...I need to use the ladies' room." My face heats when the table falls silent.

"I'll take you," Bella jumps in immediately. "I have to go as well."

"Me too," Alba adds.

"Thank you." I duck my head as I go to scoot my chair back but pause when Austin leans in close, caging me in by placing his arm over the back of my chair. "Don't do that again," he growls into my ear.

"Wh...what?" I stammer.

Austin places his finger on my jaw and tilts my face toward his. "You know what."

"I didn't want to interrupt you," I confess.

"I don't give a shit. You need somethin', you tell me. It doesn't matter. Understand?"

Swallowing past the lump in my throat, I nod.

"Tell me with words, Lelani."

"I understand."

Satisfied, Austin shifts his body and allows me to stand. A patiently waiting Bella links her arm with mine and leads me from the table. She remains quiet until we are out of earshot to speak. "Girl, brace yourself." To my left, Alba giggles.

"Brace for what?" I ask.

"You'll see," she answers cryptically, then adds, "Just know, these men are a different breed."

"In the most delicious way," Alba says in a dramatic sigh. "It's best not to fight it either. They always get what they want."

"I still don't know what you're talking about." I shake my head.

Bella laughs. "You will."

WHEN BELLA, Alba, and I return from the restroom, I take my seat beside Austin, and I instantly feel his eyes burning a hole through me. It's something I sense him often doing since the moment he carried me out of that storage pod four days ago. His presence is one I find hard to ignore. It's electric. I haven't quite figured out why he does it, but I do know I like it. I like it more than I should. Like when he sat in the room and watched me resting the night of my rescue. He wasn't aware I felt him in the room, but I did. The strange part is his presence didn't scare me. It was the opposite. Austin watching over me that night brought me peace. A kind of peace I haven't felt since my parents were alive. It didn't take me long to drift back off to sleep while he sat with me that night.

When Austin drapes his arm over the back of my chair, his hand slightly touches my shoulder. It takes all I have not to let him see the effect he is having on me. Austin and his club agreed to help me. I don't want to mess up a good thing by developing some schoolgirl crush by confusing his actions for more than what they are.

Growing up, my uncle never allowed me to date. Not that I had many opportunities. I was homeschooled and never really had any friends. My sheltered upbringing put me at a disadvantage when it comes to the opposite sex. Now is not the time to lose focus. I need to keep my head straight so that I can take back my life. I want to stop being dependent on other people and learn to take care of myself. It's time to stop letting my disability be a burden to those around me. I'm going to take the help the Kings are offering and use it to make a new life for myself.

I only hope they don't find out I'm keeping a secret. I'm afraid if the Kings find out who I really am, they wouldn't be so inclined to offer up their protection.

"Let's hit the road," Jake calls outs a short time later, when everyone has finished their meals. At the sound of chairs scraping against the floor, I stand. Austin immediately takes my hand and carefully helps me maneuver through the restaurant then outside to his bike.

As I'm putting the helmet on, Austin presses his palm against my side.

"You good, brother?" Jake asks as he approaches us.

"Yeah, Prez, I'm good," Austin replies.

Jake addresses me, "How about you, sweetheart. You hangin' in there?"

I nod. "Yes. I'm okay."

"Good. These long trips can take their toll on the body when you're not used to them. We'll be home soon."

"I don't mind it. The ride has been kind of nice," I admit.

Jake chuckles. "I'm happy to hear that, darlin'."

A minute later, I'm behind Austin. Jake's booming voice follows a loud whistle. "Roll out."

HOURS LATER, I can feel night has fallen by the temperature change and the way the wind smells as it hits my face. The air here is so fresh and clean.

"We're home," Austin announces. Lost in thought, I hadn't even realized we have stopped. My nerves start to kick in with being in a new place and of the unknown.

"Damn, it's good to have all of you home, brother!" a man

shouts, and I instinctively stand a little closer to Austin once he helps me from the bike.

"It's okay, that's Bennett. He's with his wife, Lisa. They're a part of the club too. You have nothing to be afraid of here. You have my word," Austin murmurs into my ear, and my body relaxes.

"It's good to see ya, brother." That same man, Bennett, sounds to be standing directly in front of us.

"It's good to be home," Austin tells him.

"You must be Lelani?" a woman asks, and the warm sound of her voice puts me at ease, and I smile. "My name is Lisa, and Bennett here is my old man."

"It's nice to meet you, Lisa." I stick out my hand and wait for her to take it.

"Oh, honey. We don't shake hands around here," Lisa jests, and the next thing I know, I'm engulfed in her arms. "Come on. I'll take you inside and help you get settled."

For a second, I'm reluctant to go until Austin leans in and reassures me. "Go on with Lisa, babe. I'll be in soon."

My breath catches in my throat at him calling me babe. It renders me speechless, so all I do is nod then allow Lisa to lead me away.

"Oh, my. I see what the girls were talking about when they phoned yesterday," Lisa says with a hint of a smile in her voice.

Her comment has me confused. "Am I missing something?"

Lisa laughs. "Don't mind me. I tend to think out loud."

I hear a door open, and the chatter of a couple of female voices cease.

"Hey, Lisa. Is this Lelani?" a woman asks.

"It sure is. Lelani, this is Ember, and Raine is standing beside her. These young ladies live at the clubhouse and help take care of things."

"It's nice to meet you." I give both ladies a wave.

"Ember, do you mind showing Lelani up to her room while I

37

take care of a few things? I already have her room ready. She'll be in the one next to Austin's."

"Of course." Ember takes my hand and places it in the crook of her elbow. "Watch your step," Ember halts. "The stairs begin here." She waits for me to grab hold of the rail. "There are sixteen steps. At the top is a long hallway."

I smile and nod. "Thank you for telling me. It won't take me long to memorize the layout."

Once we reach the top, Ember stops us again. "Our bedrooms are on your left. The first one is mine. The second is Raine's. If you ever need anything, feel free to knock on those doors anytime."

"Thank you."

"You're welcome. We're all family here."

After a second, she continues. "Lisa put you in the fourth room. Austin is in the one right before yours."

I nod and begin counting my steps until we stop at what I assume is the room I'll be sleeping in tonight. I turn my head when I hear heavy footsteps coming up behind us.

"Hey, Austin. I was just showing Lelani to her room."

"Thanks, Ember. I got it from here."

"No problem. I'll go help Lisa." Ember gently takes my hand and passes it to Austin. "It was nice meeting you, Lelani. Remember, if you need anything, I'm just down the hall."

"Thank you, Ember. It was nice meeting you too."

After Ember walks away, several beats of uncomfortable silence pass between Austin and me. I begin to fidget, feeling his eyes boring into the top of my head as I keep my face cast down.

Placing his finger under my chin, Austin lifts my face. "You alright, Mouse?"

My lips part, and my breathing increases with the effect he is having on me. "Yes."

I suck in a sharp breath when Austin's finger brushes away a lock of hair and tucks it behind my ear, leaving a trail of electric energy dancing along my skin, making me shiver.

"Let's get you settled," he says, guiding me into the bedroom. "In front of you is the bed." We walk five paces to the left and stop. "The bathroom is here. You have everything you need on the counter. I had Ember pick up the essentials: shampoo, conditioner, toothbrush, lotion, along with some other shit." Austin takes my hand and extends my arm until my palm comes in contact with a hard surface. "If you stand directly in front of the bathroom door and reach out to your right, there is a dresser. Ember also got you some clothes. Only enough for a few days. I'll take you shoppin' tomorrow or the next day to get you more of what you need."

"Oh, that's not necessary," I stop him. "What I have on and what Ember was kind enough to get me is enough. Please, don't go through the trouble. I can make do."

"I'm takin' you shoppin'," Austin repeats.

"Austin," I protest.

"Lelani," he growls, making his decision final.

Too tired to argue or over-analyze the situation, I keep my mouth shut.

Picking up on my fatigue, Austin changes the conversation. "Are you hungry? I can get one of the girls to whip something up for you."

I shake my head. "No. I think a shower sounds like a good idea, then lying down."

"Alright. I need to go sort some shit out, but I'll be back later to check on you."

After I hear the click of the door closing, I make my way into the bathroom. Once I have familiarized myself with the layout, I reach into the shower and turn on the water. While letting the water heat, I strip out of my clothes and untie my long hair from its braid. Pulling back the shower curtain, I slowly step into the shower and under the spray of hot water. Closing my eyes, I take a deep breath and let the built-up tension leave my body.

I'm over one thousand miles away from my past, yet it's still weighing on my shoulders. How long can I keep my true identity a secret? What will happen to me if the Kings find out? I wonder what my brother is doing right now. I want to believe he's realized his mistake and is looking for me, but a sickening feeling deep in the pit of my stomach says otherwise. How do I even begin to process his betrayal?

Shaking those thoughts away, I notice the water has turned cold, so I quickly finish my shower.

HOURS LATER, I lie awake in bed, unable to get my brain to shut off long enough to get some sleep. Thinking maybe some hot tea will help, I climb out of bed, pad over to the door and open it. Not hearing a sound, I continue to feel my way down the hall. I briefly contemplate waking Austin or maybe Ember to show me to the kitchen but decide against it. I'm sure they are all sleeping by now.

With luck, I clear the stairs and walk in the opposite direction of where I remember the clubhouse entrance is located, making it ten paces before stubbing my toe. "Shit," I hiss and catch a stool I nearly knock over before it crashes to the floor, all while ignoring the throbbing pain in my foot.

This was a bad idea.

Turning, I go to make my way back to the stairs but run face-first into a concrete wall of muscle. "Ooof." I stumble backward, but before I fall, strong arms keep me steady.

"What are you doing?" Austin asks, his voice husky from sleep.

"I couldn't sleep. I thought maybe some hot tea would help. I was looking for the kitchen."

"Why didn't you fuckin' wake me?"

I flinch at the anger in his voice. "I didn't want to."

"You didn't want to wake me?" Austin's tone changes. "What did I tell you, Lelani? What are you supposed to do when you need help?"

"To come to you. No matter what." Not responding, Austin threads his fingers through mine and leads me in the opposite direction of the stairs, and I allow him. "I'm not completely helpless, you know," I huff. "I can do things on my own."

"Never said you were helpless, babe," he says without breaking his stride. "In the mornin' I'll take you on a tour of the clubhouse so you can familiarize yourself with your surroundings."

"Oh. Well, thank you," I say sarcastically.

At my response, Austin comes to a stop and is suddenly in my space. "I still mean what I said, Mouse. The next time you don't come to me because you think needing help is a burden, I'll be inclined to place you over my knee."

I'm shocked at his words, then mortified. My face heats and my body warms at his warning. *What is wrong with you, Lelani?* Ignoring my reaction, Austin continues, "Now, let's go make you some tea."

4

AUSTIN

With her hand in mine, I lead Lelani to the kitchen. "The women usually keep girly tea around here somewhere," I say. Letting her go, I begin rummaging through cabinets until I find what I'm looking for behind a large jar of honey. "Chamomile, peppermint, Chai latte, or Earl Grey?" I ask.

"Chamomile is fine," Lelani says.

"Honey?" I ask. When she doesn't answer, I look back over my shoulder. "Babe. You want honey in your tea?"

"Oh, um, yes." Lelani answers.

"A penny for your thoughts, Mouse?" I ask, curious to know what she is thinking. Filling the mug with water, I pop into the microwave to get it hot. In less than a minute, I pull the steamy cup out, drizzle a teaspoon of honey into the water then dunk the teabag in as well.

"Why do you call me mouse?"

I shrug. "You're small and quiet, but full of a determination to survive and make it on your own."

"We only met a few days ago. What makes you see all those things in me?" she questions.

I step in close, my face mere inches from hers. "I see you, Lelani. You've been through something, and I'm not just talkin' about being sold by your fuckin' brother to some skin traders. You've overcome much more." By the way her chin lifts, I know I've hit the nail on the head. I also note her rapid breathing and wonder if I have the same effect on her as she does me. I lean in close, smelling the faint aroma of sweet strawberry on her skin. "Do I make you nervous, Mouse?"

Lelani visibly swallows. "Yes," she whispers, the tone of her voice sensual in a way that makes me wonder what my name would sound like dripping from her lips as I make her come.

My thoughts quickly shift as my eyes fall to her full lips.

I want so badly to kiss her. I want to imprint on her—leave my mark—make her mine.

The temperature in the room rises as the tension between us intensifies. Before something happens, I pull back, giving us both the space we need. "Let's get you back to your room."

I NEED a cold fucking shower by the time I get back to my room. King looks up at me from where his big ass is sprawling out on the bed. "I leave for twenty minutes..." He then proceeds to roll on his back. "You have the best dog bed on the market, that cost a fortune, and you want to take over mine." The way his mouth opens and his tongue flops out the side causes me to crack a smile. King has been in my life for over eight months. I found him one night digging in the trash out back behind the bike shop. Poor guy was skin and bones. Knowing there was no way to transport him on my bike, I managed to coax him inside the backdoor of Kings Custom with some peanut butter snack crackers from the vending machine.

Once I had him safely inside the breakroom, I found something to put some water in and laid a throw blanket Bella kept tossed across the backside of the couch onto the floor. I left him there in the breakroom long enough to drive out to the clubhouse and get my truck. He couldn't stay at the shop, but I sure as shit wasn't throwing him out on the street. I took King back to the clubhouse that night, then straight into the vet the following morning. The vet checked him for a microchip, which he didn't have. It seems he didn't have anyone, so I decided I wanted him. I had a dog once. My mom brought a puppy home for my sister and me when I was eight years old. I loved him. The problem was my dad didn't. My mom caught hell for bringing Jack, the little terrier home. I remember the day as vivid as all the rest. My dad was furious that mom would go behind his back and make a choice like that without his permission. It was always his way or the highway.

My dad walked right through my bedroom door, where I sat with my sister, huddled in the corner, and ripped the puppy from my arms. I was upset and my baby sister was in tears, but I knew he would blow his top even at that age.

Sitting on the edge of the bed, I rub King's belly. Who could throw a dog away? He's much bigger than my first dog. King is an Irish Wolfhound, and stands at nearly three feet, and weighs almost 200 pounds. He looks intimidating but is a gentle giant. King is a permanent part of the family.

"Move over," I tell him and get back into bed. Reaching over to the nightstand, I turn off the lamp. King readjusts himself, laying his head across my abdomen. I lie there forever, trying to fall asleep, but like always, my insomnia prevents it from happening. I think about the pills on my nightstand. They help most nights, but I hate taking them. My exhaustion wins, so I roll over, reach into the drawer, unscrew the top of the prescription bottle, and pop a pill into my mouth, then wash it down using the glass of water sitting nearby.

I lay my head back on the pillow, staring up at the ceiling, and watch the fan blades slowly rotate. It's not surprising when my thoughts drift to the beautiful redhead one door down the hall. Maybe thinking of her will keep other memories at bay, so I focus on the touch of her hand in mine. It doesn't take long for me to feel the pull, and my eyelids begin to grow heavy with sleep. At first, I fight it. I always do. I don't like not being in control, so I don't take the pills often. I don't have control of which memories will surface with my dreams.

I WAIT *until my sister is asleep and my mom is in her room before climbing out of my bedroom window. "Let's go," Cory whispers from the ground. Making my way across the porch roof, I access the old oak tree at the end of the house and climb down. I look back over my shoulder at the house, seeing my parents' bedroom light still on, then look at the driveway where my dad's parking spot sits empty. I don't know why she waits up for him to come home. It's Saturday, which means my dad is with the other woman. Anger boils in my gut. Why does she stay with him knowing he's a cheater? I tighten my hands into fists at my sides, digging my nails into the palms of my hands. I hate him. My mom deserves better.*

"Come on, dude. Let's get a move on. Drake is waiting for us down at the corner." My friend Cory gives me a slight shoulder shove to get my attention. One final look at the house and I walk away. There's a colossal party down at the quarry tonight. Everyone who's anyone will be there, including Raegan Richardson. I've had a thing for her since junior high. Down at the corner stop sign, Drake is in his car waiting for us. Cory and I jump into the backseat of his Jeep. Drake turns, looking over his shoulder. "We need booze," he states.

I pull a wad of cash from my pocket that I took from my dad's secret stash in his office. "I got it covered." I flash the bills, waving the cash in the air.

"Hell, yeah." Drake puts the Jeep in to drive, and we take off down

the road. We head for the Minute-Mart on the other side of town. The night clerk there doesn't give two shits if you're underage or not. As long as you line his pocket with a little cash, he looks the other way. It helps that at the age of sixteen, I look much older. Once we pull into the gas station parking lot, I stroll in, grab as many cases of beer I can carry, give the clerk some pocket money and head back outside.

Thirty minutes later, my friends and I are at the quarry, knocking beers back, listening to music, and I have Raegan on my lap. As far as I'm concerned, all the other worries in my life can go fuck themselves. Right here—right now, I'm living in the moment.

Raegan reaches down the front of her shirt. My eyes are glued to her tits as she pulls a joint from between her cleavage. Cory tosses me another beer, and I crack the tab while Raegan stokes the joint between her fingers. She takes a toke, pulls my lips to hers, and blows the hit into my mouth. I inhale on her exhale, drawing the smoke in deep, and hold it there until my lungs burn and I feel lightheaded. After a few more hits, my mind slips. I get lost in the euphoria of not giving a fuck.

I don't know how we make it home, but I soon find myself standing in my front yard, staring at my house. I sway a little. Fuck I'm wasted.

Through my brain fog, I hear my father yelling. I rush toward the front door, tripping on the steps leading up to the porch along the way. I pick myself up and burst through the door. "You are nothing without me," my dad rages, followed by an audible slapping sound.

He's hitting her again.

Something inside of me snaps.

I won't let him hurt us anymore.

Needing to defend my mom, sister, and myself, I run to my dad's office and grab the spare key to his desk drawer that he keeps hidden in his cigar box by the liquor cabinet. Rushing to the desk, I fumble to unlock the drawer. Reaching under the cashbox, I wrap my hand around the pistol, then dart out of the room.

Bounding up the staircase, I find my sister standing just outside her bedroom door in her pajamas. I hide the gun behind my back. Tears are *streaming down her frightened face. Again, I do my best to shake off the weed and booze effects I've consumed tonight. "Addilynn, it's going to be okay," I tell her just as my mom pleads for my dad to leave.*

"Bitch. This is my house. My money bought it and everything else you have."

"I can't take it anymore, Kenneth. I want a divorce." My mom cries.

"The only way you'll leave this house is in a body bag." We hear Dad hit Mom again, followed by a loud thump against the wall, causing my sister to take my hand.

"Austin." I hear the fear in her voice.

"Go downstairs," I tell my sister.

"No."

"Addy. I need you to go downstairs. Grab the phone and hide behind the couch." I look down at her. "Call the police. No matter what, do not come out of hiding. Do you understand?"

Her head shakes. "But..."

"No matter what," I cut her off. "Go."

The moment I know she's down the stairs, I make my way down the hall. My heart is racing as I place my hand on the handle.

"Kenneth, no," Mom screams, followed by a loud pop.

I burst into the bedroom and find Mom lying on her side, on the floor at my dad's feet.

"Mom?" my voice croaks, and Dad swings around to face me.

He has a gun in his hand.

The end of the barrel pointing right at me.

It all happens so fast. A chain reaction that irrevocably changes my life. I remember the gun in my hand, raise it, and without any other thought except to protect my sister, I pull the trigger.

A hot-searing pain rips through me. Gripping my chest, I look down. Blood begins to soak through my shirt. I lift my head and look at my dad. His weapon hits the floor, and his hand covers the wound in his neck where my bullet penetrated his body. His crisp white shirt turns to crimson as blood gushes between his fingers.

Nothing but pure hatred reflects in his eyes.

I feel myself swaying. Everything around me slows. My eyes drop to the floor where my mom lays, her blood seeping into the carpet beneath her. She's staring back at me, and a single tear rolls down her cheek. I don't look away because the light is fading from her eyes—life is leaving her body.

My knees buckle, and I hit the floor.

I can't breathe.

I jackknife in the bed, clutching my chest, gasping for air. I'm covered in a cold sweat, shaking, my heart trying to break free of my chest. I look around the room, filled with paranoia that the horror may have followed me here.

A warm wet nose nudges my side, and King presses his body up against mine. "I'm okay, boy." I drape my arm around him, soaking in the comfort he's giving.

I look out the window of my bedroom and take in the changing hues of dark blues to soft orange breaking through the tree line that runs along the backside of the property. I need to wash away the memories, so I climb out of bed and make my way to the bathroom. Stripping from my clothes, I step into the shower and turn on the water. I welcome the shock to my system as cold water rushes over my fevered skin until it turns hot, almost scorching. Palms pressed against the cold tiled wall, I hang my head and try to let go of the demons that still haunt me.

Thirty minutes later, I step out of the shower, wrap a towel around my waist and stand in front of the mirror that hangs above the bathroom sink. The reflection staring back at me looks a lot like the man I killed—my father.

The shot I fired that night hit him in the jugular vein. My dad bled out before the ambulance arrived. The doctors tried to save my mom, but she didn't make it either. I run my fingertip along the scar on my chest. My dad shot and killed my mom. Then he put a bullet in his only son without hesitation.

I have no remorse for taking my father's life. He wasn't a good man. He was abusive both physically and emotionally.

Kenneth Blackstone was a respected member of the community. No one knew what he was really like. If they did, they chose to look the other way. I have no doubt my mom loved him. I think perhaps she thought she could change his ways one day. My dad's heart was as black as the ink on my skin. His voice still echoes in my ears from time to time, telling me I'm worthless.

In the end, I killed him.

Now, the only demons I live with are in my head. I live with regret. If I wouldn't have been out partying with friends, getting wasted—anything to keep from being in the house of hell I lived in—I might have saved her life.

KING PAWS at the bedroom door, so I walk over, open it and let him out. "Go on. I'll be down to feed you in a minute."

I move about the room, gathering my clothes and getting dressed for the day. I push my memories to the side, not giving them another thought, and leave my past where it belongs—dead and buried.

I slip on a pair of jeans and slide a shirt over my head, followed by the leather shoulder holster I wear at my side. I slip my boots on and lace them, then snag my cut off of the hook near the door and shrug it over my shoulders, and head into the hallway.

The smell of bacon lingers in the air, causing my stomach to growl with hunger. Lelani's bedroom door is slightly ajar when I go to pass by. Stopping, I poke my head inside, but the room is empty. She must have found her way downstairs by herself again. I smile and give her credit for her determination to get around on her own, but I still don't like her wandering the clubhouse before I've had the chance to familiarize her with the layout of the building. There are spaces and rooms in the clubhouse she doesn't need to find herself wandering into. The basement is one of them.

I descend the stairs into the common room and run into Blake. "Just the guy I was searching for."

"What's up?"

"Prez just called. He said to tell you those parts you ordered for your truck finally came in." Blake shoves the phone in his hand, back into his pocket.

"Thanks, brother," I tell him.

"No problem." He turns and heads for the clubhouse front door. "Lelani is in the kitchen. Lisa is in there cookin' some grub," Blake says without looking back. "If anyone needs me, I'll be outside working on my bike." The morning light shines inside as he walks out the door. Turning on my heel, I head for the kitchen and find Lisa standing at the stove, tending to the bacon sizzling in the pan.

"Austin." She smiles. "Have a seat. I just took the biscuits out of the oven," she says, and my mouth waters. If anyone can cook, it's Lisa.

My eyes land on Lelani, sitting at the table, and King is sitting at her side. "Lelani," I brace my palms on the table and lean into her.

"Austin," she smiles up at me.

"I see you've met King." I lean down, giving my dog a scratch behind the ear, and Lelani smiles while stroking the dog's side.

"He found me first when I was making my way down the stairs a short time ago and accompanied me into the kitchen. He feels huge. What type of dog is he?" Lelani continues to pet King.

"He's an Irish Wolfhound." I pull out a chair and sit beside Lelani at the table. "He's taken a likin' to you, which is not like him."

"I like him too. You're a good boy, King," Lelani praises him, and King lays his head on her lap.

Lisa sits a cup of black coffee in front of me, along with a plate of hot food. She then sits another plate in front of Lelani.

"Here, honey. You're sure to have a long day ahead of you, so eat up. Silverware is on your right. You have scrambled eggs at twelve, biscuit at two, and bacon at eight."

"Perfect." Lelani finds her fork. "Thank you, Lisa."

Silence blankets the room as we eat our breakfast, and I keep stealing glances Lelani's way.

The past few days were long and tiresome. The road back to Montana felt longer than it has in the past. Maybe it was due to having a passenger on my bike, or it could be because of Lelani herself. As eager as I was to get back home, I found myself wishing the ride wouldn't end. Having her body pressed against my back felt good. It felt right. Holding on to her calf as we cruised down long stretches of the open road gave me a sense of comfort I'd never had before. The ride was different—more freeing. Initially, I thought traveling with Lelani would have its difficulties, that perhaps being vision impaired would make her too nervous, which would have made for a daunting task of keeping her reassured that she was okay. It turns out Lelani had no issues at all. It took her a few hours to completely relax, but as time passed, she read my body language, quickly picking up on my subtle touches and how my body adjusted to curves in the road.

I finish my meal, then take my empty plate to the sink and rinse it off. "Thanks for breakfast, Lisa." I kiss the top of her head. She's the closest thing to a motherly figure I've had since my dad ripped Mom from my life.

"It's what I do, hun." Lisa smiles.

Crossing the kitchen, I open the lid to a large bin, which happens to hold King's dog food. I scoop out some kibble and pour it into his feed bowl nearby. King lumbers over and sniffs at it, then looks at me. "Go on. Eat," I tell him and lower the lid. King barks. I stare at him, and he cocks his head. "They spoiled you while I was gone, didn't they?" I rub his head.

Lisa walks up and tosses a few bacon strips into his food bowl, and King begins devouring it and his kibble while wagging his tail. I look at Lisa, who is all smiles.

"What?" she jests, and I raise my brow. "He was moping and wouldn't eat while you were away. My heart couldn't take it. Bacon makes him happy, and King happy makes me happy." She pats his side then walks away. I say nothing about it. I want King to have a good life, and if that involves bacon for breakfast, then so be it.

Lelani stands. I move to assist her but hold back my urge, letting her find her way to the kitchen sink independently, which she does reasonably well. Lisa must have gotten her familiar with the space before I woke this morning. She washes her plate, then sits it on the rack to dry and dries her hands on a towel that Lisa hands to her.

I move across the room, coming to a stop in front of her just as she turns around. "Ready, Mouse?"

Her face lifts upward, and the beams from the morning sun coming through the sliding doors leading to the backyard dance across her face. I raise my hand, brushing my fingertips across her forehead, sweeping her wild curls to the side. I feel a jolt of electricity at the brief contact with her skin. Judging by the sharp breath Lelani takes, I'm inclined to believe she feels it too.

"Shopping?" she asks, and my eyes fall to her lip that she is biting.

"Yeah, babe." This time, Lelani reaches out. She looks unsure, and I'm curious as to why. "What's wrong?" I ask.

"Nothing." Her hand finds mine, and she gives me a less than confident smile. "I'm ready."

Once we step outside and feel the warmth of the summer sun on my skin, a thought enters my mind. "What would you say to a change of plans?" I lead Lelani to my bike.

"If you don't feel like shopping, I understand. I mean, I could get one of the women to take me," Lelani says, sounding a bit dejected.

"I'm still takin' you shoppin', but I'd like to show you something. You up for a little adventure?" I swing my leg over my bike and look at her.

"Do I get to know where we are going?" She holds her hand out, and I guide her toward me.

"Nope," I state and feel her pull back from me.

"What do you look like?" Her question catches me by surprise. "I've tried to imagine what you might look like, but..." she lets her words hang for a beat. "Can I touch you? Unless that's too weird. Crap. Nevermind," she stammers, and it's cute as hell.

"Of course. Come here." I pull her closer, and my heart starts thumping as Lelani brings her hands to my face. Her fingertips sweep across my forehead before tracing the shape of my eyes.

"What color are your eyes?"

"Brown," I tell her while her feathery touch drifts along the bridge of my nose and over the tops of my cheeks. The pad of her thumb drags across my lips. Then she gently cups my face, tracing the slopes of my jawline. She combs the length of my beard with her hands. Reaching up again, Lelani runs her fingers through my hair, her nails lightly scraping at my scalp. "It's long," she smiles. "What color is it?"

"Same as my eyes," I state, trying to ignore the effect her touch is having on another part of my anatomy.

"How old are you?"

"Twenty-six."

Lelani's hands slowly fall to her sides. Silence hangs between us for a moment, before clearing my throat as I adjust myself. "Get on," I tell her, and she places her palm on my shoulder, then settles behind me.

"Austin?" Her silky voice dances across my skin.

"Yeah, babe."

"Thank you." I can hear the smile in her voice. "And, I would love to go on an adventure with you."

That's all I needed to hear. I fire the engine and set out toward my favorite place in Polson. The warm summer heat flows across my skin as we cruise down the road. Lelani has one hand resting on my hip, with a finger hooked through the loop on my jeans. I feel her slide forward a bit in her seat, bringing her body closer to mine. Dropping an arm, I reach back, wrapping my hand around her thin calf.

Relaxed.

Content.

Free.

Those are the words I would use to describe my state of mind at the moment. I haven't felt this untroubled by life in a long time. Not that I'm unhappy. I love what I have here in Montana, with my club, Pop, and my job—everything. Lelani's presence makes me feel more at ease with myself. It's hard to explain something you've never really felt before. Women have come and gone in my life, but Lelani is different. I know nothing about her, yet it feels as if I've known her all my life. It's a strange feeling of déjà vu being around her, a magnetic force drawing me in. I'm attracted to her scent, her voice, her body, and the passion and strength she has to make it on her own.

Lelani's touch leaves my side. Glancing in my bike's mirror, I catch the moment she throws her hands to the sky. The loose curls framing her face move with the wind as she closes her eyes, and the sunlight catches her face. The smile she wears causes my chest to tighten.

There's just something about her I can't shake, and I'm not sure if I want to. All I know is there's a fire inside me that burns for her.

A short time later, I'm pulling my bike off the main highway.

We travel a few more miles until we reach a narrow trail. Keeping to one side, I avoid driving on the rougher parts left behind by off-road vehicles. I bring the bike to a stop, just beneath a group of pine trees, and help Lelani off.

"Where are we?" she asks, taking in all the sounds and smells around her.

"Faith Falls," I take her by the hand and walk us closer to the waterfall. "One of my favorite places in Polson. I come here to think, be alone, and reflect. Here I can forget about life and shut the world out for a while. Nature has a way of recharging the soul, especially out here," I tell her. Coming to a stop, I guide her to sit on the smooth surface of a large rock several yards away from the pool of the waterfall. "Come here," I pull her closer. "Give me your feet."

"My feet?"

"Yeah, babe," I chuckle. Twisting a bit, she places them on my lap, and I remove her socks and shoes. "Scoot forward a little and put your feet into the water," I instruct her as I pull off my boots and roll up my pants legs.

"Austin," she wiggles. "Are we high—will I fall?" her toes hover above the surface, afraid to lower her feet further.

I lower mine, putting them into the cool water, making sure to splash at the surface for her to hear. "You won't fall. The water is right there. You only have to lower your feet a couple more inches." I reassure her, and she slowly lowers them until the tips of her toes come in contact with the surface.

"Oh my god. It's so cold." She gasps then submerges her feet entirely. She swings her legs, moving her feet in small circles. "Describe it to me?" she asks.

"First, I want you to take a deep breath," I say, and she does. "What do you smell?" I ask.

She breathes in deep. "The air smells fresh and crisp, like clean bed sheets." She pauses, then adds, "There's a hint of mustiness though, just behind all of that. Kind of like fresh-cut grass after it rains."

"The water your feet are soaking in is so clear you can see to the bottom. We're surrounded by tall pine and oak trees. There's green grass all around us," I describe it to her, and she smiles. "Now, listen, and tell me what you hear."

Lelani takes another deep breath in, then says, "I hear birds singing. The water falling sounds like heavy rain. It also reminds me of when I was young, and my mom would fill the bathtub full of water, then let me turn on the shower. Sometimes, I would slide beneath the water and hold my breath. The sound of the water hitting the surface was loud, like someone clapping their hands." She finishes, and I stare at her. Listening to how she experiences the world around her makes me a bit jealous because the little details she takes in are the ones most of us take for granted.

"The waterfall is twenty feet high and flows fast over the edge, plunging into the water below. It's cold because the current is constantly moving." I keep my eyes on her. "Can you feel the light mist against your skin?"

"Yes." She lifts her face toward the sky, and I can see the tiny water droplets on the surface of her skin as the sunlight filtering through the branches of the trees bounces off her face.

"Tell me more about yourselves. What kind of childhood did you have?" I ask, wanting to know more about her. Lelani's smile fades. "Only tell me what you are comfortable with sharing. No pressure. If you don't want to share anything, all you have to do is say so." I try putting her at ease.

Lelani chews her lower lip. "I had a happy childhood. I never wanted for anything. Spending time with my parents was always enough for me." Her smile returns. "They were everything to me, but I guess that's the way it is when you're young," she states, and I don't dare disagree. She's giving me a piece of herself, and the last thing she needs is my tragic past casting an unwanted shadow. She sighs. "Maybe they would still be here, and I would still have my sight if I wouldn't have begged them to take me to see the Hoover Dam. I mean, we lived in Vegas, and I'd never seen it before." Lelani splashes the water with her feet. "We had just eaten lunch and were back on the road. I was sitting in the back seat of the car reading a Harry Potter book. The next thing I remembered was tires squealing, mom screaming, and feeling weightless." Lelani stops talking. I take her hand in mine and interlace our fingers. "My parents died that day, and I was plunged into a world of darkness." Tears flow down her cheeks, and I reach over, wiping them away.

"But you lived," I remind her, knowing all too well how she feels when it comes to the pain of losing a parent.

"It doesn't feel like it. I feel lost." She sniffles. "Doesn't help when I've been told for years I'm to blame for their deaths."

"Who blames you?" My blood starts to boil.

"My brother, mostly. He made it a point to never let me forget our parents would still be alive if I never would have asked to go on that stupid trip." She shrugs. "Maybe he's right." The anguish in her voice guts me.

I take her face in my hands. "Fuck your brother. Remember, he is the reason you fell victim to skin traders. He's not a good person, Lelani. Don't you dare take anything that piece of shit has ever said to heart. Don't give him that kind of power over you." I want so badly to kiss her trembling lips. Instead, I stand and pull her up with me.

"Come on," I tug on her, and she allows me to lead her through the soft grass. "It's a little slippery," I state as we start climbing the slope leading up to the cliff most people use to jump from.

"Austin, wait. Where are we going now?" she asks.

"We're almost there." I turn to help her navigate over some rocks.

"We sound so close to the waterfall," Lelani shouts after I stop.

"Do you trust me?" I look at her.

"I do," she says, looking a little panicked.

"Jump with me," I say flat out, and her eyes widen, and her head shakes.

"Austin, no. I can't." She pulls on my hand.

"Take a leap of faith with me, Mouse. Wash the past and the pain away, even if it's only for today." I pull her closer, my face inches from hers.

"I'm scared," she whispers. "My heart feels like it's about to explode from my chest."

I take her hand and place her palm over my heart. "You feel that?" I ask, and she nods. "You have that effect on me. You, Lelani." I ask her one more time, "Do you trust me?"

"Promise you won't let go?"

"I'll never let go," I say with conviction, and face us forward. Lelani's hand tightens around mine. "Ready? On the count of three," I tell her and watch her lips lift into a smile.

"Oh. My. God. I can't believe I'm jumping off a waterfall!" she screams with nervous excitement.

"One." I keep my eyes on Lelani's face, watching her smile. "Two." She takes a deep breath. "Three." With her hand in mine, our feet leave the rocky platform.

5

LELANI

I spent one of the most memorable days of my life with Austin yesterday. He took me on a ride up the mountain to a place called Faith Falls. Riding on the back of his bike is an exhilarating experience; one I will never get tired of. And nothing in this world will ever compare to the moment he dared me to take a leap of faith and jump from the top of the waterfall with him. For the first time in a long time, I felt free and safe. "Where are we?" I ask when Austin opens the passenger door of his truck. I've been so lost in memories of yesterday, that I didn't realize we had stopped.

"Grace's bakery, The Cookie Jar. Grace would chew my ass out if she found out I brought you into town and didn't bring you."

"Grace owns a bakery. That's so cool." I go to slide down from the truck only to have Austin put his large hands around my waist and hoist me out, causing a squeak to slip past my lips. "Austin, what are you doing?" I ask, gripping his shoulders.

"Helpin' you down?" he answers gruffly as he places me on my feet.

"I see that, but I could have done it myself."

"I know," he says, not offering any more. Letting me go, he then

59

SANDY ALVAREZ & CRYSTAL DANIELS

opens and closes the truck's back door, and a moment later, King is at my side, nudging at my hand. Reaching down, I rub the top of his head. Ever since Austin introduced me to his dog, he has been a constant shadow of mine. I find his presence comforting. I'm not sure why he has taken a liking to me, considering I've been told he is a bit standoff-ish around everyone except Austin and Lisa, because she feeds him bacon.

The bell over the bakery door alerts Grace to our arrival, and the smell of vanilla assaults my senses.

"Hey, you two," Grace greets us, her cheerful voice making me smile.

"How's it goin', Grace?" Austin grunts.

"Hi." I give a small wave.

"You guys came by just in time. I just pulled some fresh cinnamon buns from the oven. Why don't you have a seat and I'll bring you some. Austin, do you want your usual coffee?"

"That would be good, Grace. Thanks."

"No problem. What about you, Lelani. Would you like a coffee?"

"I'd love one, thanks, Grace."

"You're welcome. I'll be back in a minute."

When Austin and I take our seat at a table, King maneuvers his big body underneath the table and rests his head on one of my feet.

"Here we are." Grace returns to our table, and my stomach rumbles at the smell of sweet cinnamon and strong brewed coffee.

"Thank you. It smells wonderful, Grace." I bring the warm cinnamon bun to my lips and take a generous bite. "Tastes even better than it smells," I say around a mouthful.

Grace laughs. "I'm glad you think so."

The bell over the door chimes again, followed by the sound of two women giggling.

"Well, duty calls. You guys enjoy." Grace excuses herself to tend to her latest customers. A few minutes later, I'm polishing off what's left of my delectable treat when Austin hisses under his breath. "Shit."

Just as I'm about to ask what's wrong, a woman's voice rings out. "Hey, Austin."

I don't miss the sweet surgery way she says his name, and it causes burning in my belly.

"Melissa," Austin grumps, and I hear him take a sip of his coffee.

"I haven't seen you in a while."

"That's because I don't want to be seen." Austin's words are laced with irritation. Obviously, this Melissa woman hasn't caught on because she continues.

"I was going to hang out at Charley's later tonight with some friends. Maybe you can come by and have a drink with me. Then we can go back to my place like last time."

The good mood I had moments ago vanishes, and I suddenly feel the need to flee. I don't want to sit here and listen to this woman inviting Austin back to her house to have sex. I focus on her words *like last time* and grow more irritated. "Excuse me. I'm going to give you two some privacy."

"That would be great, thanks, hun," Melissa's comment drips with fake sincerity. Austin stops me when I go to stand.

"I better not see your ass move one inch from that seat," he warns, his tone lethal. "As for you, Melissa," Austin spits her name like it's left a bad taste in his mouth. "That was a careless move on your part thinkin' you could come over here and interrupt my time with my girl and start spewin' your bullshit."

"Your girl?" Melissa sneers.

"That's what I said. Now, it would be in your best interest for you and your friend to turn around and walk away."

The atmosphere around us falls deathly silent as I wait to see what will happen next. Luckily, Melissa chooses wisely and leaves, her heels clicking against the tile floor.

I'm still glued to my chair, speechless well after Melissa has fled. It's not the harsh words Austin spoke to the woman that renders me without words or action. In my opinion, the woman deserved what she got. No, what has me reeling is the fact that he called me his girl. What did he mean by that? Is it biker lingo or something?

"I can see the wheels in your head turnin' a mile a minute, Mouse." The sound of Austin's voice startles me, and I'm forced to abandon my wandering thoughts. "I'm sorry if Melissa upset you. What she and I had was never serious, and it's in the past."

"Oh, um...okay. It's not really any of my business, though. You know...um...who you see or erm...hookup with," I say, fumbling over my words as they leave a sour taste in my mouth.

Austin chuckles. "I like when you get all flustered."

"I'm not flustered," I huff, crossing my arms.

"Yeah, ya are. It's fuckin' adorable. I like that I make you nervous."

"I'm not nervous. I'm annoyed." The lie rolls off my lips effortlessly.

Austin doesn't say anymore, but I can hear the smile in his voice when he speaks again. "I'm going to hit the head before we go." The chair he's sitting in scrapes across the floor when he stands. The next thing I know, his lips are at my ear. "You should work on your poker face. You're shit at lying, Mouse."

I shiver at his words, and before I can come back with a retort, he's already walking away.

"Word of advice," Grace calls out from across the bakery. "Don't fight it. These men are persistent and always get their way in the end."

Later that day Austin and I are standing at the boutique's sales counter. I've spent the last couple of hours in a daze as Grace's words roll around in my head while the sales lady is ringing up my purchase. My style is pretty simple. I live in jeans and t-shirts. I also like the occasional skirt as long as they are not too short. I tried to tell Austin he didn't have to drag me all over town today. Heck, Bella offered to help, but Austin didn't bat an eye at refusing her offer. He mentioned it's no big deal, that he used to take his little sister shopping all the time when they were younger. I tried asking him more about his sibling, but he didn't say much, aside from her name and age, then informing me she is attending school in Texas. I wanted to ask him about his family but decided against it when he quickly changed the subject. I took the hint and let the conversation die. Besides, I know all too well what it's like not wanting people to pry.

"Your total comes to five hundred twenty-two dollars and seventy-nine cents," the lady behind the county recites.

"What?!" I screech.

"Here," Austin says, ignoring my outburst.

Reaching out, I stop his hand just as he is handing the woman his credit card. "That can't be right. Austin that is too much." I turn toward the woman behind the counter. "I'd like to put some of it back, please."

"No," Austin grunts.

"Austin," I protest.

"No."

"But..."

"Lelani," Austin says in that tone that lets me know he's not about to argue.

"Fine. I will pay you back."

"You don't owe me shit."

Clamping my mouth shut, I turn away from Austin. "Come on, King. Let's go wait outside." I give King's leash a slight tug, and, being the smart dog he is, he helps guide me out of the boutique. As soon as I step out onto the sidewalk, I take a deep breath and try to release my frustration. When Austin emerges from the store a few minutes later, he doesn't say a word. On command, King follows behind him, leading me to the truck. Once I'm settled into the cab, Austin leans in. When he goes to buckle my seatbelt, I attempt to push his hands away. "I'm not a child. I can do it myself," I lash out, letting my irritation be known. Austin ignores my behavior and continues the task. He keeps quiet even as he climbs in behind the wheel. As the minutes tick by, I begin to feel more and more like a brat.

"I'm sorry for snapping at you back there. You've been nothing but generous, and I was acting ungrateful," I admit, my voice barely above a whisper. "I have spent my whole life depending on others. I guess I'm just sick of being someone's burden."

The moment I utter the last word, I feel the truck come to an abrupt stop. My seatbelt is unfastened, and I suddenly find myself in Austin's lap. "Austin," I gasp.

Trapping my face between the palms of his hands, Austin demands my full attention. "This is the last time I'm going to repeat myself. You are not a burden. A good man would never think takin' care of his woman as a burden. A man takes care of his woman because he wants to because it gives him purpose," Austin finishes, leaving me speechless.

Once I can collect myself enough to string a sentence together, I ask, "Your woman? Are you calling me your woman, Austin?"

"Now she's starting to get it," he murmurs, tucking a strand of hair behind my ear. *Getting what? Why do men have to be so confusing?* For a split second, I think he's going to kiss me when he runs the pad of his thumb over my bottom lip. Instead, he bypasses my mouth, and his lips land on the tip of my nose. "Come on. We're late. I told Prez we'd be at the garage ten minutes ago." Austin helps me settle back into my seat. I don't want to show my disappointment, so I just smile and nod.

· · ·

"Austin, Lelani! What are you guys doing here? Austin, I thought you had the day off?" Bella calls out when we walk into the garage.

"I do. Prez asked me to bring Lelani by. Is he in the back?"

"You'll find him in his office."

Keeping in step with Austin and with King at my side, we make our way toward what I presume is Jake's office.

"Prez." Austin knocks on a door.

"How's it goin', brother. You two come in and take a load off."

Austin takes my hand and guides me to a chair. Once I'm seated, King lies at my feet.

"Good boy," Austin praises his dog in a low tone.

"I'm still in fuckin' shock at how well that dog has taken to your girl," Jake remarks. "I guess the sayin' is true. That dogs choose their people and not the other way around."

"I've never had a pet before. It's nice having King around. Animals have a way of making you feel less alone." I smile. And as if King knows I'm talking about him, he sits up and nudges my hand with his nose. Leaning forward, I give him a rub down his back and kiss the top of his head. "Such a good boy, aren't you?"

Jake chuckles then continues, "I asked Austin to bring you in to discuss the job offer I mentioned the other day."

"Oh, yes. I remember. I'm very anxious to start. Although I'm not sure what I could do to help out in a garage. I promise I'm willing to try anything and work hard."

"I know you will, sweetheart. After talkin' with Bella and Reid, I think we have come up with a solution to help not only you but Bella and the garage."

I nod. "Okay."

"Well, ever since Sara up and quit a few months ago, Bella has been back here full time. If we bring you on, it will take some of the load off Bella, and she can go back to part-time like before. She's missing being home more with the kids."

"How is Lelani going to do Bella's job, Prez?" Austin asks.

"Bella's job is to take inventory, place orders, and schedule appointments. All those things are done on the computer."

"Actually," I cut in. "There are computers specifically designed for the visually impaired. There are also Braille keyboards."

"Really?" Austin sounds intrigued.

"She's right," Jake adds. "And fuck if I didn't know that shit either, until this morning."

"Believe it or not, I can do just about everything a person with sight can," I laugh.

"Fuck, Lelani. I didn't mean it like that," Austin says regretfully.

I wave my hand and smile. "I know you didn't. Unless someone is around a visually impaired person a lot in their life, I don't expect them to know all there is about our world. Though it is nice when people take an interest and want to include us. Most people assume I can't work a regular job. I appreciate Jake looking into how to help."

"I can't take all the credit. It was mostly Reid. He's going to come in tomorrow with a computer system designed specifically for Lelani. It'll be voice-activated and have all the features she will need. If you are interested, you can come in at the end of the week. Reid will show both you and Bella how to use the new system, then Bella will show all of you the ins and outs of what your job will consist of. How does that sound?"

"It sounds perfect! Thank you. I promise to pay you back for the computer. I know something like that wasn't cheap."

"There will be no paying me back. That's not how we do things around here," Jake says. "We're family. We take care of our own."

Jake's word hit straight to my core. I haven't felt like I was a part of a family or had people who care about me the way the Kings do in a long time. It feels good.

6

AUSTIN

"Ready?" I find Lelani waiting downstairs in the common room, sitting on the sofa, with King laying at her feet. She stands and wipes her hands nervously down the front of her jeans.

"Is what I'm wearing okay?" she asks, and I take in her attire. Lelani is wearing black boots, ripped jeans, and a Kings Custom tank. I smile because she kept her hair down, the red curls spilling down her back. I notice the soft pink lipstick she's wearing.

"You're perfect," I tell her, and she smiles.

Taking her hand, we walk outside, and I open the truck door. "We're not taking the bike?" she asks as I help her into the cab.

"You like riding on the back of my bike, babe?"

"It's not bad."

"I usually take the truck into work because King rides with and hangs at the shop all day," I explain, and her face lights up.

"Oh."

The truck isn't much to look at. It's an old 1978 Ford crew cab that belonged to my grandad. He mainly used it back when he raised cattle on the land he owns. This big heap of metal was the first vehicle I was given and called my own. I open the back door, turn, and slap my leg. "Come on, boy. Get in." I give King the command, and he jumps into the empty space where the backseat once was. I ripped it out a few months after rescuing King. With his size, taking it out made traveling with him easier. I close both doors, walk around, climb behind the wheel, and fire up the engine.

A ways down the road, we pass by the exit leading to my grandad's place. "I need to make a quick stop," I tell Lelani and turn right onto the long dirt road. King starts to bark the instant my grandad's ranch-style home comes into view. "Simmer down," I tell the dog.

"Is everything okay?" Lelani becomes alert.

I place my hand on her knee. "Yeah, babe. He's just excited to see my grandad is all." I stop and turn off the truck. "He had a pacemaker for his heart put in just before our New Orleans trip. I usually make it a point to check on him a few times a week, and this is the first opportunity I've had since being back home." King paces in the back, eager to get out.

"I'll just wait here," Lelani says and finds a loose thread on her ripped jeans to pick at.

Opening the door, I slide out. After freeing King, I walk around and open the passenger door. "Come inside. I'd like to introduce you to him."

"Really, I can wait here, Austin."

"Take my hand, Mouse," I order and wait for her to place her palm on mine.

With her and King at my side, we walk to the front door. "Pop!" I yell as we stroll inside.

"I'm back here!" my grandad calls out, and I head for the screened-in porch, just off of the kitchen. We find him sitting in an old recliner, with his feet up, sipping on a cup of coffee.

"Pop. You've got to stop leavin' the door unlocked."

"What for?"

"Anyone could waltz in here. You can't trust everyone."

"Son, I know who my neighbors are, and I've lived here long enough to know just about every man and woman in this town. Those that know me, also know to announce themselves. If they don't, I know to greet them with the barrel end of my shotgun." Pop lowers his feet, puts his coffee on the table beside him, then stands. He notices Lelani standing at my side. "Well, hello, young lady. Seems my grandson here has gone and lost his manners. My name is Warren," Pop greets her, and Lelani reaches out to find him. His face softens as she takes his weathered hand in hers, realizing she can't see him.

Lelani smiles. "It's very nice to meet you. I'm Lelani."

"It's a pleasure to meet you as well." Pop grins, then turns his attention to me. "Austin has never brought a young lady home. You must be special." Pop's comment causes Lelani to blush. "You got time to sit and have a cup of coffee, or is this a drive-by to make sure the old man is still kickin'?" Pop asks as he lets go of my woman's hand.

"Sorry, Pop, but we need to be at the shop soon. I open this morning and would like to show Lelani the ropes before the doors open. How are you feelin'?"

Pop nods, running his hand through his gray beard. "Hell, Son. I'm feeling just fine. The doctor says I can get back on Sarge this week. As a matter of fact, I'm glad you came by. Do you mind helping me unload the feed I picked up yesterday before you go?"

"Sure," I tell him. Pop leads the way as he swings open the screen door. Taking Lelani by the hand, I help her navigate down the narrow steps.

"What needs to be fed?" Lelani whispers as we stroll across the yard toward the stables. King keeps pace at my woman's side.

"Well, I'll be. Would you look at that; King doesn't take a liking to just anyone," Pop observes as we walk down the gravel road that leads to the stable.

"He hasn't wanted to leave Lelani's side since the moment she got to town," I mention.

"How long have you been in Polson, sweetheart?" Pop asks.

"Not long. I hitched a ride from New Orleans with the Kings," Lelani answers.

Pop looks at me and raises his brow but doesn't ask any questions. He knows how the club operates and knows if we traveled with an extra person back to Montana, it was with good reason.

"No better place to call home than Montana. This here is God's country, child. I've been to a lot of places throughout my life, and you can't beat the sunsets or sunrises here in Polson," Pop tells her.

"I wish I could see the beauty for myself." Lelani's face falls, her voice sounding somber.

We come to a stop at the tailgate of Pop's truck. "Sweetheart, you don't have to see the beauty to experience it." Pop touches her arm. "Come here." He looks at me, and I let go of her hand. Pop turns her body to face the sun. "What do you feel?" he asks her, and Lelani answers.

"Warmth."

"Exactly. And what would you associate warmth with?" he asks her, and Lelani takes a moment to answer.

"Love." Her lower lip trembles slights.

Pop nods. "Good answer. I'm going to tell you the same thing I told Austin not long after him and his sister came into my life. Focus on your advantages, darlin', not your disadvantages in life— it's all about perspective. Only then will you get a different outcome."

Lelani draws in a deep breath of air, closes her eyes, and tilts her face upward toward the sun again. She smiles. "Warren?"

"Yes," Pop looks pleased with himself, and he should be.

"Thank you," Lelani says.

"No thanks needed," Pop tells her, then faces me. "Now then, what do you say we get this load off the back of my truck and feed some horses."

An hour later, we are at the shop. "Hey," Bella greets us as we walk through the front door.

"Prez in?" I ask her.

"Not yet, but Logan and Reid are in the back unboxing the new equipment needed for Lelani."

"You guys are spending way too much money on me," Lelani says.

"Nonsense." Bella gestures with a wave of her hand. "We are going to make sure you have all the tools you need to work on your own as well as navigate through the building." Bella looks from Lelani to me. "You cool with me taking it from here?"

As much as I wanted to be the one to show Lelani around and familiarize her with the place, I need to finish the final touches on the custom Bobber a customer is picking up later today. "I'll come to get you at lunch," I say to Lelani before leaving her in Bella's hands.

I stroll into the garage and open the bay door, letting in the fresh air and sunlight. Walking toward the backside of the garage, I take inventory of the tools I left lying on top of my workspace before getting to work. The mechanics of the bike itself are already solid. I finished working on all of that before we left for Louisiana. I run my palm along the side of the gas tank. The customer wanted the entire body blacked out, including the frame. All that is left is to airbrush and hand paint the ghost flames and skull in a pearl white finish. I get to work setting out all my equipment and color. I'm good at what I do. Building bikes, hell, anything to do with mechanics comes naturally to me, but I love to express my passion for art through custom work like I'm doing now.

When I was younger, as far back as I can remember, art has been an outlet for me—a source of comfort. I find quiet in my time spent crafting any work I do. When I've finished a piece, whether on a bike or paper, I feel a deep sense of satisfaction. I hear my mom's voice telling me I have talent and that I'm going to make it big someday. My mom and my sister were the two people I could count on growing up to make me feel like I would amount to something—that I would do more with my life than I thought was possible. I wish I could say the same for my old man, but I can't. He hammered into my skull daily that I was nothing more than a delinquent screwed up kid and that I would never amount to anything. My old man wanted a son who played on the varsity football team—the jock. He wanted a son who followed in his footsteps. I wanted none of those things. I like working with my hands, art, tattoos, heavy metal, and piercings. I didn't want to be eclipsed by him or his fucked-up ways. I wanted to walk through life casting my own shadow, not his. He hated me for it and had no problems making his disappointment known.

Boots smacking against the concrete floor yank me back from my past. "How's it goin', brother?" Logan strolls in, and an old beat-up truck pulls into the bay, with Charley behind the wheel.

"About to get crunchin' on this paint job. How's Lelani fairin'?" I ask.

"She knows her way around assistive technology. Bella is at her side in case she needs anything," Logan says, filling me in on her progress.

The truck door squeaks as Charley opens it and climbs out. "I'm happy to see you, men, back in town. How was New Orleans?" Charley walks up and shakes Logan's hand.

"Eventful," Logan tells him. Charley knows the club, so he doesn't pry.

"Enough said. Listen, I just bought this lunker a few days ago.

Been waitin' on you to get back and take a look at her for me."
Charley turns around and lifts up the rusted hood.

"You just bought a brand-new truck a couple of months ago.
What happened to it?" I get in on their conversation.

"Nothin' happened to it. I bought this fixer-upper for Kinsley.
That shit car of hers finally gave out. As you know, she has a little
boy to support, and, well, I can't stand to see her struggle with
ways to get to work," Charley explains.

Kinsley is a young woman who has been working at Charley's
bar, waitressing for some time now. The most we know about her
is she's a single mom who busts her ass daily to take care of her
kid. For now, that's all the club needs to know. Charley, being the
good man he is, because he has a heart the size of Texas, helps the
young woman out.

"Shit," Logan clamps his hand on Charley's shoulder. "You're a
good man, Charley. If anyone ever says otherwise, I'll stick my size
twelve boot up their ass," Logan states, and Charley chuckles.
"Come on, let's take a look at her and see what we need to do to get
it runnin' better than it sounds."

While Logan works on the truck, I get started on the painting.
Reaching into my pocket, I take out my earbuds and place them in
my ears. Finding a playlist on my phone, I crank up the music. I'm
in the zone as *Wrong Side of Heaven* by Five Finger Death Punch
filters through the speakers. I find my stride after the first stroke of
paint goes onto the gas tank, and the outlines of the ghost flames
start to take shape.

A few hours later, the artwork is completed, and we are closing
up shop for the day. The bike owner called, explaining he's still
out of town and will be by the shop later in the week. I clean my
work area, then chug a bottle of cold water before making my way
to the front of the store to get my woman and take her home.

"How was your first day?" I ask Lelani after getting her and
King into the truck and climbing behind the wheel.

"Better than I hoped," she tells me, wearing a smile as I pull out of the parking lot. "I think Bella put braille labels on everything." She giggles, and I glance at her. It's the first time hearing a genuine laugh out of her, and I feel myself grinning over it. "Alba showed up to help. Everyone has really outdone themselves, trying to make life around me feel accessible. I really appreciate it," Lelani says, slumping back on the seat. "I'm exhausted."

I clear my throat. "I hope you're not too tired. The club is having a family cookout this evening. So, there will be kids runnin' about, lots of food, and music. I think Logan's dad will make an appearance too."

"It actually sounds great. I love hanging out with the women and their kids." She sighs. "I wish I had a family with a bond like the club seems to have." Lelani becomes quiet. King rises from the backseat and nudges her cheek with his nose. "Hey, King." She reaches to pet him.

The rest of the ride is spent in silence. I thought about asking Lelani tons of questions about her life back in Vegas, and further digging into her story but decided against it. Today has been good for her, and I don't care to be the one to fuck it up. Before long, we are pulling up to the clubhouse. "Will your grandad be here too?" Lelani asks as I help her out of the truck.

"No. Pop knows that he is always welcome, and he likes the club, but it's part of my life, not his," I tell her. Grabbing her hand in mine, we walk into the clubhouse.

"I like him," she admits.

"Who, Pop?"

She smiles again. "Yeah."

"I'll take you back for a visit soon." I stop at the foot of the stairs.

"I'd really like that," she tells me. There she goes biting that lip again. Raising my hand, I run the pad of my thumb across it to make her stop. "Umm, I think I will freshen up before the rest of your family arrives."

"I'll be in the back yard. If you need me, just let one of the girls know." Her breathing increases when I sweep the back of my knuckles across her cheek.

"Okay," she says but doesn't budge.

I grin. "Go on," I tell her, and Lelani turns to make her way up the stairs.

"Are you watching me walk away?" she asks but keeps moving up the staircase.

"Yep." I don't take my eyes off her until she enters the hallway and can no longer be seen.

MOST OF THE family have arrived. With the last of the tables set up outside, I pull my hair back, secure it with the elastic band around my wrist, and pluck a cold beer from the nearby cooler. I down almost half the drink, then take in a deep breath of air. I fucking love Montana. The sky is blue, and the sun is warm. A westerly wind blows, and with it carries the sweet smoky aromas from the food Reid and Quinn are cooking.

It's always a competition between the two of them. One always tries to out grill the other. This evening they have us judging who makes the best Kansas City style spareribs.

I scan the yard. It doesn't take but a second to search out Lelani. I find her sitting with the women gathered around the firepit. She's different today, happier. She seems to be less guarded than usual too.

Perhaps it has something to do with her dishonesty. We all know she's keeping something from us. Reid has been doing some digging but still has nothing to report except that there is no Lelani Davis. She provided us with a false identity—lied to the club. For now, the only thing keeping Lelani from being put on the

75

hot seat is Jake giving her the benefit of the doubt due to the trauma she experienced days ago. Knowing she's lying puts the entire club on guard. I've known about all of this since the second day of our road trip back to Montana. After a brief talk with my brothers, Jake felt it was best not to confront her on anything just yet.

Her laughter pulls me from my thoughts, and I watch her get down on the ground and play with one of the kids.

Blake walks up to me. "She fits in pretty well," he says, and I nod while drinking my beer.

Quinn stops, and I feel him eyeing me before following my line of sight. "Man, I've seen that look before. You've got it bad."

"I hardly know her." I try to brush off their unwanted prying. I know they see past my bullshit.

"Did any of us know our women for long before stakin' our claim? I sure as shit know I marked my property before lockin' her down." Quinn puffs out his chest.

It's not long before all my brothers are gathered in one spot, having a beer together. Lucky for me, the conversation of my attraction for Lelani dies.

The back door behind us opens, and out walks Glory, Grace's best friend and Demetri's woman. In her hands, she's carrying cocktail mix and tequila. "Hey, bitches. I brought margaritas!" The women hoot and holler as Glory makes her way across the yard to the firepit.

"She always has to make an entrance," Demetri says, not too far behind her. Logan hands his dad a beer and, after a beat, us men decide to join the women.

"Where's Nikolai and Leah?" Logan asks as we stroll across the lawn.

"They just landed and will be here soon," Demetri informs Logan. "Now, where are my grandchildren?" He looks over at the women and children. His body language changes drastically, and his face hardens. "Lelani Mancini." He takes a step in her direction.

Lelani stops laughing and having a good time at the sound of her name. Her body stiffens, and her smile disappears.

Instinctively, I take a step forward, blocking his line of sight. "What the fuck?" I stand between him and my woman, guarded.

"Austin, stand down," Jake barks, but I hold my ground.

Demetri eyes me, unflinching by my actions. "That woman is Lelani Mancini, the niece of Arturo Mancini—Italian American Mafia."

Quinn speaks, "Oh shit."

7

LELANI

My racing heart feels like it's about to beat out of my chest, and Bella's reassuring words do nothing to calm my nerves. "Everything is going to be alright, Lelani." She gives my hand a squeeze. Moments ago, a man showed up and turned my world upside down, and once again, the universe has proven I'm not safe no matter where I go.

"Somehow, I don't think so. I recognized that man's voice."

"Who?" she asks. "Demetri?"

I nod and swallow past the lump in my throat. "Yes. He's a Volkov." Just saying his name out loud sends a chill down my spine. I will never forget the conversation I overheard between Demetri Volkov and my uncle four years ago. The Volkov's threat was toward my uncle, but even I felt the dangerous energy that surrounded him that day. I also know the Mancinis and the Volkovs are enemies. The question is, why is he here?

"You don't have to be afraid of Demetri," Bella tries to reassure me once again, reading the fear that must be written all over my face. "Demetri and Nikolai are part of our family."

"What?!" I shout as I stand and take a step away from Bella.

These people are not only associated with the Russian mafia, but they are family.

"Lelani," Bella says in a calm tone. I hear footsteps shuffle closer to me. "Demetri is family. He's not here to hurt you."

"I don't believe you." I step back until my foot catches on the edge of a chair, causing me to stumble.

"Lelani! Watch out!" Alba calls out, but it's too late. Losing my balance, I trip and fall to the ground. Ignoring the pain in my hip and embarrassment, I stand. "I need to leave."

"Sweetheart," Lisa is the next to speak. "You should try and calm down."

"No! I will not calm down. I want to leave. I don't want any trouble." With tears streaming down my face, I begin to panic.

"Nobody's in trouble. I promise," Bella tries again to calm me down.

I shake my head frantically back and forth. "I won't go back." Turning away from Bella, I run. I don't know what direction I'm headed; I just know I have to get out of here. I can't let them send me back to my uncle. My attempts to run away are short-lived because I don't make it far before a set of muscular arms wrap around me from behind. I immediately know it's Austin. "Let me go!" I kick and flail against his hold.

"No," Austin grinds out.

"Yes. I want to leave."

"You're not leavin'."

Tightening his hold on me, Austin lifts me off the ground. I feel him moving forward until he has me pinned against a brick wall, my front against the wall, and his large frame caging me in. He then sets me down and angles my body to face him.

"Austin, please let me go," I plead once again. "I don't want to stay here."

Using the pad of his thumb, Austin brushes away the tears that are steadily falling down my cheeks. "You're not goin' any fuckin' where Mouse."

The way my nickname slips past his lips is my undoing, and I lose the will to fight against his hold, and I slump forward into his waiting arms. Without hesitation, Austin wraps me in his embrace. "I got you, babe."

"Please don't send me back," I sob into the crook of his neck.

"I already told you, you're not goin' anywhere."

Off in the distance, I hear sniffling coming from some of the women. "Is she okay, Austin?" Mila asks.

"She will be," he answers, then turns his attention back to me. "Prez wants to talk with you."

I stiffen in his arms, and he quickly adds, "Nothing bad is going to happen. He only wants to talk."

"Austin," my voice shakes. "I..."

He cuts me off. "You have my word, babe. You are safe here. Nobody is going to hurt you or send you away."

Hearing the sincerity in his voice, I give him a small nod. Knowing there are several sets of eyes on me and feeling embarrassed at my current meltdown, I put my head down as Austin leads me through the clubhouse.

"Head up, Mouse," Austin orders without breaking his stride.

I know the moment we enter the room where all the club members and Demetri are because the air tension is so thick it's suffocating. So much so, I tighten my hold on Austin's hand and try not to panic.

"Take a seat," Jake orders, followed by the sound of him lighting a cigarette. After Austin and I sit, there is a long pause before Jake speaks again. "Is your name Lelani Mancini?"

"Yes," I answer, my voice small.

"Is your uncle Arturo Mancini?"

"Yes."

"Are you the daughter of Massimo and Nalani Mancini?"

I nod. "Yes."

"Fuck," a man across from me curses under his breath.

"I'm a little lost, Prez. What exactly does all of this shit mean?" Quinn asks.

Demetri Volkov is the one to answer, and I realize he is sitting right beside me. "It means all of you are about to have a war brought directly to your front door should her uncle find where she is."

"Well, shit," Quinn huffs.

"When you said your brother was the one who handed you over to the skin trade, was that true?" Jake continues to grill me.

"Yes. Derrick is my brother. His friend Bobby helped him hand me over to those men."

"When Arturo gets wind of what his nephew has done, he will cease to exist," Demetri adds.

"If that's the case, then why not go back to your uncle and tell him what happened? If he is willing to kill his nephew to keep you safe, why run?"

"My uncle doesn't want to keep me safe because he loves me. It's because of who I am and what I am to the family."

"I'm not following," Sam remarks.

All the men wait for me to answer, but I'm unable to form the words. If I say any more, it will make my worst fears a reality. I was so stupid to believe I could start over, that I could escape what I was born into and have a life of freedom.

"Babe, you need to tell us," Austin urges.

Ripping my hand from Austin's, I stand abruptly, making the chair crash to the floor. "I never meant to cause trouble. Please," I plead for the hundredth time. "I can just leave. I'll do anything." I turn to where I know Demetri is seated. "I know who you are. I remember your voice. I'm not who my family is. I'm not them," I choke on a sob.

The sound of a chair scraping against the floor, followed by footsteps heading in my direction, has me holding my breath as I try to back away. Austin is at my side the same moment Demetri's presence fills my space. The room falls silent, and I feel as though there is a quiet conversation happening between Demetri and Austin.

A moment later, Demetri speaks, "I see my presence has caused you alarm. Let me be clear on something, Lelani. I wish you no harm. I speak on behalf of myself and my son, Nikolai, when I say you have no reason to fear us."

"Sweetheart," Jake addresses me. "When I offered you my help back in New Orleans, I meant what I said. I'm a man of my word. But my men and I cannot help you if we don't know what we are up against. I didn't bring you in here to scare you. I brought you in here for the truth. Now, I can get the truth from Demetri because I gather he knows what kind of shit-storm my club is up against by havin' you here, but I'd prefer to hear the truth from you."

I let Jake and Demetri's words roll around in my head, and though I'm uncertain about my future, my gut tells me to trust the club. So, gathering all the courage I can muster, I put my faith in these men. I have nothing to lose. "When I was thirteen, my parents, Massimo and Nalani Mancini, died in a car accident. The same accident that took my eyesight. After the accident, I went to live with my uncle. Uncle Arturo is the head of the Mancini family now. A couple of months ago, I went to my brother and asked for his help. I wanted to get away from my life. A life that was being forced upon me."

"What do you mean forced on you?" Austin asks.

"My uncle wants to form an allegiance with the De Burcas."

"The fuck," Jake's voice echoes off the walls. "The De Burcas are dead," he states, and I feel the energy in the room shift.

"Cillian De Burca is the man I met. He and my uncle want to merge the two families, only there is one condition..."

"Mierda," Gabriel grinds out, knowing what I'm about to say next, followed by Austin's apparent mood change.

"Don't fuckin' say it."

Wrapping my arms around my middle, I say the words anyway. "I'm to marry Cillian De Burca. We were officially engaged three weeks before I asked my brother to help me escape. The day the wedding invitations were sent out was the day I left." The room erupts with cursing and chairs scraping across the floor. I sit unmoving, feeling like a caged animal, but push through the fear gripping my inside and continue to tell them my story. "I've met Cillian once." I pause a moment as the room settles and the men quiet. "I don't want that kind of life." I turn, reaching for Austin. The energy I feel radiating off his body can only be described as murderous. "If you send me back, I will be forced to marry him. I'd rather die than live in a gilded cage." I fist the front of Austin's shirt and feel his body shaking at my confession.

"Lelani, you speak nothin' of this to no one. The name De Burca stays in this room. Do you understand?" Jake's voice is sharp enough to shatter glass.

I take a deep breath, feeling small under all the pressure. "I understand."

"Prez," Austin growls, and the room has gone so quiet you could hear a pin drop.

Finally, Jake speaks. "You claimin' her, son?"

"She's fuckin' mine," Austin declares just before his mouth crashes down on mine.

8

AUSTIN

I kissed her.

I claimed Lelani in front of my brothers. I needed them to know, without doubt, she is mine, no matter what the cost.

"Goddamn. Now that's how you do it," Quinn boasts.

"Now that we have our answer let's get down to business. Austin, take Lelani back to the other women. We've got further business to discuss," Jake orders.

My hand never letting go of hers, I escort Lelani out of the room. The old ladies have their kids occupied with an animated children's movie and snacks at the common room's far side. Sofia is the first to lay eyes on us as we make our way over.

"Are you okay?" Sofia asks Lelani.

"Could you maybe ask me that after I find time to breathe and process everything?" Lelani's voice shakes with emotion. I palm her cheek and look down on her red-rimmed eyes and splotchy tear-stained cheeks.

"I'll come to get you soon," I tell her, then go to pull away, but Lelani doesn't let go of my other hand. It pulls at my chest, and I regret having to leave her side. I feel several sets of eyes on me as I lean in, kissing my woman for a second time. "Everything will be okay. I promise. I need you to believe in me—in the club," I say, doing my best to reassure her fears, and Lelani nods.

"Words, Mouse."

Lelani closes her eyes and takes a deep breath. "I believe in you, Austin," she tells me. Only then does her hand release mine, and I walk away.

Back in church, the men have waited for my return before beginning. I take my seat at the table. "What's the plan?" I ask.

"Demetri, what can you tell us about the Mancini family?" Jake inquires.

Demetri leans back in his chair while nursing a glass of whiskey. "The Mancini are one of the largest syndicate families in the Las Vegas area. The Italian American mafia. Their roots run deep in the world of organized crime. Before Lelani's father died, Massimo Mancini ran one of the largest drug industries in North America. He also had his hands in extortion, corruption of public officials, and gambling. He was a force to reckon with, ruthless in his own right. His hands were stained with blood like most of us. You didn't piss off the Mancini family."

Curious, I ask, "How'd you come to know the Mancini family?"

"Keep your friends close but your enemies closer," Demetri states. "I've always operated under the rule of, you respect me, I respect you. At one point, both our families had more than one American investment in common, so we crossed paths on several occasions. Even had dinner at his house once. Despite his ruthless side, Massimo adored his wife and his children. The way he treated them was one of the reasons I respected him." Demetri places his drink on the table then reaches for the cigar burning in front of him, resting across the top of an ashtray. "Unfortunately, respect and the mutual understanding amongst us died with him years ago. Once his brother took over, the family got into bed with many gangs and even had dealings with the now annihilated MC, Los Demonios." The mere mention of that club's name makes my blood boil. Looking around the table, I can tell by the scowls on their faces that my brothers share the same invoked emotion.

Logan reaches for his beer sitting at the table. "Did Mancini start doin' business with human traffickers?" he asks, and his father nods. Logan continues, "And what about De Burca. You know anything about their connection to the Mancini?"

"No."

"We need to approach this situation knowing both families will come lookin' for her," Jake states.

"Mancini prefers to keep his hands clean. If he goes looking for his niece, it will only be to save his own hide. As for De Burca, if he's anything like the rest of his family, he won't let this go," Demetri states. "Speaking from personal experience, arranged marriages, though not talked about outside the two respective families, are practiced more than society realizes. Their sole purpose within the Mafia world is to merge two empires." Demetri pauses, and we all let his words sink in. I know all about Demetri, not just from the club doing business with him, but parts of his life story mimic what Lelani is running away from. He met Logan's mom before his father sealed his fate with an arranged marriage. It was done to merge the Volkov empire with another. That marriage was one of obligation, not love, and he went through with it because it was expected of him to do so. That marriage came with a high cost, including years lost not knowing he had another son.

I won't let my woman suffer the same fate.

A cold shiver shoots through me, gripping my spine as if the devil himself reached out and grabbed it. There is no way in hell I'll allow someone to take my woman from me. Not now—not ever. I feel my anger rising, a fire in my gut burning out of control.

"The club and our entire family will have a target on their

backs once both families find out where Lelani ran to," Logan says, his voice heavy with concern, and rightfully so.

"Arturo is a loose cannon, and has been since he took power. He'll do whatever it takes to maintain the control he holds, and at any cost. The Mancini family will come for her. If De Burca doesn't find her first," Demetri adds.

"You willin' to start a war for this woman?" Gabriel, who is usually quiet, eyes me.

Something dark moves through me as I rerun the load of information dumped in this room this evening. Lelani lost her parents and sight in a horrific crash. She was being groomed to one day marry a man she doesn't know or love. The same family who caused Grace to run and hide for two years is also after her. When she was the most vulnerable and needed someone on her side, Lelani's own brother betrayed her trust and sold her like cattle.

A rage like no other I have felt seeps deep into my bones. I don't run from it. I welcome the feeling like a warm blanket. "I'll spill blood for Lelani. No cost is too high—not even my life if that's what it takes. Arturo and De Burca will have to pry her from my cold dead hands," I confess, and Gabriel's devilish smirk shows his approval.

"And the club stands behind you," Jake confirms, then turns to Reid. "I want to know every piece of intel you can get your hands on. Names, locations. Find out what rock this new De Burca roach crawled out from under. I want to know why his existence was kept secret and what other allies he may have. And use all your resources and connections to run down Lelani's brother." He then looks around the room. "We're about to stir up a shit storm like no other. It's not one but two organizations we are dealing with here." Jake blows out a breath while running his palm over his beard. "Demetri, are you willing to stay for a spell? I need to pick that brain of yours some more. Also, are you willin' to use your long reach within the channels of organized crime to gather more information on the men we are dealin' with here?"

Demetri nods. "I'm at your disposal."

Jake reaches across the table, offering his hand to Demetri, who accepts. "Thanks, brother."

"We are family. The Volkovs stand behind the club."

With nothing more to go over, Jake slams the gavel, ending church. Before walking out of the room, he stops me. "Austin."

Turning around, I eye my president. "Prez."

"Keep your eyes on her at all times. I have a feelin' if Lelani gets the chance, she'll bolt."

I sigh. "She wouldn't get far," I tell him.

He eyes me. "Don't underestimate Lelani because of her handicap, son. I recognize the same fight or flight spirit in Lelani as my Grace once had, and right now, your woman is teeterin' on the edge of fear. Her inability to see has nothin' to do with her will to survive. She'll bolt, risking everything if she feels for one second the club will betray her the same way her brother did. All rationality goes out the window when fear takes complete control of someone's actions."

I stare at Jake for a beat, letting his words sink in. I'd like to think everything he said is untrue, but it holds more weight than I care to admit. I've only known Lelani for a few weeks. If she for one second believes her life is less valuable to us or her presence will pose a risk to others, she'll find a way to run. I search for words to say in return, but there are none. Instead, I give him a tight nod of understanding before walking out of church, closing the door behind me, leaving him and Demetri to talk.

Glancing around the commons, I spot Lelani seated between Bella and Grace. The expression on her face tells me all I need to know—she's feeling defeated. Striding across the room, I come to stand in front of her. "Mouse," I hold my hand out for my woman to search for, and she doesn't hesitate in seeking me out.

"Austin," her voice trembles.

"It's okay, babe. Trust me." I pull her up, then place my finger beneath her chin, tilting her head back to see her beautiful face.

"I trust you, Austin." Her eyes are reddened from tears, and her lips swollen for the same reason. In front of the other women, I kiss Lelani. I press my lips against hers, tasting the saltiness of her tears that still linger on her skin. She's mine, and I need everyone to know it. Lelani melts into me, her hand gripping my forearm as my palm slides down her lower back before grabbing a handful of ass, giving it a firm squeeze. She moans into my mouth, and I deepen the kiss.

A throat clears, and my lips lose connection with Lelani's, leaving her flushed and breathless.

"That was hot," Glory breaks the silence in the room.

"Hell, yeah, it was," Quinn says from the chair he's dragging across the floor at the nearby table. "Fuck, don't stop now." He pats his thigh. "Emerson bring that pretty ass over here and sit on my lap," he says to his woman, who rolls her eyes but glides across the room anyway. She lowers herself to his lap. Quinn takes a sip of the beer in his hand. "Cupid done shot another brother in the ass. That makes you part of the lucky fucker club. Where we worship our women, spoil their asses, and sometimes let them believe they are in charge. All in the name of love," Quinn states and Emerson shakes her head.

"You're delusional," Emerson laughs, and my woman smiles at the lighthearted banter between the two.

"Don't let her sass fool ya," Quinn directs his words at Lelani and me. "She loves me." Quinn grins.

"Let's go for a ride." I guide Lelani to the front door, with King close to her side. "Let Prez know I'm out and that Lelani is with me," I announce before stepping through the front door. The sun is almost down, and the sky has faded from a deep purple to midnight blue. I lead us to the truck, open the door, and help my woman inside the cab.

"Where are we going?" Lelani asks.

"To the lake," I tell her. Closing her door, I open the back, and King jumps in.

Behind the wheel, I fire up the engine and pull away from the clubhouse.

Reaching across the seat, I take hold of Lelani's hand as we cruise down the road, with the windows down.

It's not long before we reach our destination. I back the tail end of the truck along the water's edge and throw it in park. My boots crunch against the rocky bankside as I walk around and open my woman's door. She takes a deep breath. "The air is so crisp out here." After letting King out, I pull a blanket from beneath the seat then walk toward the truck's end. I've parked so close to the lake that small waves of water almost touch my boots, and I have to lift Lelani onto the tailgate after spreading the blanket out to avoid her feet getting wet.

I sit beside her and watch King sniff around the perimeter of the truck before he jumps into the back with us. I stare out at the surface of the water, letting the silence hang between us for a beat.

"I needed this—the quiet. Thank you." Lelani swings her legs. "I'm sorry I've caused so much trouble."

I run my fingers through my beard. "We suspected you were lying to us about your true identity," I admit.

"You did?"

"Yeah, babe. But we sure as shit wasn't expectin' you to be a mafia princess."

Lelani scoffs. "I'm far from royalty, Austin." She goes silent again, and I glance at her. Lelani picks at the rip in her jeans, pulling loose threads out. "My father was a great man. I know who he was and accept that he did some bad things, but he was kind too. I never walked through life while he was alive, not knowing I was loved." Lelani smiles. "Family was everything to him."

I don't know what comes over me, but I began sharing parts of my life story without thought. "I grew up in the suburbs of Los Angeles. My life was about as cookie-cutter as you could get. Nice home. Two car garage. Kid sister. My parents were still together. Women admired my mom for her volunteer work in the community, and men respected my dad for his position and power."

Lelani sighs. "Sounds perfect."

My head shakes. "Far from it, babe. It was all a façade, a veil of lies. Behind all that perfect hid the truth. My father despised me."

'Why?" she asks,

"Because I wasn't him." My woman threads her fingers together with mine, and I feel her support, so I continue. "My dad wanted a clean-cut, white collar son. Someone he could mold in his likeness." My face heats as I talk about him. "Instead, he got me. I'm defiant, headstrong, tattooed, pierced, and hung out with kids he disapproved of. I was nothing he wanted in a son." I breathe deep. "I lived in a home where I witnessed my father physically and verbally abuse my mom." I pause a moment as I think of her. "She was a beautiful soul."

"Was? Meaning she's..."

"Yeah, Mouse. My mom is dead, and my father is the one who took her life." My voice thickens with emotion, and Lelani reaches out, her palm finding my cheek. I lean into her touch, then confess, "I killed him."

"Your father?" Lelani questions.

"Yes. I saw my mom on the floor at my dad's feet, blood seeping into the carpet beneath her." I close my eyes and focus on Lelani's warmth against my skin. "He turned the gun on me and pulled the trigger. My finger pulled the trigger at the exact moment he tried to kill me as well." I don't know if she can feel it, but sharing my story isn't something I often do. Most days, I walk through my life ignoring my past, as if someone else lived it, and I was merely a spectator to the destruction. The therapist I saw for a short time after my parents' death said it is my way of coping with the trauma.

"I'm so sorry you had to live through so much pain." Lelani leans her forehead against mine.

"It took me a couple of years to come to terms with my mom's death. For the longest time, I blamed myself for not being there to save her. Depression and guilt took hold of my life, and the darkness wouldn't let go. My demons were determined to devour what was left of me. I was drowning. The thought of ending it all began to appeal to me more every day."

"Austin," I hear nothing but sadness in her voice.

"Pop saved me. That old man never once gave up on my sister or me. From the moment we walked through his front door, he loved us like our mother would have, unconditionally. That love helped me step out of the shadows of despair. He saw me and never gave up." Emotion swims through my veins, and I fight to keep them from overwhelming me.

"I may be blind, Austin, but I see you," Lelani whispers, and I pull my woman onto my lap, her legs straddling my thighs. I push wild curls away from her face, where the moonbeams reflect her flawless skin. Lelani runs her fingers over my face, using touch to map out my features. Her breath caresses my skin as she presses those full lips of hers against my ear. She softly whispers, "Is it possible our souls knew each other in another life?"

Her words sink beneath my skin, deep into my chest where they take root in my soul. "That's impossible," I whisper back, kissing my way down her neck.

"Nothing is impossible, Austin." Lelani threads her fingers through my hair.

"I could never forget someone like you, Mouse."

9

LELANI

It's been a few days since the club found out the truth I had been hiding and since Austin claimed me in front of all his brothers. The thought of belonging to Austin both excites and terrifies me all at the same time. I managed to escape a life where a man wanted to own me, only to land myself in a situation where I actually want to belong to Austin.

"Okay, spill. What's on your mind?" Bella asks, snapping me out of my inner turmoil.

"What?" I turn on my stool toward her voice.

"Girl, you've been sitting at the computer for more than twenty minutes, entered the same specs for the same order three times."

"Oh my God. I'm so sorry." I wince at my careless mistake. "I'll fix it."

"Don't sweat it, Lelani. I wasn't fussing about the mishap. I'm concerned about what's going on inside that head of yours. These past couple of days have been a lot on you."

"Honestly," I sigh, "my emotions are all over the place. I don't want anyone to get hurt because of me, and anytime I ask Austin a question about what's going on, his response is things are being handled, or it's club business."

"Unfortunately, that's something you'll get used to. The guys are pretty tight-lipped when it comes to club business. Just know they will do whatever is best for you in this situation. Keeping you and the club safe is their top priority. You have to learn to trust them."

"I get it, and I do trust the club. I just can't help but worry."

"Worrying comes with the territory of loving one of these men. That part never goes away. Remember, it's a two-way street, though. Those men love their women fiercely and will go to the ends of the earth to keep them safe. I have no doubt Austin will do the same for you."

Bella's words cause a knot to form in my stomach behind the butterflies that flutter whenever Austin is on my mind, which is often. Her statement solidifies my inner struggle with how to feel about what is going on between Austin and me.

"There's something else bothering you. I can see it," she pushes.

Closing my eyes, I rub my temples. "The other day, when everything went down, Jake asked Austin if he was claiming me. Austin answered by saying I was his."

"Okay," Bella draws the word out. "We all knew that was coming. I saw it on his face the first time he laid eyes on you back in New Orleans." Bella falls silent a second before she continues. "Wait, I thought you felt the same way about him."

"I do," I'm quick to answer, and my face heats. "I really like him. He makes me feel beautiful and confident. He makes me feel like I'm the most precious person in the world."

Bella's voice turns soft. "Then what's the problem?"

"Well, I escaped a life where my uncle controlled every aspect of my life, then wanted to hand me off to another man who would be doing the same. Then I come here and have Austin claim me, announcing to the world I'm his. To be honest, it's a bit crazy and scares me."

"Oh, Lelani." Bella places her hand on my arm. "Austin doesn't want to control you. When one of these men decides to claim a woman, it means that she is the one he wants to spend the rest of his life with. It means you are his to love, to protect, to take care of. To control and to claim means two completely different things, Lelani."

"That's what Austin said," I reply softly.

Bella gives my arm another squeeze. "What does your heart say about Austin?"

"My heart says to let go and give in," I tell her the truth.

"There's your answer. I promise if you follow your heart and allow yourself to fall, you won't regret it. There is no greater reward this life has to offer than the love of one of those men. I speak from experience. I don't regret one single moment of the life I have with Logan. Take my advice, Lelani; take a leap of fate and don't ever look back."

An hour later, Bella and I have completed most of the day's work at the garage and are sitting behind the counter at the shop's front when a voice rings out. "I'm in the mood for tacos but don't want to go to Fernando's alone, so I'm taking you, ladies, to lunch," Glory announces, her heels clicking on the concrete floor as she walks into the garage.

"I'm down," Bella answers. "What about you, Lelani?"

"Sounds good. Just let me go to the back and tell Austin."

"Tell your man Victor will have us covered while we are out," Glory adds.

Nodding, I hop down from the stool and make my way from behind the reception area and toward the back of the shop where Austin is working. As I'm about to clear the hallway and step into the stockroom where Austin said he would be earlier, I'm halted by the sound of a familiar female voice. "Come on, Austin. I've missed you, baby."

"Melissa," Austin grunts.

"Don't tell me you don't miss this. You used to fuck me all the time in here. Your little friend doesn't have to know."

Shocked at what I'm hearing, I cover my mouth with my hand to muffle the gasp that just escaped past my lips. Not wanting to stick around and listen to what happens next, I quietly back away, turn and head back up to the front where Bella and Glory are waiting. Before I get there, I pull myself together and fight back the tears that threaten to spill. I should have known better. Now I feel like an even bigger idiot, especially after the talk I had with Bella this morning. I was ready to jump in with both feet when it came to Austin and me. Turns out listening to your heart will only break it.

"That was fast. You ready?" Bella asks.

"Yup. Let me grab my purse."

Like always, King is at my side when I make my way to the parking lot with Bella, and he climbs into the vehicle behind me. On the way to the restaurant, I plant a fake smile on my face while listening to Glory and Bella discuss plans for one of the kid's birthday parties they are having at the clubhouse in a few weeks. I try to forget what I heard back at the garage and engross myself in their conversation, but it's not working. All I can think about is what Austin and Melissa could be doing right now. I think back to the day at the bakery when Austin swore that what they had was in the past. I think how he claimed me in front of his club, yet so quickly turned around to have sex with another woman. Why would he do it? Why would he parade another woman around right under my nose? The more I think about it, the more it makes me angry. I'm sick of people thinking disability equals stupidity. Or that someone like me would feel I'm worth nothing. I'm not a doormat.

By the time we reach Fernando's, I'm on edge. Sensing my mood change, King paws at my hand and insists on laying his head in my lap. Taking a few deep, calming breaths, I try releasing some of the pent-up tension.

"You okay, Lelani?" Glory asks

Smiling, I lie. "I'm good. Just hungry."

As soon as the words leave my mouth, a cell phone rings, followed by Victor speaking. "Hello." There is a small break of silence before he says, "She's with me." Another pause. "It was my understanding you knew. I apologize." More silence fills the car as the telephone conversation ends. I have a good guess as to who Victor was talking to.

My suspicion is proven correct when Bella asks, "What was that about?"

"That was Austin. He was beside himself looking for Ms. Mancini," Victor supplies.

"I thought you told him where you were going?" Bella's next question is directed at me.

I shrug. "I couldn't find him. I assumed he'd figure out I was with you."

"Oh," is Bella's only reply. Luckily, the subject is dropped.

Five minutes later we are walking into the restaurant when a man stops me. "That dog can't be in here."

King places his body between the guy and me and lets out a low growl.

"Oh, I'm sorry," I say.

"No, she's not. That's her service dog," Glory interjects.

"Service dog, huh? That doesn't look like no service dog to me. Besides," the guy adds, "he's not wearing anything that identifies him as a service animal."

Victor, who was parking the car, finally joins us. "Is there a problem?"

"Like I was telling your friends, the dog is not allowed in here."

"The dog stays," Victor tells him.

"Sir."

"I said, the dog stays with the lady." This time Victor's tone delivers a warning; one the host decides to heed. There is only a brief moment of pause before he instructs us to follow him to our table.

Once we are seated, I apologize. "I'm sorry for the trouble. I'll leave King at the garage next time."

"Don't be ridiculous," Glory says. "That man was a dick."

I smile at Glory's choice of words.

"Now, who wants a Margarita. You two aren't going to let me drink alone, are you?"

Bella laughs. "Since when do I ever?"

"I guess I could have one," I chime in. Having a drink sounds like a good idea right about now. When the waitress returns a few minutes later with our drinks, I pick mine up and take a hefty gulp, then choke as the taste of sweet and salty alcohol explodes on my tastebuds.

"Are you okay?" Bella pats the middle of my back.

Clutching my chest, I nod. "I'm okay. This is my first time drinking alcohol. I guess I was a little overconfident when taking my first sip."

"No shit?" Glory jests. "You've never had a drink before?"

I shake my head.

"Well, consider your cherry popped. Drink up."

I go to take another sip when Bella hisses. "Bitch."

"Who?" Glory asks.

"Melissa," Bella announces. My stomach drops at the mention of that name.

"Great, she's walking this way. Don't let me get arrested, Glory. And if I do, you better have bail money ready."

"I got your back, sister."

"Ladies," Melissa's voice drips with so much fake kindness I'm surprised she doesn't choke on it.

"Bella, Glory, it's good to see you. And it's Lucy, isn't it? You're Austin's little friend, right? I just came from the garage. You guys ducked out before I could say hi. Then again, I was a little tied up, if you know what I mean."

"I know this gutter trash did not just roll up on our table and pretend to talk to us like we are friends," Glory's voice raises, and the restaurant falls silent.

"Excuse me!" Melissa screeches. "Who are you calling gutter trash?"

"You, bitch." Bella jumps in. "You don't get to come over here, interrupt our lunch, then try to low-key insult Lelani. Quit trying to stir shit up by pretending you and Austin are together. He's been done with you for months. Austin is going to have your ass when he hears about the stunt you just pulled in front of his woman."

"He wasn't acting like he had a woman when I was with him earlier," Melissa's snarky retort churns my stomach. She must have stepped closer, invading my space, because King darts out from under the table and starts growling. I jump out of my seat while keeping a tight grip on the leash.

"Oh my god!" Melissa cries. "Your dog is trying to attack me."

"Down, King," I demand at the same time Glory pipes in. "Bite her tits off, King."

"What's going on here!" Victor yells over all of the commotions. At this point, King is barking nonstop. "King, down," I command, and finally, he complies but doesn't move from in front of me.

"I should call the police. That dog should be put down."

I gasp at the notion of doing such a thing. "King is not a danger. He's protecting me."

"Miss, I'm going to have to ask you to leave," Victor states.

"This is a public place. I don't have to do anything."

"Leave," Victor's tone takes on one that makes me nervous, and he's not even talking to me.

"Whatever." Melissa tries to act confidently through her fake bravado, but there is no mistaking the fear in her voice. "It's not like I don't have better things to do."

"Mhmm. The street corner is missing its resident whore," Glory sneers. "You better get on that."

I can't help the snort that escapes my mouth at the jab while Bella bursts out laughing. Victor, however, lets out an audible sigh. "I swear I can't take you anywhere."

After the run-in with Melissa, we end up cutting lunch short and coming back to the garage. The moment I step out of the SUV, a hand wraps around my arm, and I'm steered away. I sense the anger coming off Austin in waves as he leads me through the building. Once we stop, he slams the door, and I'm proud of myself for not flinching. "Care to explain why you left the shop for lunch and didn't tell me where you were going and with who?"

I cross my arms over my chest. "Not really."

"You know you don't go anywhere without me knowin'."

"I know the rules, Austin. I tried to tell you I was going to lunch with Glory and Bella but you were a little busy at the time."

"What the hell are you talkin' about?"

"I'm talking about you and Melissa. So, excuse me for not wanting to stick around while you two were getting ready to do whatever it is you were going to do."

"Babe," Austin goes to say, but I hold up my hand, cutting him off.

"Being blind doesn't make me stupid. It also doesn't make me a doormat. Also, my ears work just fine."

"Not once have I thought of you as stupid. I sure as shit don't expect you to become someone's doormat. Had your stubborn ass stuck around, you would have heard me tell Melissa to fuck off."

"Funny, her account on how things are between you two are

different. Melissa had a lot to say when she ran into us at Fernando's."

"Tell me you are fuckin' kiddin'. What did the bitch say?"

"Look, Austin," I sigh, wanting this conversation to be over because the more we talk about it, the harder it is to hold back the hurt. "You don't owe me an explanation, and I don't want to recount the scene that went down earlier. Somehow, I misinterpreted this thing between us. I may not have experience when it comes to being in a relationship, but I do know I'm not the kind of girl who can handle being with a man who is also with other women. If that is what you are looking for, I am not the woman for you." As I say those last words, I lower my head and close my eyes to try and hide the tears that threaten to spill.

"Babe," Austin rasps into my ear, then places his finger under my chin, bringing my face to his. "I'm so fuckin' sorry you heard what you did, but I give you my word when I say nothing happened. I told her to leave and that I didn't want to see her back around the garage again. My guess is she saw you leave with Bella and Glory, then followed. Trust me when I say I'm pissed as fuck. Melissa will be dealt with. I told her to stay away, and she clearly failed to heed my warning."

"Austin." I shake my head.

"Babe, do you really think I would be so hateful?" I hear the anguish in his voice.

I don't have to think about the answer. The truth is, I believe him. He's been upfront with me about Melissa from the beginning and has never given me a reason to think otherwise. "No," I whisper. "I was hurt, and I acted on that hurt. I'm sorry." I step forward, wrap my arms around Austin's waist, and bury my face against his chest.

"I'm the one who is sorry, babe. I should have come to you after I talked to Victor. I knew something was off but decided to wait until you got back, and because of that, Melissa was able to get to

SANDY ALVAREZ & CRYSTAL DANIELS

you first. This situation is on me, not you." Pulling back, Austin takes my face in the palm of his hands and brushes his lips across mine. It doesn't take long for our kiss to turn heated. The moment I open for him and his tongue tangles with mine, and the taste of him explodes in my mouth, causing me to whimper. The next thing I know, Austin picks me up and presses my back against the door the same time my legs wrap around his waist. His hips grind against my core, allowing me to feel just how turned on he is when he presses his very hard, very large erection into me. I gasp, "Austin."

"Fuck," he growls, breaking our kiss. "Unless you want the first time we fuck to be right here against this door, we'd better stop," he says, grinding his erection against me again making me whimper.

"I think we should stop," I pant. "I don't think my first should be at work," I say, my face heating from embarrassment.

"Fuck," Austin grunts again.

"I'm sorry. I don't know why I just told you that. It's kind of a mood killer. I didn't plan on telling you like that. It kind of just came out."

"Lelani." Austin fists the hair on the back of my head, and peppers kisses down my neck. "Finding out you are untouched is not a mood killer. In fact, it's having quite the opposite effect on me. I'll spend the rest of the day with my cock hard as a rock thinking about your tight little pussy and the fact it's all mine."

"Oh," is all I manage to say. What does a girl say to that?

"Are we good?" he asks.

I swallow and nod. "Yeah, we're good."

Austin gives me one last kiss before letting me down. "You can go on back out there. I'm going to need a few minutes."

When I walk back out front, Bella and Glory stop talking, and I can feel their eyes on me. Finally, Glory breaks the awkward silence. "You're looking a little flushed there, girlfriend. I think I'm

102

about to go home and pick a fight with Demetri just so we can make up."

"Makeup sex is the best," Bella laughs.

"Austin and I didn't have sex!" I sputter.

"Hey, this is a judgment-free zone. You do you, girl," Glory says. "And on that note, I'm out of here, ladies. I'm off to start a fight with my man."

"Bye, Glory," Bella and I say in unison.

"She's nuts." I can't help but laugh.

"Glory is one of a kind," Bella agrees.

10

AUSTIN

It's been one hell of a day. Thank fuck, it's Friday. To celebrate Lelani's first successful week at the shop, the club decided to introduce her to another place we frequent and kick our feet up at; Charley's. After the other men secured sitters for their kids, we all met up at the clubhouse and rode together, heading for the other side of Polson.

Vibrant orange hues start to slowly fade away as the sun sinks below the waterline as we drive past the lake. Lelani's palms rest lightly at my sides as I lean back in my seat. Reaching back, I caress the exposed skin on her bare leg. Having her on the back of my bike has fast become my favorite activity, and I take her riding every chance I get. When I'm not around Lelani, I can't stop thinking about her. I absorb the energy she brings to a room, and the electricity between us shoots through my fingertips every time we kiss. She's like a high, her lips laced with my drug of choice, and like an addict, I can't get enough. Love at first sight was never a concept I believed in until Lelani's path crossed with mine. I hardly love myself. How the hell could I be capable of loving someone else? At least, those are the thoughts floating around my head for all these years. I'm not falling for Lelani. I've already fallen for her.

I fall into a tranquil state of mind listening to the hum of the bike tires turn against the asphalt as we cruise northwest down the open highway. The landscape around us changes to open fields of green pastures, with tall pine trees and distant mountain peaks as the backdrop. The wind carries the scent of wildflowers as it whips at my face. A calm washes over me, watching the horizon shifting from soft pastels of tangerine and indigo. Dusk blankets the Montana sky as the warmth of Lelani's body seeping into mine soothes the workday away. Looking toward the east, I notice grey storm clouds gradually casting dark shows over the mountain tops. In no rush, I set my sights ahead, keep my speed steady, and enjoy the ride.

WE ROLL into the gravel parking lot of Charley's bar located on the outskirts of town and back our bikes in our usual spots along the side of the building. I notice several rigs across the street where truckers passing through usually park when stopping for the night. "The music is loud," Lelani says, wearing a smile on her face as we walk through the front door.

"Friday nights tend to be busy for Charley," I speak above the music playing from the old jukebox at the front of the bar.

"Well, hell." Charley throws the rag he was using to clean onto the counter and steps from behind the bar. "Good to see ya, Jake." The two shake hands. "The place is lively tonight. A small convoy rolled into town. You men get settled in. I'll send Kinsley over to take your orders in a moment."

"All we require is a cold beer, shot glasses, and a full bottle of whiskey, my friend," Jake tells him.

"You got it."

Several sets of eyes follow us as we walk to the back of the bar, taking a seat at the large round table Charley usually leaves the table open if we decide to drop by. A group of men seated in three of those seats all stop talking mid-conversation as we approach. "Thanks for keepin' our seats warm." Quinn pulls out an empty chair.

"Find another seat; this one is taken." The prick with a pencil-dick mustache laughs, and his trucker friends join in.

Gabriel moves Alba to the side. "Move." his deep voice and tall stature make one of them jump to his feet.

"Come on." The guy's eyes stay fixed on Gabriel as he pulls at his friend's jacket. "Let's go," he says again to his stubborn friend. Reluctantly, the other two assholes vacate their seats. Their bloodshot eyes hint at their drunken state as the one who smarted off sways and eyes my girl far too damn long.

"Take your fuckin' eyes off my woman," I warn. Lucky for him, his buddies lead him away. There is always that one brave bastard willing to test his luck. Damn whiskey will do that to some people, make you feel ten feet tall and bulletproof. In other words, stupid.

"Come here." I take a seat and pull Lelani onto my lap. Kinsley walks up, carrying our drinks on her tray, and sits everything down on the table.

"How's it going, Sweetheart," Jake asks her.

She tucks the empty serving tray beneath her arm. "These truckers are keeping me busy."

"How's your boy?" Bella asks, and she smiles.

"He's doing good. Oh, and thanks for the new clothes. You have no idea what it means to me," she tells Bella. "Well, better get back to work. I'll check on you guys later," Kinsley says, then walks away.

"She sounds nice," Lelani notes.

"She and her little boy are good people," I say while Emerson pours whiskey into shot glasses. Lelani fidgets, wringing her hands together while they rest on her lap. "You okay?" I notice her nervousness.

She bites her lower lip. "A little worried those men really wanted to pick a fight with you guys," she admits, and I chuckle.

"Babe, they've had too much to drink. The only harmful thing about those dipshits is their mouths and inflated egos the liquor gave them." I rub her arm. "Relax. I won't let anything happen, nor will the rest of the club. Most people know to leave us alone. They give us our space and respect us, and we do the same." Lelani sighs, her body still not relaxing. "Forget about those assholes. We are all here to let loose and have a little fun," I tell her.

Lelani finally smiles again. "You're right. I'm supposed to enjoy my first time in a bar. I'm here to listen to some good music and laugh with friends."

"I'll drink to that." Mila smiles and raises her glass.

"To family," Reid boasts, doing the same.

I place a shot glass in front of my woman to find, and she takes it in her hand. I lift mine. "To new beginnings," Lelani states, and as she brings her shot to her lips, we all follow suit, downing the shot of whiskey. Lelani shivers as the liquid amber coats her throat.

The rest of the night goes by without any more excitement. We all sit around the table, take a few shots, and laugh our asses off at the endless jokes Quinn has filed away in that head of his. "Wait, I got another one." Quinn downs a shot. "What's the difference between hungry and horny?" He glances around the table, waiting for one of us to guess. "Where you stick the cucumber." He delivers the punchline, and Lelani loses it again. Across the table, I even watch Gabriel's face crack a smile and his shoulders shake.

"Stop. I can't take it anymore." Lelani laughs hard, wearing a smile that lights up the room. "I've never laughed so hard in my life." She takes a deep breath trying to regain her composer.

"Would someone please show me to the restroom before I pee myself?"

Grace stands, still laughing herself. "Come on. I'll show you. I need to go too." She takes Lelani by the hand, and they walk through the crowded room toward the bathrooms near the other end of the bar.

"I say we call it a night," Jake suggests, then digs some cash out of his wallet and lays it on the table. The rest of us men do the same.

After about five minutes, I stand. "I'm going to hit the head." I stroll toward the restrooms. Before entering the men's bathroom, the door to the back exit ajar grabs my attention. I go investigate. "Where are your biker men now?!" I hear a man shout the moment I step outside. My blood runs cold as I catch the fuckers from earlier with Lelani and Grace pinned against the side of the building. Grace spots me, her mouth covered by the fuckers hand, trying to muffle her screams. I reach for my weapon. Something cracks across my head, and I stumble a couple of feet before the side of my body slams against the metal dumpster.

"I'm going to fuck you up," a man sneers, then swings at me with a goddamn baseball bat. I dodge the blow, then rip it from his grasp and bring the bat across his face, and watch his big ass hit the ground.

I throw the bat and draw my weapon. "Get your filthy motherfuckin' hands off the women." I fire a warning shot into the sky. The bearded fucker holding Grace raises his hands and backs away. The bald motherfucker with his hands on my woman does the same, and Grace grabs Lelani's hand. "Inside." As much as I'd like to hold my woman and wipe that terrified look off of her face, her and Grace's safety is more important. "Inside. Now," I order, keeping my gun aimed at the men in front of me, their buddy still out cold on the ground. Grace tucks Lelani at her side and walks back into the bar, and soon after, my brothers burst through the back door.

"Which one?" Jake growls, and I know what he's asking. "Beard there," I tell him, and before I blink, Jake has his gun drawn and fires a shot. The guy who laid hands on his woman goes down with a bullet in his leg.

"You're only brave because of the gun in your hand." The bald bastard whose filthy hands touched my woman squares his shoulders, looking for a fight.

"And only a small-dick pussy puts his hands on a woman, but rest assured, I don't need this gun to hurt you." I hand my weapon to Logan for safekeeping. I step up, ready to go one on one with the motherfucker. He hesitates. "Figures. The only thing your mouth is good for is talkin' shit and suckin' dick." My words hit a nerve.

"I should have taken that redhead back to my rig and shown her what a real man feels like." He grabs his crotch, smirking.

"You fucked up, boy," Logan states just as I bury my fist in the fucker's face. I don't give him time to recover and deliver several blows to his face, his front teeth cutting at my knuckles. I don't stop until he falls and his face is broken. I stand over him, my fist coated in his blood, but I don't feel satisfied. Grabbing my weapon from Logan, I aim it at the bastard's head.

"Fuck, man. Don't kill him." The one guy who cracked me over the head with a baseball bat has come to and pleads for his buddy's life. I spot the one Jake shot sitting against the dumpster, his hand pressed against his wound. I turn my attention back on the busted motherfucker lying at my feet.

"Prez?" I question, waiting for direction.

"We don't need to deal with dead bodies tonight," Jake orders, and, as hard as it is for me to follow, I stand down. "Now, I suggest the three of you get the fuck out of my town. If we see your faces again, you won't live to see another day."

My brothers and I stand there as the two able-bodied men pick their beaten friend off the ground and struggle to carry his large ass off Charley's property. Reid and Gabriel follow them to the road in front of the bar, making sure they get to their rigs. What they do from there is up to them, as long as they don't return.

Without speaking, I holster my weapon and walk inside to get my woman. "The women are in the break room!" Charley shouts when he sees me.

In the breakroom, the women are seated on a small couch together. I kneel on the floor in front of Lelani and place my palm on her cheek. She leans into my touch. "You okay, Mouse?" I run my eyes over her, finding no visible marks.

"I'm okay." Her voice shakes a little, and I regret not getting to kill the motherfucker. I take her by the hand, stand and pull her body into mine, needing to feel her warmth. Her hands slip beneath my cut, wrapping around my waist, holding me tight. "Did you kill them?"

"Would it bother you if I did?" I ask and wait for her reply, but she remains quiet. "I'm no saint, Mouse. I'm not here to judge a man on his sins while he stares down the barrel of my gun. I'm setting up his appointment for judgement day." I pull back, lift her face to my, and drag the back of my knuckles across her cheek. "Can you live with that?" Lelani answers with a nod. "I need your words, babe."

"Take me home," my woman says and it's the only words I needed to hear.

11

LELANI

Austin leads me out of the bar in a rush. The air around us crackles the second I declare my acceptance for the man he is. It's a monumental moment. I can feel it and know my fate is sealed. If there was any doubt I belonged to this man before, it has been washed away by my vow to accept all that he is.

"You know there's no goin' back?" Austin states, and there is no missing the edge in his tone. "You get on the back of my bike now, that's it. I won't let you go even if you begged me."

I place my hand on Austin's chest. "I don't want you to let me go. I want you to make me yours." I pause for a beat to gather the courage to speak my next words. "I want you to make me yours in every way." I wait with bated breath for Austin's response to my bold statement. My palms become sweaty, and my face flames. "Austin," my voice quivers.

"Let's go." He tugs on my hand. That's it? He's seriously not going to acknowledge what I just said?

Masking my features, I tamp down my embarrassment, and place my hand on Austin's shoulder and climb on the back of his bike. I shouldn't have put myself out there like that. That goes to show just how inexperienced I am.

The ride from Charley's to the clubhouse doesn't take long. As soon as Austin cuts his bike engine, I climb off and set the helmet on the seat. Neither of us says a word as we walk into the clubhouse.

"Hey. How was Charley's?" Ember asks as we walk through the door. I offer her a small smile as I keep in step with Austin. "It was good," I supply and toss a wave over my shoulder and hear Ember respond with a giggle.

Once Austin I and make it to the top of the stair, I attempt to pull my hand free of his. "Well, uh...goodnight," I say awkwardly. Only Austin doesn't let me go. Ignoring me, he keeps walking. "What are you doing?"

"Takin' you to my room."

"But I thought..."

Austin stops, and I feel the heat of his breath as he brings his face within an inch of mine. The smell of his cologne and whisky invades my senses. "Not twenty minutes ago, you stated you wanted me to make you mine in every way. Unless you tell me no, I'm not goin' to bed alone."

My tummy dips, and the space between my thighs tingles. "Oh."

Austin dips his face closer, brushing his lips across the shell of my ear, "Are you ready to have your pussy claimed? For me to mark you as mine?"

My breathing becomes shallow, and my panties flood at the thought of having Austin inside of me.

"You like the idea of my cock inside that tight pussy of yours, don't you? I bet you're wet right now at the thought of me filling you." Forcing me back, Austin's six foot two inch stature cages me in against the wall, right there in the clubhouse hallway, then he proceeds to unbutton my jeans. Slowly, he slides his hand inside the front of my panties, his touch leaving a trail of burning flesh in its wake as his fingers find the evidence of my arousal. I gasp when the cold steel of his knuckle piercing brushes across my clit.

"Austin."

"So fuckin' wet," he growls, sliding his fingers further down. "I want you to come on my fingers." I hold my breath when he slips one finger inside of me, then two, stretching me the same time his thumb presses against my clit. "Breathe, babe," Austin says, reminding me to release the breath I'm holding. Soon my legs begin to quiver, and a warm sensation starts to flood my body. "That's it, babe. Feel it and let go."

"Austin," I pant.

"Come, Lelani," he demands. "I want to feel you come all over my hand."

As soon as the command leaves Austin's mouth, my pussy clamps down around his fingers. Before I have a chance to scream his name, his mouth crashes down on mine, swallowing my cry of pleasure as the orgasm surges through my body. I don't know how much time passes, but I'm faintly aware of the rise and fall of Austin's chest, caused by his heavy breathing. He shocks me by gingerly removing his hand from the inside of my panties, followed by the sound of his gruff voice. "You taste just as good as I imagined."

Wait...did he? Oh my god!

Not giving me time to respond, Austin hauls me against his chest, grabs my butt in the palms of his hands, and lifts me up. On instinct, I wrap my legs around his hips as he carries me into his bedroom and kicks the door shut with his foot. Not wasting any time, he takes three strides before my back hits the mattress of his bed. The second that happens, it's like a spark ignites, and we both are in a race to get each other's clothes off. "Austin," I call out just as he slides my cutoffs down my legs.

"You okay, babe? Want me to stop?"

I shake my head. "No. I want to touch you. Will you let me?"

"For future reference, babe, you never have to ask permission to touch me."

With a shuddered breath, I sit up on the edge of the bed to where Austin is standing right in front of me. Reaching out, I come into contact with his bare torso. Somewhere in the middle of him undressing me, he rid himself of his shirt. Not wanting to waste a single second of this moment, I take my time exploring every inch of his skin. Starting at his navel, I slowly glide my hands up Austin's abs, counting three on each side. "Do you have any tattoos here?" I trace my finger along his ribcage.

"Yes." Austin's response is gruff.

"What is it?"

"It's a skull wearing a crown and it's surrounded by flames."

"Hmm," I hum, not missing the way his muscles ripple at my touch. Standing, I continue to explore. Leaning in, I lightly flick my tongue over the barbell pierced through his nipple. The grip Austin has on my hips tightens as he tries to keep a handle on his control. Next, I glide my hand up toward his left shoulder. "What about here?" I allow every ridge, every bump, and every scar to be ingrained into my memory. I don't ever want to forget the first time I got to put my hands on the man I love.

"The grim reaper," Austin grinds out when I nip at his skin.

I glide my palm over the scar on his chest, then lean in and kiss it. "You're beautiful." I don't miss his sharp intake of breath at my statement.

Deciding to be bold for the second time tonight, my hands travel south to Austin's belt buckle. "I want to touch all of you," I whisper. Austin's breathing accelerates, but he doesn't say a word. I take that as a yes and continue by dropping to my knees in front of him. Keeping my face aimed up at his, I hook my fingers into the waistband of his jeans and tug them down. Swallowing past the nervous lump in my throat, I take his cock into my hand. It feels different than I imagined it would. It's long, thick, and smooth like silk. It's also very hard. When my thumb brushes over the tip, a hiss escapes Austin's mouth.

"Fuck."

Liking the effect I'm having on Austin by touching him, I decide to take things a little further. Leaning forward, I swipe my tongue over the head of his cock just before I take as much of his length in my mouth as possible, making him jerk forward. I may not be experienced, but I can damn sure make up for it with enthusiasm. My enthusiasm pays off because just as I'm getting into the task of making Austin feel as good as he made me, he frees himself from my mouth. "Fuck, babe. As much as I like your lips wrapped around my cock, I don't want this to be over too quickly. The way you are working my dick will have me comin' like a damn teenager."

In a flash, Austin has me up off the floor and straddling his hips as he sits on the bed, his hard cock pressed against my center. I can't help but silently curse the scrap of material separating us. As if he can hear my thoughts, Austin fists my lace underwear in his hands and rips them from my body. Next, he reaches behind me and unclasps my bra. Chest against chest, I hum at the sensation of my hardened nipples scraping against the sprinkling of hair on his chest. "That feels good," I rasp when he palms my butt and guides my hips forward, which causes his cock to rub against the seam of my wet pussy. My skin prickles when his hands make their way up my back until his palms hook over my shoulders, pulling me back so that he can dip his head between our bodies and close his mouth over my nipple.

Austin licks and nips at the hardened peak before moving onto the next, giving it equal attention. I moan as I thread my fingers through his long hair, loving the feel of the soft strands. "Austin, I need more," I rasp while I continue to grind myself down on his cock. I'm dangerously close to coming again and desperate to have him inside of me. In one fell swoop, I'm on my back with Austin hovering above me. He's silent for a long moment, and I can feel his eyes on my exposed skin, drinking me in. Surprisingly he makes me feel sexy. I always thought this moment, the moment I give myself to a man, would be scary, but it's not, because I'm giving myself to the right man. I've spent a long time fantasizing about finding a man who makes me feel the way Austin does. It almost feels like a dream, like I'll wake up and realize none of this is real, that this kind of happiness doesn't exist.

"What are you thinkin' about?" Austin asks, his face inches away from mine.

"I'm thinking I love you and how happy I am."

"Baby," he breathes. "I don't know what I did in a past life to deserve a fuckin' angel like you, but I promise to God, I'll spend the rest of my life makin' sure you don't regret sayin' those three words to me 'cause I love you too." With that, Austin's hips surge forward. I cry out as he claims what is now his and only his. Austin's lips cover mine in a gentle kiss as he mummers. "You're so gorgeous, babe. My sweet, Mouse." Austin's loving words, adoring touches, and soft kisses help take my mind off of the pain. I relish the feel of his large hands skimming my body to the point where I can think of nothing else but the way he is worshiping my body. Soon the pain subsides into a dull ache. Once Austin feels me relax, he begins to move. And though there is some discomfort, the pleasure starts to work its way to the surface with every thrust. There is something to be said about the amount of restraint Austin is showing right now, and that act makes me fall in love with him a little more. Before too long, I start to feel my orgasm build. Austin reaches between our bodies and his thumb zeros in on my clit. My release crashes through me out of nowhere. "Austin!" I cry out the same time he rests his forehead against mine. The sound of my name on Austin's lips as he finds his release has to be one of the most beautiful things I have heard.

THE NEXT MORNING I wake with a steel band wrapped around my waist. Last night was the best night of my life. Just thinking about it causes my body to heat, and I rub my thighs together to elevate the tingle between my legs. My movements cause Austin to stir behind me, and his sleep-filled voice fills the room. "If you don't stop rubbin' that sweet ass against my dick, I'm going to spread your legs and give you somethin' to rub."

"Sorry," I giggle. "Can you let me up, though, so I can use the restroom?"

Austin gives my waist one last squeeze before he releases me. When I climb out of bed, I note the soreness between my legs and wince. Then it suddenly dawns on me, something that I stupidly didn't think about last night. *How could I have been so careless?* Sensing something is wrong, Austin's sleep filled voice is more alert.

"What is it, baby?"

"Um..we didn't use any protection last night and I'm not on anything." My voice comes out a little panicked.

"Okay," is all Austin says.

"Okay? That's all you have to say? I just told you that I'm not on birth control after having unprotected sex last night and all you have to say is okay?"

"Baby, calm down." I hear Austin climb out of bed and a second later he's in front of me. "I'm sorry I fucked up and forgot about protection. If something happens then we'll deal with it."

"How come you're acting so calm? I mean, I could get pregnant, Austin. And pregnancy is not the only thing there is to worry about."

Austin's arm around me tightens. "If you are concerned about whether or not I'm clean, then don't be. I get tested regularly. I would never put you at risk, Lelani. Besides, you're the only woman I have been inside ungloved."

The thought of Austin sleeping with other women causes my stomach to churn, but I do believe him when he says he wouldn't intentionally put me at risk.

"We good?" He kisses the tip of my nose.

"Yeah. We're good."

He holds me for a long moment before asking, "You sore?"

"It's not too bad but do you have some pain reliever I can take?"

"Yeah babe, I'll get you some."

On my way to the bathroom, I step on Austin's discarded shirt. Leaning down, I swipe it off the floor and tug it on over my head. Just as I'm about to continue my trek to the bathroom, a pair of hands land on my hips, halting me in place. "I fuckin' love seeing you in my shirt, Mouse," Austin rumbles into my ear, then I feel his lips against the crook of my neck. I lean back into his embrace and sigh. The two of us stay locked together in that position for a beat before he delivers one last kiss to my temple. "Go get cleaned up."

Twenty minutes later, I emerge from the bathroom feeling refreshed from my shower to find Austin has returned, and the smell of bacon assaults my nostrils, making my tummy rumble.

"I have that pain reliever and some breakfast. Lisa cooked," Austin supplies.

"Thank you. It smells delicious." Climbing back on the bed, Austin hands over the plate, and we sit in comfortable silence as we tuck into our food.

"Noah's birthday party is today. I have to run to Charley's to pick up an order Prez placed. You want to ride with or stay here?"

"I'd like to stay if that's okay. I promised I would help set up."

"Yeah, babe. That's cool. I like that you want to help the women. They like you."

"I like them too." I smile. "I've been looking forward to helping.

I didn't have a family like yours growing up. There were no birthday parties or cookouts. My family didn't get together just because. I like being included here."

"Babe." Austin cups my face. "The club is your family now."

"I'm starting to see that," I whisper. "It feels good to be surrounded by so many people who care. I haven't felt that since my parents died."

Not wanting to start the day on such a sad note, I lean on my tiptoes to give Austin a kiss. "I'm going to get dressed, then go downstairs to see if Lisa needs any help in the kitchen."

"Alright, baby. I'm going to run to town, but I shouldn't be but an hour. You need anything while I'm out?"

"Not that I can think of."

LATER THAT AFTERNOON, the yard behind the clubhouse is abuzz with the children running around laughing and music playing in the background. The day has been filled with birthday cake, presents, and family catering to the birthday boy. Grace was kind enough to describe to me everything in detail. I wasn't surprised to find the party was biker-themed. The cake was decorated with tiny little motorcycles, and the gifts were wrapped in motorcycle themed wrapping paper. There was even a motorcycle-shaped piñata. Now that the presents have been unwrapped and the cake has been eaten, all the children are in the bouncy house the club rented, burning off some of their sugar high, except for Quinn and Emerson's little girl, Lydia, who has taken a liking to me. She's been perched on my lap for the last thirty minutes, content as can be while submerged in a cup of ice-cream.

"Callan was an asshole. I can't fathom how he believed that ho bag over Denver."

The sound of Alba's exasperated tone knocks me out of my

wandering thoughts, and I can't help but listen to her and Leah's conversation.

"Yeah, I was mad at him for that too. Especially the part where the cops showed and Denver was begging Callan to believe her," Leah adds. "Denver forgave him too easily. She should have made him grovel a little longer."

"I don't know," I cut in. "I think Denver realized that Callan was truly sorry, and she didn't seem like the kind of person who would prolong the groveling process with the sole purpose of hurting Callan. I mean, really, what does that truly say about a person's character? Denver was hurt, and she held Callan accountable for his actions, which he took responsibility for. He also gave her the space she needed. He did everything right and followed her lead on their road to reconciliation. I never saw Denver as weak for forgiving Callan as quickly as she did. In my opinion, it takes more strength to forgive someone than it does to hold a grudge. Denver loved and wanted to be with Callan. She wanted to move on with their life together. Had she continued to keep him at a distance and make him continue to grovel, she would ultimately be allowing her life and her happiness to be held, hostage." I shrug. "Why would anyone purposely miss out on happiness?"

Alba and Leah are silent for a moment before Alba breathes, "Oh my god! A fellow book nerd! You've listened to Keeping Denver?"

I laugh. "Yes. It's one of my favorites."

"This is so awesome," Leah chimes in. "How long have you loved books?"

"I fell in love with them when my mom introduced me to Harry Potter as a kid. But my love of romance started a few years ago. I'm even a member of an online book club." I sigh. "I miss my audiobooks, though. I haven't listened to one in what feels like forever."

"What?!" Alba makes a choking sound. "There is no way I could go even a day without reading."

I shrug. "I don't have my Kindle. It will be a while before I can save up to afford one."

"Why haven't you said anything?" Leah asks. "I have a few laying around. Here," she says, and I hear a rustling sound. "I have one in my bag. You can have it."

"Oh, no." I hold up my hand. "I couldn't. It's too much."

"No, it's not. I insist. Plus, Alba and I get together at least twice a week to discuss what we have read. We would love it if you joined us."

"Really?" I ask. "Are you sure?" I can't help the giddiness in my voice.

"Absolutely!" Alba exclaims.

"We can meet at Grace's bakery later this week. Have you read..." Leah goes to ask me a question, but her voice is suddenly drowned out by the sound of rapid gunfire, followed by women and children screaming. Without hesitation, I cocoon Lydia in my arms and throw myself to the ground. Bullets fly past me as I use my body to shield the scared and crying child beneath me. For as long as I live, nothing will erase the memory of the terrifying screams coming from all around me.

12

AUSTIN

One minute I'm watching Lelani from the opposite side of the back yard, playing with Quinn's little girl, Lydia, then suddenly all hell breaks loose. The next several seconds of my life happen so fast I only have time to think about protecting those closest to me—the kids. "Get down!" I shout in the middle of diving for Remi and Logan's little boy Jake, whom she was helping into the bounce house nearby. Grabbing the two of them, I pull them to the ground, shielding them with my body as bullets pelt the ground, ripping at the grass around us. A hot-searing pain tears at my upper arm, but I hold my position, creating a barrier between the gunfire and the kids. The deafening sound of women screaming and children crying makes it nearly impossible to decide which direction the bullets are coming from. Remi does her best to console Jake, who begins calling for his mom Bella.

Who the fuck shoots at women and children?

As quickly as the gunfire started, it abruptly stops.

I wait for a beat before moving, then lift my head, looking down into the frightened faces of my brother's kids. "It's okay," I keep my tone calm. Remi's hair sticks to her tear-stained face, but she doesn't make a sound. Instead, she pulls Jake closer. "Are you okay?" I ask her as I look them over for any injuries.

"I think so," she says, then her eyes widen. "You're bleeding," she points out, and I look down at my arm. Blood is trailing down my bicep, but I don't have time to think about it. I glance over my shoulder, scanning the yard.

"Inside. Now!" Jake yells as he swiftly moves across the yard and the rest of my brothers work at getting their families to safety.

Women are scrambling to gather children, and my brothers are helping. Checking my surroundings once more, I quickly scoop up Jake, tuck Remi into my side, and run toward the clubhouse, getting the two kids to safety. "Take him to the main room. Stay away from the windows," I tell Remi when I have them safely inside the back door leading into the kitchen.

Turning, I head back to get my woman. I spot Lelani being assisted off the ground by Quinn, and I take off in a sprint across the yard. As he lifts Lelani to her feet, I notice Lydia clutched in her arms. Emerson gets to them the exact moment I do.

"Oh my God!" Emerson cries as Lelani loosens her hold on my brother's little girl and takes their child into her arms.

"Lelani." I quickly pull her body into mine.

"Austin." I hear the desperation and panic in her voice as she clutches my cut. "Is Lydia okay—are the kids okay—are you okay?" she asks while rushing her back across the yard to the safety of the clubhouse.

Inside, the family gathers in the common room, and the women try their best to calm the kids, keeping them huddled against the wall away from the windows. "Lock the place down," Logan orders, and most of the men fly into action to secure the building.

"Babe, are you okay?" I give Lelani all my attention and run my palms down her arms, looking her over to make sure she has no injuries. I ignore the pain shooting down my arm when she grabs it before feeling her way upward to find my face and palms my cheek.

"I'm not hurt." Her voice shakes. "Who would shoot into a crowd of kids, Austin? They're babies." Lelani's eyes pool with tears that begin falling down her cheeks.

I pull her head against my chest, embracing her. "I don't know, baby." I press my lips to her forehead when she lifts her face to mine. "But I plan on finding out."

"Everyone accounted for?" Jake asks, glancing around the room. Suddenly the clubhouse's front door bursts open, and Doc rushes in with Lisa cradled in his arms. "She's hit!" Doc lays Lisa on the nearest flat surface, which happens to be one of the pool tables. Doc peels his shirt from his body and presses it to her chest. "Shit-shit!" he shouts. "There's too much blood. She needs to get to the hospital." Doc lifts his head, his eyes filled with unshed emotion. "They shot my woman, brother." He eyes Jake.

"Austin, bring the fuckin' truck around," Jake orders. I give Lelani a quick kiss then jump into action, leaving her with the women. As fast as my feet will carry me, I get to my truck, flinging open the driver's door, and get behind the wheel. It takes me seconds to pull my vehicle to the front door. Gabriel holds Lisa in his arms while Doc climbs into the back seat then Gabriel hoists Lisa inside, and Doc applies pressure to her chest wound again once more.

"A few of us will be right behind you, brother," Gabriel tells me, then slams the door.

Not waiting for them, I peel away from the clubhouse, my tires kicking up loose rocks, creating a cloud of dust behind me as I race against time.

"Come on, baby. You hold on. Don't you fuckin' leave me, woman," Doc pleads.

As I hit the open highway heading toward town, I catch sight of Jake, Logan, and Gabriel tailing me on their bikes in my rearview mirror. I press my foot into the gas pedal, pushing my old truck harder than ever before to get us to the hospital in time to save Lisa's life.

Doc is on the phone with the hospital moments before we arrive, relaying his woman's injury and stating she has a pulse, but it's weak. My tires squeal as I bring the truck to a stop outside the emergency room doors. Several staff members rush out with a gurney, and Doc lays Lisa on it. Abandoning my vehicle, I run inside behind the team of nurses and doctors, whisking Lisa away.

As his woman disappears behind closed doors, Doc hits his knees. He peers down at his hands, breathing heavily as he stares at the blood coating them. "I'm not ready," he whispers. I grip his shoulder, letting him know I'm here. Lisa is his world. Her life means more to him than his own.

"Shit." Jake appears along with Logan and Gabriel. "Come on, brother." He gets Doc to his feet. "She'll make it. Lisa is a fighter. She's stared death in the face before and won. She can do it again," Jake tries to reassure Doc.

Doc looks at him. "I'm nothin' without her, Jake." His voice cracks.

AFTER ABOUT TWENTY LONG MINUTES, our heads lift to the sound of automatic doors clicking open and shoes clacking against the floor. Doctor Lawrence, someone we have dealt with in the past, approaches, his eyes taking in our tattered appearances. Doc stands. "Tell me what's goin' on with my woman," Doc demands.

"Bennett." Doctor Lawrence regards him. "Your wife is losing a good bit of blood, so she is receiving a transfusion as we speak. X-rays show bleeding coming from a laceration of her heart, just fractions from her aorta. I'm preparing her for emergency surgery now."

"Don't let her die," Doc tells him, doing his best to school his emotions.

The doctor nods then he glances at me. "You should get that looked at," he points to my arm before walking away.

AT THE FAR end of the parking lot, I'm standing outside next to my truck, smoking a cigarette, with Logan, Jake, and Gabriel beside me.

Almost two hours later, we can breathe a sigh of relief, knowing Lisa made it through surgery and is heavily sedated, resting in recovery, with Doc by her side. As for me, a bullet grazed my skin, leaving a decent gash that required a few stitches.

The bandage on my upper arm tugs at the sutures underneath the cotton wrap as I roll my shoulders to loosen the built-up tension in my muscles.

"Doc is stayin' with Lisa until visiting hours end. He'll call a brother for a ride back to the clubhouse in a couple of hours," Jake informs us, then his phone rings. He pulls it from his pocket. "Talk to me." His features harden, putting my brothers and me on alert. "Move the women and children upstairs. Tell Reid to hold his position. We're on our way." He quickly ends the call, and our full attention is on our Prez. "That was Quinn. Security measures around the compound's perimeter were compromised, explaining why someone got the drop on us earlier. Reid also found the trail cameras along the wooded area missing."

"Which means whoever fired on our family gained access from the north. They would have traveled on foot," Logan states.

"There's more," Jake adds. "Reid also found evidence of a campsite as he traveled deeper into the woods. That's a lot of land to trek. That gives reason to believe the fuckers could still be out there somewhere."

My blood turns red hot, and my hands clench at my sides.

Gabriel suddenly slams his fist through the driver's window of my truck, raging with anger. "The fuckers lay in wait, watching us, then when we're at our most vulnerable, they attacked!" he roars. "I need to kill someone," he breathes, blood dripping from the cuts on his knuckles. I can't even be mad at him for his outburst. The rage inside him needed somewhere to go.

"You'll get your chance. We all will," Jake states. My brothers walk to their bikes, and I swing open the truck door, brush the glass shards from the seat and climb behind the wheel. "Everyone packin' heat?" Jake asks, and we all check our weapons then nod. "Austin, we need to access the north side of the club's property from your Pop's. If they are still in there, hiding like fuckin' cowards, I want to find them."

"That shouldn't be an issue." I slam the door shut and start the engine. "Let's go huntin'."

A short time later, we drive down Pop's driveway, approaching his house at high speeds before coming to a stop. The commotion has the old man stepping out the front door with a hunting rifle in his hands. The moment I step out of the truck's cab, he lowers his weapon. "Shit."

"Sorry, Pop."

"Damn, Son. I was ready to put lead in someone's ass." He looks past my shoulder as my brothers walk up beside me. Jake passes by, heading for the porch. "Warren." He extends his hand, and Pop gives it a firm shake.

"Jake. I'm assumin' this isn't no social callin'," Pop hedges.

"Have you noticed any strange activity around your property lately?" Jake leads with questions.

Pop rubs his trimmed beard. "Can't say that I have. About all the excitement I've had as of late was the other night, my horses were making a commotion. I didn't find anything of concern when I investigated, so I chalked it up to coyotes snoopin' around the stables." Pop looks at me, then back to Jake. "Why?"

"We had an incident at the clubhouse earlier today, during a birthday celebration for one of the kids. There is reason to believe the suspects are still in the woods between our property and yours," Jake tells Pop without divulging too much club business.

Pop's eyes trail over me then he notices the bandage on my upper arm. "Gonna tell me what happened?" Pop directs his question at me.

"I'm alright, Pop. That's the only thing that matters."

He nods. "Well, I guess I have no choice but to live with that answer. Everyone else okay?"

"Doc's woman, Lisa, was injured. He's with her at the hospital now," I tell him.

"I'm sorry to hear that. Lisa's a sweetheart of a woman," Pop comments.

"Warren, we need to conduct a search of the grounds between the two properties. You okay with us conducting business on your land and taking the appropriate action should we come across uninvited guests? Should we find them?" Jake is vague with his question, but the lines are crystal clear as to our intent.

"You have my permission to take any action necessary when it comes to trespassers." He looks to the sky. "There's a storm rollin' in. You'll find some rain gear and flashlights in the stables. I keep a few extra rifles locked up in a trunk up in the loft should you require extra protection," Pop tells Jake.

I walk up onto the porch. "Thanks, Pop."

"You stay safe, Austin. My old heart can't take losin' a grandson, you got me? I'm taking a wild guess when I say the men you're after fired shots?" I say nothing, but he reads my expression loud and clear. Pop's face hardens, and so does his voice. "If these bastards can pull the shit they did with babies and women amongst you men, then they won't hesitate to kill you. You copy?" Pop's words of warning don't go unheard by any of us.

I give his shoulder a squeeze. "Copy. You keep that gun beside you, old man," I tell him as I walk away.

In the stables, we find some raincoats hanging on rusty horseshoes turned into wall hooks. I walk over to the toolbox nearby, where Pop keeps a couple of flashlights, before climbing the wooden ladder leading up to the loft overhead. In the corner, up against the wall, is Pop's old military trunk. I haven't been up here in years. It's where Pop first caught me smoking a joint not long after my sister and I came to live with him. He didn't scold me. Instead, we talked. I open the trunk lid. Lying beneath an army green jacket are two rifles. I lift them from the trunk and grab a box of ammo. We spoke more that day than I'd ever talked in my life. I shared things with him I'd never spoken of since. That day I learned I could trust not only him but myself.

Pushing thoughts aside, I call for Gabriel. He plucks a roll of tape from the toolbox, looping a small rope through it and shrugging it over his shoulder. I toss the rifles and ammo down to him.

On the ground, I throw my gear on. Before walking out of the barn, I spot a shovel leaning against one of the stables and grab it.

"Only take what we need," Jake says.

"Can't leave bodies lying around for anyone to find," I tell him.

He smirks. "Good thinking. Let's get going," Jake says, then I fall in alongside my brothers, and we enter the woods.

Pop has plenty of land stretching between here and the clubhouse. It could take a couple of hours to reach the other side of the property. It's not long before thunder booms above the tall pine trees. Keeping a steady pace, Logan, Gabriel, Jake, and I keep the course, heading in the direction of the club's property line as dark gray clouds begin to gather in the sky, blocking out the sun. The droplets of moisture began to pelt the leaves on the trees before feeling the first droplets against my uncovered head. Just as quickly, the rainfall becomes more intense. Rain is falling so fast and hard it sounds like the rotor blades on a helicopter.

Thirty minutes into our trek, the storm passes. "We're losin' daylight," Jake mentions, then he stops and falls to one knee. "You hear that?" he asks, and I strain my ears to listen. Murmured voices. It's faint but there. "Two, possibly three." He states as the rain starts falling again. Jake signals for us to keep moving. It doesn't take long before we walk upon their location. Tucked beneath a large oak tree are two men with their backs pressed against the trunk. Jake signals for him and Gabriel to move in one direction as Logan and I move in the opposite direction.

Twigs snapping catches my attention. I glance over my shoulder and find myself staring down the barrel of a semi-auto shotgun. My ears ring as a shot rings out, and in that hair second, I prepare for a bullet to rip through my body, but it never happens. Instead, the man who had me in his crosshairs drops to the ground. At my side, Logan keeps his rifle raised, prepared to fire another shot if need be. I give him a look of gratitude for saving my ass.

"Don't fuckin move," I hear Jake's voice above the sound of rain. After sweeping the perimeter for others, Logan and I approach the oak tree where he and Gabriel stand, holding the two men at gunpoint.

"Third one is dead," Logan reports.

"One down, two to go," Jake presses the rifle tip against the man wearing a camo ski mask.

"Prez?" the tone of Gabriel's voice is sinister, and without using words, we all know what he's asking.

"We only need one alive," Jake announces, and it's all the clarification my brother needs to lower his gun, lift his pant leg and pull his blade from his boot. Gabriel rips the mask from the man's head in front of him, giving us a good look at the dark-eyed bastard's face. The fucker glares up at Gabriel before spitting at him but says nothing. Reaching down, Gabriel pries open the man's mouth, pulls out his tongue, and slices his blade through it. The bastard screams, but Gabriel stifles his cries by shoving the severed body part down the man's throat, causing him to choke. Keeping his large hand over his mouth, Gabriel presses the knife against the throat of the man he is about to kill. "Decirle al diablo que dije hola, *Tell the devil I said hello.*" Then slits his throat.

Unphased by the death of his man, the one we plan on keeping alive keeps his face forward. "Get the fuck up," Jake orders, and he stands.

Logan rips the mask off the asshole's face. "You get to dig the dead's graves," he tells him, and I slam the shovel against the guy's chest.

As day turns to night, we watch the bastard dig two shallow graves, then he rolls the lifeless bodies of his men into the holes. When the last shovel of loose dirt and pine straw hit the top of the mounds, Gabriel binds our prisoner's hands behind his back using the rope he thought to bring earlier, then uses duct tape to cover the bastard's mouth, wrapping it around the circumference of his head a few times.

The four of us head back the way we came. After another thirty minutes of walking, the horse barn's side comes into view, and we emerge from the woods. I notice Pop sitting in a rocking chair on the front porch, facing our direction. He stands, the dim porch light reflecting off the extended barrel of his rifle in his hand. Jake takes notice of him as well. "Toss this sack of shit in the back of the truck while I have a quick chat with Warren."

Without question, we do as instructed. For good measure, I take the tow straps in the back of the truck bed, secure one end around the guy's ankles, then clasp the other end to an eyelet welded to the sidewall. If he decides to get the bright idea to take a leap of faith, he won't go too far. Instead, he'll earn himself one bad case of road rash after being dragged along the asphalt.

Jake returns, mounting his bike. "Take him to the old barn house. We don't need to expose our family to any more trauma. Quinn and Reid will be there waiting on us. Let's ride." He fires his engine, and I climb into my truck, doing the same

A short time later, we're rolling through the compound gates, where Sam lets us in. Outside the old barn, Quinn and Reid are waiting to unload our guest as I back the truck up to the doors. Quinn grabs the tow strap, using it to pull the fucker toward him, unties the binding around his ankles, then, with one hard jerk, throws him to the ground. Not finished, Quinn pulls a set of brass knuckles from his pocket, grabs a handful of the guy's hair, hauls him to a standing position, then proceeds to bury his fits in the bastard's face repeatedly.

"Enough," Jake orders. "Take his ass inside."

The barn doors close. Producing a knife, Logan slices through the duct tape covering the man's lower face, cutting into the flesh of his cheek in the process. He rips it from the bastard's mouth, taking facial hair and skin with it. Then gripping the man's chin. Logan stares him in the eyes as he drags the edge of the blade down his other cheek. Logan tosses the man to the floor. "String him up."

Reid drags the guy to a massive hook, attached to a thick rope, hanging from the rafter in the center of the barn. With force, Gabriel hoists the fucker off the ground. The strength my brother uses to lift him dislocates both of the fucker's shoulders, breaking the man's silence. He wails in agony, his body swaying from side to side. To the left sits a little worktable, with a variety of tools scattered across the top.

Quinn, Reid, Gabriel, Logan, and I gather around the man, forming a circle, waiting for the chance to inflict pain. "Who are you workin' for?" Jake asks our guest.

"Fuck you." The man grinds his teeth, trying to avoid the pain he's in. Jake eyes Quinn, who removes the man's boots, along with his socks. Beneath the man, bolted to the top of the floor planks, are two heavy-duty, industrial vices. One at a time, Quinn places the fucker's bare feet into the contraptions and holds them in place as Gabriel cranks the wheels until the man's feet are pinned between the metal plates.

"Are you workin' for the Mancini family—did De Burca send you here?" Jake asks, and the bastard spits his reply. Gabriel and Quinn give the wheels a few turns, applying crushing pressure on the guy's feet. The sound of bones breaking is as satisfying as his screams.

"You motherfuckers!" he roars as my brothers crank the vices a few more times. "Fuck," he flails, but his movement causes more pain to his dislocated joints as his body slightly sways again.

"The pain will only get worse if you don't talk," Jake states, then cuts his eyes at me. I walk up to the table. "Can I borrow that?" I ask Logan for his knife, slice down the man's pants legs, and expose his knees and shins. I lift the Hilti gun off the table, which is used to drive nails into concrete or steel beams under normal circumstances. Sweat rolls down the bastard's face as I look him in the eye, press the tool into the first kneecap and pull the trigger, embedding a nail into his bone. His wails mean nothing to me as I repeat the process, driving one into his other knee.

Outside we start hearing the sounds of another storm rolling in. The rafters over our heads creak from a strong gust of wind, and a low rumble of thunder is followed by the percussion of heavy rain pelting against the tin roof.

I turn my head at the sound of the heavy barn door opening, feeling the rush of damp night air wafts in, and notice Doc standing there. He strides to the center of the barn, taking in the scene. Doc's tired, red-rimmed eyes narrow to slits as he stares down one of the men responsible for the attack on our family.

Jake clamps his hand on Doc's shoulder before directing his attention back to the guest of honor. "We can keep going' or end your suffering now. The choice is yours." Jake drags an old stool nearby across the dust-covered wood planks that make up the bar floor. Sitting, he crosses his arms over his chest, demonstrating the fact he is willing to go all night until the man breaks.

Breathing heavily, the man sputters through clenched teeth. "The devil himself is coming for you and your men."

Doc looks to Jake, who gives him a nod before drawing his weapon. Taking a few steps forward, he presses the end of the barrel between the man's eyes. "I'd like to see him try." Doc pulls the trigger.

We stand silent for a beat before Doc speaks again. "Are there others?"

"The other two met untimely death earlier," Jake tells him.

"He give up a name?" Doc questions as he stares at the man he killed.

"No, and if I thought for a second, he was going to, he'd still be breathin'," Jake states. "How'd you get here?" He looks at Doc.

"Took a cab home. Had to clean myself up. I'm not havin' my woman see me covered in her blood when she wakes." Doc sighs and scrubs his hand down his face. "I couldn't find my phone, so I drove Lisa's car out here to let someone know I'm camping out at the hospital until further notice."

"Alright. We'll touch base with you first thing in the mornin'. If anything changes before then, let me know," Jake tells him, then looks at the rest of us. "Cut the bastard down and get rid of the body. We'll start fresh tomorrow. I think I speak for everyone when I say we all need to embrace our women and children tonight and thank fuck we still can."

At his statement, all I can think about is getting back to Lelani. With her on my mind, I help Gabriel with the disposal.

My brother, Gabriel, and I are the last to walk through the clubhouse door. It's quiet, and after the day we've had, I welcome the calm. After making a final sweep of the building, I drag my tired ass up the stairs, where I find Lelani sitting with her back against the headboard, her eyes shut, listening to a book.

"Austin," she breathes, removing her headphones.

"I could have been anyone, babe."

She gives a small smile. "I felt you the moment you entered the room."

I strip from my clothes. "I need to grab a quick shower." I step into the bathroom and turn on the hot water. As the bathroom fills with steam, I step into the shower. The hot water scalds my skin as I wash away today's filth. Slender hands pull the shower curtain back, and Lelani feels her way along the tiled wall. Reaching for her, I help guide her to step inside. My eyes travel over her body. I didn't realize until now how much I need to feel her close to me. I pull her naked body against mine, bringing her beneath the spray of hot water.

"I was worried about you," she admits as her hands travel across the tops of my shoulders, then down my biceps. Her fingertips travel over the bandage covering my wound. "You're hurt."

"It's nothin', babe." I lower my lips to hers and kiss her with fervor, losing myself in the way her skin feels as my hands trail down her spine. I follow the curves of her body, my palms skimming over the flare of her hips. The entire time I keep my eyes closed, using my other senses to map out every inch of her body. One of her hands travels down my chest and over my abs. I hiss as she drags her fingertips the length of my dick. Taking me in her palm, she strokes my cock. My hand covers hers. "Harder, babe." I instruct her to squeeze a little tighter and guide her hand, showing her how I like it. I then slip my hand between her thighs and gently rub her swollen clit, manipulating her bundle of nerves.

"Austin." With her other hand, Lelani grips my hair at the base of my skull.

"Fuck. You're going to make me come, babe." With every stroke, I grow more sensitive. I feel Lelani's body shiver, and I know she's close too.

"Oh God." Lelani keeps rhythm as her hand slides down my shaft, and her nails graze ever so slightly against the head of my cock.

"Let me have it, Mouse. Come for me." My mouth crashes down on Lelani's, swallowing her cries as her orgasm washes over her. After two more strokes with her hand, the most intense release of my life takes hold, curling my toes against the shower floor.

"Jesus. Watchin' you come is the hottest fuckin' thing I've ever seen." I struggle to catch my breath. I take her face in the palms of my hands, tilting her head back to look down on her face. "Where have you been all my life?"

"Waiting for you."

13

LELANI

Taking a sip of my coffee, I close my eyes and imagine how beautiful the sky must be as the start of a brand-new day rises from behind the Montana mountains. I imagine the sky being aglow in bright orange and a beautiful shade of pink and painted in the promise of a new day. When I was a kid, I called them flamingo clouds because the color reminded me of pink flamingos. My mom told me to never wish on a star, to always wish on a sunrise. A sunrise is the start of a brand-new day, and it is up to us to make our hopes and dreams come true. She always told me if I want anything out of life, it was up to me to make it happen, and the sunrise was there to remind us.

I haven't thought about my mother's wise words in a long time, but I feel her here with me today. I feel her in the warmth on my face, and though I can't see them, I know she is in the flamingo clouds reminding me not to give up.

I lay awake last night long after Austin drifted off to sleep, with my mind racing. I kept playing the events of what went down, over and over again, in my head. Soon, guilt began creeping in, and I couldn't help but think how it was all my fault. My being here has put the people I've come to care about in danger. Lisa is in the hospital after almost losing her life. Austin was injured when a bullet grazed his arm. When I think about all the innocent children that could have been hurt or, God forbid, killed, my stomach knots. All because of me.

"I know what you're thinkin, darlin', and I'm goin' to tell you now, to not let that pretty little head of yours go there."

The sound of Quinn's voice knocks me out of my wandering thoughts, causing me to jump out of my skin.

"Sorry, didn't mean to scare ya."

"That's okay." I smile. "I didn't realize anyone else was awake."

"I'm always up early. I like the quiet before the chaos," he tells me, then continues, "I have to say, I don't like comin' out here seeing that look on your face, doll."

"What look?" I play stupid.

"You can't bullshit a bullshitter, darlin'. I'm the biggest one here. Just ask," he chuckles. I sigh and shake my head but don't say anything. Quinn is right. "Yesterday was pretty fucked up, not gonna lie. What I will do is tell you that shit is not your fault."

"Isn't it, though?" My words bite back a little too hard. "If not for me and the baggage I bring, yesterday would not have happened. Children, Quinn. Your daughter." I choke on a sob, and the lump in my throat won't let me finish my sentence.

"You saved my daughter's life, Lelani." Quinn's emotion is not something I have heard from the fun-loving man before, and it gives me pause. "I saw what you did yesterday, sweetheart. You threw yourself over the top of my little girl and guarded her life with your own. You were prepared to sacrifice yourself to save Lydia." Quinn shuffles closer to where he is kneeled down on the ground in front of me. "My family and my club are everything to me, but my daughter," Quinn pauses like he is trying to gain control of his emotions. "My daughter is the air I breathe. Without her, I would be dead. Because of your actions yesterday, I will forever be in your debt, Lelani."

"I did what anyone would do, Quinn. I would do it again. All of you have come to mean a lot to me."

"That answer is why this club has your back, darlin'. You are not responsible for what happened. So, no more fillin' your head with that shit," he finishes.

Nodding, I take a shuddered breath. "I'll try."

I hear the opening and closing of the sliding glass door. "Everything okay out here, brother?" Austin asks. King, who is lying at my feet, moves at the sound of his owner's voice.

"We're good, brother. I was just enjoyin' a cup of joe with your girl before Em and Lydia wake up."

"That's cool, man." I feel Austin sit down beside me. "Mornin', Mouse." His lips touch mine in a soft kiss.

"Good morning," I return.

"Well, I'm going to make my girls some breakfast before hittin' the road. Em and the other women want to go to the hospital to see Lisa today," Quinn remarks.

"I'd like to go too if that's okay?" I ask.

Austin grips the back of my neck. "I'll take you, baby. Quinn, what time are we rollin' out?"

"An hour. Blake and Grey are stayin' behind along with Rain and Ember, who will look after the kids. Sam and Sofia agreed to stay too, but Prez doesn't want to be gone for long."

Austin lets out a sigh, weariness heavy in his tone. "Alright, man. We'll be ready."

When I hear Quinn walk back into the clubhouse, I go to stand. "Babe." Austin grabs my hand, halting my sudden rush to leave. "You okay? Why didn't you wake me when you got up?"

"I'd been up for a while. You were tired, and I didn't want to bother you."

"You never bother me, Mouse. If you can't sleep, I want you to wake me. We could have talked, or I would have put you to sleep another way," Austin's voice drops, and flashbacks of just how he can work my body pop into my head.

"I'll remember that for next time." I smile, but it doesn't quite reach my eyes, and I can tell Austin wants to press me further, but thankfully he doesn't. "I'm going to get ready."

Reluctantly, Austin releases my hand. "Alright. I'll meet you upstairs in a minute. I need to talk to Prez about something first."

I'm doing my best to hold onto the words Quinn spoke to me earlier when walking into the hospital an hour and a half later.

"Girls," Lisa's weak but cheerful voice calls out as we all file into her hospital room. "You guys didn't have to come to see me. I'm going to be out of here and back home in no time."

"Nothing could keep us away," Bella says with evident emotion.

"Yeah," Alba adds. "If it were any one of us, wild horses wouldn't be able to keep you away."

Lisa lets out a little chuckle. "Damn straight. I love my girls. Even you, sweetheart." At her words, Austin gives my hand a squeeze, and I realize Lisa is talking to me. Out of nowhere, I burst into tears. Here is this lovely woman, laid up in a hospital bed after being shot, knowing it's my fault, and she calls me one of her girls. "Oh, child. Come here, come here," Lisa orders, her tone soft.

Austin leads me over to the hospital bed, where Lisa pulls my head down to her shoulder and begins running her fingers through my hair.

"I'm sorry this happened to you," I cry.

"Why are you sorry, pretty girl? You didn't put me here."

"No, but it was my mess that did."

"Child." Lisa lifts my face from her shoulder and uses her hand to dry my tears. "You may not know this, but every person in this room has had to deal with similar circumstances. We all know what it's like to face the kind of evil that sets out to destroy us. But you know what?"

"What?" I ask.

"We come together and do whatever is necessary to take down those who try to destroy us. Our men will do whatever it takes to keep us safe. That is what family does. You are a part of this family, Lelani. Being a part of this family means every one of these men and women will go to hell and back for you." Lisa wipes away another tear. "Now, no more crying, at least not for me. Ya hear?"

I nod. "I hear you."

AFTER A SHORT YET EMOTIONAL visit with Lisa, the doctor came in and ordered everyone out so she could get some rest. We are currently in the waiting room down the hall, waiting for the guys to finish talking to Bennett. A minute ago, Bella, Alba, Mila, and Grace mentioned something about getting coffee. With everyone distracted, I decide to slip into the nearby restroom. I overheard another woman earlier asking a nurse where the ladies' room was and decided to seize the opportunity to slip away and hope my departure is not noticed. Once I make it into the stall, I retrieve the cell phone Austin gave me a few days ago and call a number I know by heart but hoped I'd never have to use again.

Placing the phone to my ear, I nervously wait for the person on the other end to answer. "Hello," is the greeting barked into the receiver.

Just as I'm about to open my mouth, the door to the ladies' room burst open, making me panic and hang-up.

"Lelani!" Austin's deep baritone voice echoes off the walls.

"Yes?" I call out then flush the toilet for good measure before exiting the stall.

"Babe, you can't just disappear like that."

Feeling my way to the sink, I go about washing my hands. "I had to use the bathroom," I lie, turning the faucet off and searching for something to dry my hands, and grab a paper towel from the dispenser.

"Lelani, you still can't go off by yourself like that while we are in public. Shit with the club is not good right now. You wandering off alone puts you in danger."

At the mention of the club having to deal with my "shit," as Austin put it, I press my lips together and turn away from his watchful eye.

"Baby." Austin hooks his arm around my waist and forces my chin up. "I didn't mean it like that, so get out of your head."

"It's okay. I know you didn't," I say in a whisper. The thing is, he only stated the truth, whether he meant it to come out like it did or not.

"Come on." Austin kisses the top of my head. "The guys are ready to hit the road."

By the time we get back to the clubhouse, I'm settled more in my decision to reach out to my uncle to see if he is behind the shooting that happened yesterday and see if I can talk him into leaving the club alone. Though I took to heart what Quinn and Lisa told me about the club not blaming me for what happened, I still feel I should try and do something to help the situation. I can't just sit back and do nothing without cleaning up my mess, and before another person gets hurt. It is time for me to take some kind of responsibility.

"I'm a little tired, so I think I'm going to go upstairs and take a nap," I tell Austin as soon as we walk into the clubhouse.

"You sure, babe? The girls were about to make some lunch. You don't want to hang with them?"

"Yeah, I'm sure."

"Okay. I need to handle some shit for Jake, then I'll be up to check on you." Austin cups my cheek and kisses the tip of my nose before sealing his mouth over mine. I feel him step away, and he lets out a whistle. "King," he calls, and a few seconds later, the gentle giant is at my side, nudging my hand with his head. Without missing a beat, King follows me up to Austin's room.

Closing the door behind me, I make my way across the room and sit on the edge of the bed, where I retrieve my cell phone from my purse. Taking a deep breath, I hit redial. My uncle answers on the second ring.

"Hello?"

My voice shakes as I speak. "Uncle Arturo."

The other end of the line is silent for a moment before my uncle utters, "Lelani?"

"Yes. It's me."

"Tell me where you are."

That's it? No, where have you been? How are you? Are you okay?

I'd like to say the fact that my uncle doesn't even ask about my well-being after I disappeared for weeks doesn't hurt, but I would be lying. I also don't miss the fact that he is demanding to know where I am. Does that mean he's not behind what happened yesterday? Or is he playing stupid?

Suddenly I'm fuming. "Are you not going to ask how I am? I have been missing. I could have been dead in a ditch somewhere? Also, what about Derrick? Maybe you should ask him about my whereabouts?" I snap.

"Don't forget who you are speaking to, Lelani. Obviously, you are fine, seeing as you are talking to me now," he says curtly. "As for your brother, he will be dealt with."

"I'm not going to tell you anything and you can quit acting like you don't know where I'm located, Uncle Arturo. I'm not coming back. I just called to tell you that and to tell you to call your goons back home and to leave my family and me alone."

"Family? I'm your family, and I'm ordering you to tell me where you are this instant!" my uncle barks, losing patience.

"I already said no!" I shout. "Call your men off, Uncle Arturo."

"I don't know what this nonsense you keep going on about is, but my men are here in Vegas with me. Now, I am not going to tell you again, young lady. You are a Mancini, and as a Mancini, you have an obligation to this family. It is time for you to come home." I hear his fist slam against a hard surface.

At the mention of my "obligation," my stomach drops. "I am home, Uncle Arturo. I'd rather die than marry Cillian De Burca." With those parting words, I hang up the phone. It's also the same moment I hear a loud gasp at my back. Standing, I face whoever is at the door.

"Did you say De Burca?" Grace asks with a tremble in her voice.

14

AUSTIN

"Grace, wait." Lelani's distraught tone catches not only my attention, but every brother gathered downstairs as we wait for Jake to call church. Lelani holds tight to the stair railing while trailing behind a visibly upset Grace.

"Grace?" Jake pushes his chair from the table where he sits and crosses the room as I rush toward Lelani. "Grace, babe. What's wrong?" Jake grabs hold of his woman.

"Grace. I can explain. Please," Lelani says, her voice trembling.

"Someone better fuckin' explain what the hell has my woman upset," Jake booms.

"I thought I would never hear the De Burca name again," Grace cries.

"Where did you hear that name spoken?" Jake asks her.

"From me," Lelani admits, her hand tightens around mine for support as I lead her to the center of the room where Jake and Grace stand.

Jake peers at Lelani, his eyes hardening and his face contorted with anger. "I ordered you to never speak the name De Burca around the women," he storms.

. . .

I STEP in front of Lelani. "Prez." I do my best to check myself, but the anger Prez is directing at my woman has my defenses up, for her sake.

"Austin. You'd do best to remember the peckin' order around here," he warns.

Grace stops a foot before walking into Jake's embrace. "I thought De Burca was dead, along with him and his family legacy. And don't go blaming Lelani for everything. In her defense, I was walking by when I overheard a phone conversation she was having with someone."

My brothers, minus Grey and Blake, are standing about the room. The women quietly usher the kids out of the commons into the kitchen with the promise of ice cream. Dialing back on his anger, Jake looks at Grace. "Babe. Shit. I promise you, Ronan De Burca is dead." Jake's eyes soften as he looks at his wife. "He is in hell where he belongs."

"Then explain to me why I heard the De Burca name again and why you are not as surprised as I am right now?" Grace snips.

"Jake. I'm sorry." Lelani's voice cracks as she attempts to keep her emotions in check.

All eyes in the room shift to Lelani, and even I'm curious. "Babe. Who were you on the phone talking to?"

Lelani takes a deep breath, gathering herself. "My uncle." The moment she says it, I close my eyes.

"Fuck," I hiss. "What were you thinkin', Mouse?"

"I was thinking of you—of The Kings," she admits. "I can't take it!" Lelani almost shouts, and it's the first time I or any of us have heard her raised voice. "Guilt is eating at my insides." She pounds her chest with her fist. "It's my fault men attacked the compound and shot at innocent people." Lelani's voice wobbles. "Something awful could have happened to the kids that day. My presence is putting everyone I've come to care for in danger. I called my uncle to confront him and ask about his involvement. Like many of you, I want answers too." Lelani steps forward and pushes her shoulders back, standing tall. "At the end of the day, I'm Massimo Mancini's daughter, and it's high time I start acting like it. My uncle is not what the Mancini name stands for. If he committed an act of violence against The Kings, I want him to pay."

I admire my woman for having the strength to speak up like she is. Not many will stand toe to toe with Jake during a heated moment. It also guts me to know she blames herself for the action of spineless men whose corpses are rotting in shallow graves. They are the ones who committed a crime against us, and they paid the ultimate price for doing so. Looking at the faces of my brothers, I can tell they feel the same.

"Damn it!" Jake's voice is harsh. "You may have had the best intentions, but it was careless. Your action could lead them right to our doorstep."

"What did your uncle have to say?" Logan asks.

"Nothing, other than he wants me home and that I'm to fulfill my obligation to the family by marrying De Burca."

"Someone needs to explain what the hell is going on," Grace says, still looking for answers.

"Grace, I'll explain later. All you need to know is you and Remi are safe. You don't have to be afraid," Jake tells her.

"I'm angry, Jake. Not afraid. Two completely different emotions. I stopped running and living in fear a long damn time ago. Because of you and this club—my family, I get to live. If Ronan is dead, then what De Burca would Lelani be referring to?"

Divulging club shit isn't something Jake does. We keep information from our women for their safety. The less they know, the better. Should shit go south, and the law is up to our asses, that's one less worry. Keeping the club's business between the men keeps our families' hands from getting dirty.

"Turns out Ronan has a younger brother, Cillian," Jake tells her. Grace opens her mouth to say more, but Jake cuts her off. "Nope. That's all you get. You know how we operate. I won't be tellin' any more details." Jake pulls Grace to him, and she lets him, sinking into his chest. "You have to trust my brothers and me."

"I do," she tells him, and he kisses the top of her head.

"I'd never put you or our daughters' lives in harm's way, Little Bird. Never."

"I know." Grace pulls back. "I would feel better if I knew more about the situation."

"I love you, babe." Then he looks at Lelani, then back to his wife. "If you need answers, then perhaps you should speak to someone else," he raises his brow, and Grace looks back over her shoulder in our direction. Her face softens as she glances at Lelani. There is no judgment in her eyes, only understanding.

Releasing Grace, Jake steps closer to Lelani and me and directs his full attention to her. "I'm not goin' to apologize for my anger."

"And you shouldn't. This is your family, and you need to keep them safe," Lelani tells him.

"Sweetheart, you need to understand one thing. The moment Austin claimed you as his woman, you became part of our family. I will do whatever it takes to keep our family safe. Do you understand?" His voice is less harsh but still sharp with his message.

"Yes," Lelani's voice breaks, and a tear slips down her cheek. I pull her to my side.

"Don't let something like this happen again. You go to your man first, then he'll bring your concerns to the table for all of us to handle. Got it?" Jake states, and she nods. Jake then looks at me and rubs his forehead. "You good, son?"

"Good, Prez." I lift my chin.

"Alright. Kiss your woman. You and Logan need to hit the streets. Start puttin' a bug in people's ears. I want to know if anyone remembers seeing strangers in town that fit the profiles of the shooters." Jake turns, kissing his woman. "I've got a Russian to visit." He walks out of the room.

Everyone else disperses, and I face Lelani. "You okay?" I tuck a loose curl behind her ear.

"Yeah."

"Austin, let's roll out," Logan calls.

"You going to be alright?" I ask, hating to leave her side.

"I'll be fine. My feelings were hurt more than anything." She lightly laughs it off. "I felt like I was being scolded by my father," she claims, and I chuckle, finding her statement relatable.

"Jake has that effect on many of us. He's rough around the edges, and his words can be a bit abrasive, but he means well. His actions have a purpose," I reassure her.

"I think I'll go upstairs for a bit," Lelani mentions, so I walk with her to the stairs. "Be careful," she speaks. Leaning down, I kiss her lips.

"Always."

WE'VE BEEN RUNNING DOWN possible leads all day, and not one panned out. We have three dead men, and now this junkie says he talked with a couple of unknowns several days ago. "Yeah, man." The guy picks at one of several scabs on his face. I've fucked with a variety of drugs in my life but never once touched meth. I look at the poor guy and a couple of his junkie friends sitting on the ground behind him, eating the fast-food Logan and I bought them. "They were asking around about The Kings specifically," he tells us.

"You remember what they looked like?" Logan questions.

"Oh, yeah, sure," the guy says around a mouth full of his burger. "They wore black suits and dark sunglasses." He shuffles his feet.

"Anything about their voices stands out to you—accent?" Logan continues to throw out questions.

"Like, were they from another country or something?" the guy questions, then thinks for a beat. "I'm not sure where they are from, but they aren't from Montana." He takes another bite of his food, and I can tell Logan is running out of patience. "The one doing all the talking maybe sounded Irish or Scottish. I don't know. The two accents sound the same to me."

Logan gives me a look, and right away, I know he's put together the same puzzle pieces. Irish can only mean one thing—De Burca. Then my thoughts shift to Lelani and the fact a De Burca is resourceful enough to track her down in a small town like Polson, bringing the war right to our doorstep.

"If you ask me, those men are working for the government. You know the ones who look for extraterrestrials," the guy adds, and his buddies join in.

"They exist, man. Beings from other worlds are walking among us," one speaks.

The junkie standing in front of us nods his head, then looks at Logan. "What he says is true. We see weird shit out here on the streets, man." The guy looks around then leans in close to me, his breath reeking from rotted teeth. "Aliens are real. I've seen them myself."

I tilt my head back and run my hand through my hair. "Jesus."

Logan turns. "Let's go." Without another word, we walk away.

"Thanks for the meal," the guy calls out, and Logan responds by throwing his hand in the air.

"That was interesting," I said tonelessly. The junkie's statement has holes in it. What parts are real, and what are figments of his drugged-up imagination? "How the fuck does an Irishman suddenly become a secret government official who hunts down aliens?"

"Let's focus on the Irish part of his story. The De Burca are like cockroaches. They could be anywhere," Logan says, swinging his leg over his bike. "Let's get back to the clubhouse and fill the others in on what we know so far."

FINALLY, back at the clubhouse, my brothers and I gather in church. Logan fills them in on what the junkie had to say, leaving out the extraterrestrial part. Jake leans back in his chair. "So, De Burca knows Lelani's location." He peers out the window. "As you know, Demetri is using his clout to find out what he can about the Mancini-De Burca merger. Unfortunately, he didn't have much to report. Turns out no one knows about any Mancini marriage announcement, and no one has heard of Cillian. Demetri believes if he's been in the States for some time, he is most likely operating under an alias. De Burca had several overseas accounts set up to funnel money. Those accounts have gone untouched since his death, until a year ago," Jake states. "Demetri's connection confirmed that Cillian stepped forward as sole heir of the family fortune." Jake scrubs his graying beard.

"And what about Arturo?" I ask, then add, "and his piece of shit, nephew?"

"I can tell you everything about the man, right down to his shoe size. Demetri gathered enough intel on that asshole to fill a warehouse."

There's a knock at the door, and Quinn stands to answer. Raine is standing on the other side when he pulls the door open, holding a tray of whiskey glasses and two bottles of Jameson. Quinn steps aside, and Raine quickly sets what is in her hands on the table. She turns and walks back out of the room without saying a word, closing the door behind her. The once silent room fills with Jake's voice once again.

"Arturo is a piece of work. The man has his hands in every seedy pocket Las Vegas can offer. Bad business has led to an extensive amount of debt. He owes several associates large sums of money. Many of the people Lelani's father did business with cut ties with him years ago because his sloppiness was a liability."

I reach out for one of the whiskey bottles and glass, then pour myself roughly two shots worth. I take a drink and the warm amber liquid coats my throat on the way down. "Lelani's uncle marrying her off is a means to an end. De Burca has money, which would settle any debts owed, saving Arturo's ass." I begin trying to analyze the situation out loud. "De Burca needs power and a stronger foothold in the States to better establish the family empire. He's swooping in and low key plannin' a coup. He's about to take complete control of the Mancini empire?"

"You may have hit the nail on the head, son," Jake states, "and here's another kicker. Years ago, Oren De Burca, their father, was to wed Lelani's mother in an arranged marriage."

"This shit is fucked up." Quinn pours himself a drink.

Jake continues, "Her mother was already secretly in love with another man and ran away with him. Lelani's mother married Massimo Mancini, which caused the would-be alliance between the two families to dissolve." Jake reaches for the bottle and a glass.

I tilt my head back, downing the remaining whiskey I'm drinking. "This is a lot to dissect," I state, realizing how much of a clusterfuck this all is. Nalani, Lelani's mom, was meant to be a De Burca, who instead wed a Mancini. Then a next generation De Burca married Grace, which ultimately led her to the arms of our Prez, and that led to the downfall of the entire De Burca family— so we thought. It just goes to show that no one's future is set in stone. Destiny can change by the simple choices we make, and those decisions can affect the future lives of so many others. Jake and Grace's paths in life may have never crossed if Lelani's mother hadn't chosen love over obligation, then I may have never known a life with Lelani in it.

"What about her brother. Any leads?" I ask.

"Demetri hasn't any information on Derrick to report," Jake answers.

My brothers pass the bottle around the table. Jake lets out a heavy sigh. "There's more." He sits his glass on the table. "The crash that caused the death of Lelani's parents and took her sight was no accident." He looks around the table, his eyes stopping on me. "Arturo murdered her parents—his only brother."

"We know this for certain?" My fingers tighten around the glass in my hand.

"Arturo wasn't as thorough as he thought when covering his tracks years ago. Don't ask me how, but Demetri found concrete evidence of the murders. Arturo is a selfish bastard, hungry for power, and loathed playing second fiddle to Lelani's father," Jake finishes.

All I can think about is my woman. She has no idea her uncle killed her parents, and for years she's felt like it's her fault they are dead. The truth will hurt her more than I care to witness. "Do we tell her?"

"For now, no. We keep all information you've heard today within these walls. Let's eliminate the threats against her and the rest of the family before breakin' her heart with yet another betrayal."

I'm afraid it will do more than break her heart. I fear it will crush her spirit.

15

LELANI

It's been two days since I messed up and called my uncle, which led to Grace overhearing me then freaking out when I mentioned the name De Burca. I still don't know the whole story behind why that name affected her like it did, but I have no intentions to pry. What I have been doing is keeping my distance from her and pretty much everyone else. I don't like that my actions made Jake upset with me and, more so, somehow hurt Grace. While sitting outside at the clubhouse, I find it impossible to pay attention to the audiobook I'm attempting to get lost in. Instead, I'm drowning inside my own head as thoughts of the week's events run rampant through my brain. It's not until King lifts his head from my lap, alerting me to someone's approach, that I pull myself out of my stupor. When I remove the earbuds from my ear, Grace greets me. "Mind if I join you?"

I give her a small smile. "Sure."

"Here, I brought some cold iced tea. It's pretty warm out today, and you've been sitting out here for hours."

Grace hands me the glass, and I take a sip before setting it on the table beside me. "Thank you."

"You're welcome," she says gently, then adds, "I wanted to talk about what happened the other day and my initial reaction."

"Grace," I protest. "You don't owe me any explanation."

"Yes, I do. I have been wanting to talk to you for two days but had a feeling you were trying to avoid me."

Oh, no. Now I feel like an even bigger brat. "Grace. I'm sorry. I didn't..."

"No." She cuts me off. "I know why you were doing it, and I'm not mad."

"I feel terrible for upsetting you. I thought it was best to keep to myself for the time being."

"Oh, Lelani. That's not what I want at all. You didn't upset me. It's just that name...hearing it again." Grace lets out a heavy sigh. "I was married once, before Jake."

I straighten and tilt my head to the side. "Really? What happened?"

"Long story short, I married way too young to a man I thought I knew but didn't. I married a man who was not only emotionally abusive but physically. A man who was the definition of evil. His name was Ronan De Burca."

My hand flies to my mouth, and I suck in a sharp breath. "What?"

"You heard right. I was married to Ronan De Burca. Apparently, his brother is Cillian De Burca."

"Oh my god, Grace. I had no idea."

"Neither did I. Not until two days ago."

"What happened to Ronan?" I ask.

"He's dead," Grace supplies, her tone a little clipped. "I won't tell you the details of how he met his demise, but what I will tell is that being married to Ronan De Burca was the stuff nightmares are made of, and I'm lucky to be alive today."

"I'm so sorry, Grace. I promise I had no idea."

"I know you didn't, sweetheart. You have nothing to be sorry for."

Grace continues, "And I'll tell you something else. When I met Jake, I was living a life in hiding and constantly looking over my shoulder. I had the weight of the world on my shoulders, and more baggage than any person should have to carry. But Jake didn't care. He didn't care that I had a crazy husband who was out to get me, that I had a daughter, or that getting involved with me meant putting himself and his club in the line the depth of hellfire. All that man cared about was keeping me safe and making me happy." It dawns on me why Grace is sharing this particular story. "I understand feeling guilty for allowing other people to carry your burdens, Lelani."

"It's not easy. I've spent years feeling like I'm either a burden or in the way," I confess. "My own brother hated me merely for existing then tried to get rid of me, and to my uncle, I was simply a means to an end; a pawn he could use for his own gain then try and pass it off as me filling my family obligation."

"Speaking as a parent, I can tell you that children are not burdens," Grace says with conviction. "It's not your fault your uncle and brother made you feel otherwise. When it comes to Austin, I can tell you right now he doesn't consider you one either. The same goes for me and for the rest of the club."

I shake my head. "You and everyone else must be really tired of giving me the same speech. Even though all of you keep telling me the same thing, I still have a hard time believing in it."

"Well, we'll just have to keep saying it until you do." She chuckles. "Trust me, sweetie. I have been in your shoes. I know what you are feeling. Accepting help and learning to let go is not an easy task. Putting all of your trust into someone can be daunting. Especially when you've been let down many times before." Grace puts her hand on my arm with a reassuring squeeze. "Everything will be okay. You'll see."

Giving Grace a shaky smile, I place my hand over the top of hers. I sigh. "I hope you're right."

"Babe!" Jake calls, alerting Grace and me to his presence.

"Hey. When did you get back?" she asks.

"Just now. What are you ladies up to?"

"You know, girl talk."

"That's good." Jake then addresses me, "Lelani, how ya doin', sweetheart?"

"I'm doing good."

"Glad to hear it, darlin'."

"Where is Austin?" Grace asks. "Wasn't he with you? Oh, there he is," she adds.

"Hey, babe. I was lookin' for you," Austin says, and I hear his footsteps as he approaches.

"Looks like you found me." I smile.

"Yeah, I did." Austin kisses me, and my skin prickles when his lips graze space below my ear. "You feel like gettin' out for a bit? Prez wants me to make a grocery run."

"Yes!" I jump from the chair, and Austin chuckles. "I've been going a little stir crazy."

"Alright, babe. Let's go."

ON THE WAY back to the clubhouse after leaving the store, I start to think about the conversation Grace, and I had and what Lisa told me the day we visited her in the hospital. "You've been extra quiet today, Mouse," Austin notes.

"I've just been thinking."

"Yeah?"

I angle my body in the passenger seat toward him. "I get it now."

"Get what, babe?"

"What the definition of family truly means. I get it now. For weeks, I have been beating myself up and letting guilt tear me up inside. I have spent weeks questioning whether or not the club would regret taking me in and helping me out."

"Lelani..."

"No." I hold my hand up. "Please, let me finish." Austin stays quiet, allowing me to say my piece. "It's hard to go from a life where the people around you make you feel as though you are an inconvenience. That taking care of you is a chore. After my parents died, I learned to stay out of my uncle's way. I spent my days keeping to myself because I didn't have anyone who cared. Then I met you." I beam. "And I met the people you call family. All of you treat me like I'm somebody. You make me feel like I'm not invisible and like I'm not an inconvenience. I haven't had that since my parents were alive. I think on some level, I didn't trust it. It was as if all the love and support I was receiving was too good to be true. I kept waiting for you to wake up and realize I wasn't worth the trouble." Once the last word leaves my mouth, the truck lurches to the right before coming to a complete stop.

"Baby." Austin grips the back of my neck. "That is something that will never fuckin' happen. Do you hear me?"

"I know that now, Austin. It's taken me awhile to see it, but I do. I see that a real family sticks by your side no matter what, and their words mean something. A real family will do whatever it takes to make sure you wake up every day feeling your worth. They never make you feel less than, no matter how many times you screw up or in my case, no matter how much trouble your former life brings to the table."

Austin kisses my forehead, my cheek, the tip of my nose and then my lips. "Yeah, now my woman is gettin' it," he murmurs, and soon it doesn't take long for our kiss to turn heated. Gripping the back of my neck, Austin angles my head to accommodate the assault he currently has on my mouth. Moaning at the taste of him, I eagerly slip my tongue in his mouth, desperate for more.

Unfortunately, we are interrupted by the sound of Austin's phone. With a growl, he reluctantly releases me, leaving me breathless.

"Shit," he curses a moment later.

"What is it?"

"The alarm at the garage is goin' off again. Reid is asking me to deal with it."

"You think something is wrong?"

Austin shifts in his seat and I hear him put the truck in gear. "Naw. Reid checked the cameras and didn't see anything. It was probably just a stray cat or something. I need to stop by and reset the alarm, though, because he said it's not lettin' him do it from where he is."

Ten minutes later, we pull up to the garage. "You and King stay here while I secure the shop. Keep the doors locked."

"Okay."

"I'll only be a minute." As soon as the truck door closes, I reach for the door and engage the locks. In the back seat, King climbs through to the front and plants himself in Austin's vacated seat. Reaching over, I start stroking his fur while the two of us wait patiently. Maybe only five minutes have passed when King suddenly becomes agitated. I feel his posture go rigid under my palm before he goes from sitting to standing on all fours. When he starts to growl is when I go on high alert. "What is it, boy?" I continue to stroke down his back to see if that calms him. Only it doesn't. In fact, he becomes more agitated and starts to paw at the driver's side door. Worried that something could be wrong with Austin, I decide to go check on him. Disengaging the locks, I open the door and jump down from the truck. I feel King at my back with a snarl the second my feet hit the pavement, but before he can follow, a hand clamps down around my bicep and yanks me away from the truck. The door slams closed. I can hear King barking like crazy and his paws clawing at the glass in a desperate attempt to get to me. I try screaming, and a hand covers my mouth, then shoves me up against the truck, knocking the wind from my body. "Shut your fucking mouth," a familiar voice hisses into my ear.

Derrick.

"How's it going, sister dear?" Derrick takes his hand from my mouth, and I suck in a much-needed breath of air.

"What are you doing here? Let me go." I try to wrench my arm from his hold.

"I'm here because once again, you screwed me over. Because of you, I can't go back home. I have Uncle Arturo looking for me, and because your new friend fucked up and hijacked the shipment that was supposed to make its way down to Florida, I now have Diaz on my ass. I literally have nowhere to go. All thanks to you," he snarls. I have no clue who this Diaz person who he is talking about is. No doubt just another person my brother crossed.

"You're crazy. I didn't do anything to you. You're the one who tried to sell me. You got yourself into this mess. You're the one who has screwed over the wrong people. Now you have to suffer the consequences," I say through clenched teeth.

Without warning, my brother backhands me across the cheek, making the whole left side of my face explode in pain. "Fuck you, Lelani," he grinds out then hits me again, this time the blow so hard I cry out as I fall to the ground. As I'm laid out on the gravel, the steel toe of my brother's boot connects with my stomach, causing pain like I have never felt before to radiate through my entire body and a strangled cry to escape past my lips. "Austin!"

16

AUSTIN

Once in the back, where the security equipment is located, I punch in the code to disarm the alarm, but it doesn't work. After it fails a third time, I pull the phone out of my pocket and call Reid.

"Hey, brother. Everything alright?" he asks.

"Yeah, nothing looks out of place, but the code to disarm the damn thing won't work!" I shout above the blaring noise.

"You see the black box near the ceiling, just above the control panel?" he asks, and I look up.

"Yeah."

"You see some wires running into the ceiling?"

"Yep."

"Remove the housing and disconnect the wire bundle plugged into the top side. It's hardwired into the shop's electrical system. That will completely disarm it," he instructs, then says, "I'm home, so I should be there in fifteen minutes to sort shit out."

"Thanks, brother," I say, then disconnect the call. Needing a ladder, I leave the room and make my way to the storage closet.

"Austin!" Lelani screams my name, and I bolt for the front

door. Outside I find her struggling with a man who has her back pinned to the ground next to my truck. King is clawing at the closed window, snarling and barking to be set free. I rip the motherfucker off my woman, tossing him like a bag of trash to the asphalt. I don't allow him to recover, and bury my boot in his side, then follow it up with a kick to the back of his head. "You picked the wrong woman to fuck with, asshole." He tries crawling away on all fours. I snatch him by the hair on his head and shove his body against the roll-up doors.

"Austin!" Lelani yells desperately.

"Get in the truck," I order her, then grab the piece of shit by the neck and squeeze. His eyes bulge from their sockets as I constrict his airway. Out of nowhere, a sharp crippling pain radiates across my thigh. I look down to see his hand wrapped around the handle of a small blade currently embedded in my flesh. A headbutt to the nose causes him to release his weapon, then I reach down and rip it from my thigh. Blood pours from his nose, now contorted at an unnatural angle. Finding some fight in him, the bastard brings his arm up then down across my forearm, breaking my stranglehold, his elbow clocking me in the left temple. I stumble back a few steps before shaking off his blow, then deliver a kick to his kneecap, hear the snap the moment my boot makes contact. He falls to the ground once more, screaming in agony. While the bastard withers, I pull my gun from the holster. He looks at me, breathing heavily. Spittle mixed with blood runs down his chin. "Stay down, motherfucker, or I'll put a bullet in your skull," I demand. Keeping aim, I move toward Lelani.

"Babe, you okay?" I run my eyes over her, checking for injuries.

"I'm okay."

Movement pulls my attention from Lelani, and I catch the fucker scrambling to his feet, attempting to take off. I open the door to the truck and set King free. "Go get him, boy," I command, and he tackles the piece of shit, taking him to the ground.

"He's going to rip my fucking arm off. Lelani, please," the man pleads, but it's his use of my woman's name that grabs at me.

"You know this dickhead?" I ask just as the rumble of a bike approaches, and Reid pulls into the parking lot.

"He's my brother."

My blood boils at her admission. Putting her safety above my need to murder her brother, I pull her to me. "I need you to get back in the truck."

"But—" she goes to argue.

"Back in the truck, Mouse." I open the door and help her slide onto the seat. "Don't open this door."

"Austin."

"Stay put," I demand and close the door.

It's not long after I have Lelani back in the truck that Reid parks his ride and takes in the scene. "What the fuck happened here?"

"That's Lelani's brother." I walk up to the motherfucker laying on his stomach, trying not to move. "King, let go." On my command, my dog releases his arm and wags his tail. "Good boy." I pat his head.

"Shit. How'd you get King to take the bastard down and hold him there?" Reid says, impressed.

I shrug. "He likes to fetch. It's basically the same thing, right?" I jerk the asshole off of the ground. "Watch Lelani for a moment?" I ask Reid.

"You got it. I'll place a call to one of the brothers and have them bring another cage around." He strides over and stands beside the truck as he pulls a phone from his pocket.

I drag Lelani's brother into the shop and shove his broken, bloodied ass onto a metal chair. Walking around the counter, I dig through drawers, finally finding a roll of duct tape.

"You'll pay for this," he spews, still breathing heavy.

I secure his hands behind his back, then wrap some around

his ankles. "Looks like you're the one who fucked up." I cover his mouth, shutting his trap, being sure to apply extra pressure to his busted nose. I leave him there and return to my woman. "Thanks, brother."

"No problem. Gabriel and Sam will be here soon with the van, and Prez was made aware of the situation," Reid informs me. "I'm going to go take care of the alarm system before we have Polson's finest coming to check shit out. You headin' back?"

"Yeah." I let King into the truck, then walk around to climb in. I grip the steering wheel, taking a breather, before turning the engine over.

"You mad?" Lelani questions fiddling with the hem of her shirt.

"I told you to stay put."

"I know." Her voice is small. "King was having a fit, and I started to worry something was wrong."

"I appreciate your concern, babe, but your safety comes first. Period. If I tell you to stay in the truck, I mean it." I press my point.

"I get it." Lelani remains quiet for a beat as I begin to drive. "How did he find me?" she finally speaks again.

"I don't know, but I plan on finding out." My hands tighten on the steering wheel.

"What will happen to him?"

"That's for the club to decide."

After arriving at the clubhouse, I had Emerson help Lelani get settled and leave her to soak in a warm bath, listening to one of those romance novels she loves so much, then get Doc to take care of my knife wound.

"You're lucky it was a small blade and that the dipshit didn't have the force to drive it in any deeper," he says, flushing the wound with saline. "It's a clean cut. I'll have you stitched up in no time." He pulls out a needle and injects the numbing solution around the wound.

"I'm sorry we dragged you away from the hospital," I tell him.

"Shit. I was threatened with bodily harm if I didn't leave."

I grin. "Sounds like Lisa."

"Damn woman is feistier than ever." Doc makes quick work on the stitches. "Done. Now put some pants on. Lelani alright?"

"She's a little busted up. The fucker clocked her in the face and she said he nailed her in the stomach with his foot and she was nursin' her wrist. Em thinks it's just a sprain, so she wrapped it up for her."

"You got you a strong one. Hard-headed too." I give a little chuckle at his statement.

"Women like her, like all the old ladies around here, they love hard though," Doc states with a gleam in his eye.

My phone chimes. Swiping the screen, I read the text from Reid.

Reid: Our guest has arrived

Me: On my way

I slide my phone into my back pocket. "You stickin' around?" I ask Doc before walking out of the room.

He continues to clean up. "I'm sittin' this one out and heading back to the hospital."

Stitched up, I head for the barn, where the club has to conduct questioning since the use of the basement for brutality is out of the question with the women and children present. The basement wall is thick but not enough to muffle screams of torture or gunfire. Not to mention getting someone down there unnoticed then disposing of the body.

I walk the long way out, taking the extra time for myself, smoking a cigarette along the way. My mind goes to dark places, imagining all the ways I want to make her brother pay for what he did to her. By the time I walk through the barn doors, finding him sitting in a chair front and center, my blood is pumping, itching for another go at him.

"Austin. I'd say let's get started, but by the looks of our friend here, you got a head start on the rest of us," Jake states. "Your girl okay?"

"She's good," I say as Quinn rips off the tape covering Derrick's mouth.

"How's the dog?" Quinn asks. "I heard he got a piece of the action too." He prods at Derrick's broken nose causing him to wail. "Don't be such a pussy. Something's wrong with your nose," Quinn flicks the tip, and I suppress my amusement. He can have a warped sense of humor, but I like it.

"That's because it's fucking broken dickhead," he spews at Quinn. Then his eyes fall on me. "Fuck you and your dog." He spits, and Quinn backhands him across the face.

"Thanks," I tell Quinn with a grin.

"Happy to be of assistance, brother." He tugs at his cut.

Derrick squirms in his seat as Jake approaches him. "Did your uncle send you, or was it De Burca?"

"De Burca can go fuck himself. The only reason he wants my sister is to take control of what is rightfully mine. I wouldn't help him if you paid me." His eyes dart wildly from face to face, not keeping eye contact with anyone. "As for my uncle, I'll be there to help the gravedigger bury his body when he dies. Because of Lelani, I have nothing." His sob story falls on deaf ears.

Jake looks at me. "It's your call what we do with him."

I draw my weapon, willing to put a bullet in his head just to get back to my woman.

"Wait—wait. Wha—what," Derrick stutters, "What if I help you out? I'll give you the information I know about my uncle in exchange for my life," he tries to bargain, and I balk.

"We know all there is to know about Arturo." I look at Jake, who gives me a nod to continue and then take a few steps forward. "I tell you what. You give us information on Cillian De Burca and what he is doing in the States, and I just might make your death a little less painful."

"Please. I don't know anything. This is stupid. If I did, why would I talk if you still plan on killing me anyway?" Derrick goes from begging to being cocky.

Unable to hold my anger back, I draw my weapon and shove the end of the barrel in his mouth, fighting like hell to not pull the trigger. "You sit here, pleadin' for your worthless life after sellin' your sister—your flesh and blood—to the highest bidder for greed. Men like you aren't suited for power. You are nothin' more than a spineless coward lookin' for a way to save his own ass." I shove the cold steel down his throat until he gags.

A phone rings inside his pants pocket. Unmoving, Gabriel steps up, pulling it from his pocket, and passes it to Jake.

"Just the man I'd like to speak with. I'll let your uncle know you're a little tied up at the moment." Jake swipes the phone screen. "Arturo," Jake says with distaste. "Your threats mean jack shit to me. Shouldn't you be askin' about the wellbeing of your nephew?"

Derrick garbles and gags around the barrel of my gun, trying to call out to his uncle.

Jake scrubs his beard. "I see you've done your homework. You'll have my answer within the hour." He disconnects the call and slips the phone into his pocket. "Change of plans." I feel his hand clamp down on my shoulder. "I need you to stand down," he orders. When I hesitate to follow through, he repeats himself. "Austin. Stand. Down." His tone is more authoritative.

I pull my weapon from Derrick's mouth. "Seems Arturo was trackin' his nephew for some time and believed he may go lookin' for Lelani, so he waited him out."

"You motherfucker!" I growl. Needing to release some anger, I bury my fist in Derrick's face. Blood gushes from his nose again. "You dumb piece of shit!" I shout, but he doesn't hear my words because the force of my blow knocked the fucker out cold. I start pacing.

"Arturo requested a sit-down," Jake states.

"When?" Logan asks.

"Tomorrow," Jake informs us. "Give our friend here somethin' to keep his ass asleep until then. We'll see if his uncle values his life in exchange for De Burca's."

I stop in my tracks and look at Jake. I'm mad as hell. "Fuck Arturo. I say kill the piece of shit now and be done with it."

"No," Jake says flatly.

"You know what he did to Lelani. He doesn't deserve to breathe." My nostrils flare, and my face heats.

"All of us in this room know what happened, and your time for retribution will present itself. Now is not that time. We need information on Cillian De Burca, and we will use her brother to obtain what we need to know in hopes it will put us one step ahead of a threat this club can't see." Jake's tone is harsh, but his expression is one of understanding. I give his words a beat to sink in and let my temper come down a few levels before giving him a tight nod.

Before nightfall, Jake sends word back to Arturo that the club agrees to a sit-down. Our terms are, the meeting will take place on neutral ground, keeping any threat away from the clubhouse and our families. Tomorrow morning, we ride across town to Charley's bar and finally come face to face with Arturo himself.

I, for one, can't wait.

THE DAY ENDS with me lying in bed with my woman draped across my body. Her fingertips trace down the long scar on my chest. I can tell she has been itching to ask me questions since I walked into our room after dealing with her brother. "Spit it out, Mouse." I rest my palm on her ass cheek.

"Is he dead?"

I sigh. "It's hard for me to wrap my head around your concern for the man who did you wrong," I admit.

"Dead or alive, he's still my brother."

I thread my fingers through Lelani's hair. "He's alive—for now," I tell her, then pull the comforter over our bare bodies. I kiss the top of her head. "Try and sleep. It's been a long day."

The room falls silent. As I stare at the ceiling, the shadows filling the room seem to move in on me, then I realize it's only my eyes closing as I drift off to slip. Before letting slumber pull me under, I tell Lelani, "I love you," and feel her lips lift in a smile against my skin.

"I love you too."

I'M WOKEN the next morning by a sharp knock on my bedroom door, followed by Sam's voice. "Rise and shine, lovebird. Prez wants us on the road within the hour."

Lelani moans, snuggling deep in the blankets, tossing her leg across my thigh. "Don't go," she groans.

"Sorry, babe. I can't skip this one." I reluctantly peel myself from under her soft warmth and stride across the room. I enter the bathroom, turn the cold water on, splash it on my face, then quickly take care of my other business.

"Will you be gone long?" Lelani asks, still in bed snuggled with the dog instead of me.

"I don't know how long this trip will take."

"Are you going to share with me where you are going?" She's rubbing King's belly. I cross the room and dig clothes from the dresser drawers.

"Sorry, Mouse. You know I can't do that." I slide on my jeans, then pull a black shirt over my head. Sitting on the bed's edge, I step into my boots. Lelani reaches out to find me and runs her palm up my spine.

Twisting around, I face Lelani, lean down and cage her in. I brush my lips across hers, and as she drags her palm down my chest. I kiss the tip of her nose. "Why don't you take it easy today. Soak in the tub and listen to one of your books." I stand and stride across the room, retrieving my holster hanging on a wall hook.

"I guess. I am still pretty sore." Lelani adjusts herself and leans her back against the headboard, grimacing a little as she moves. I begin to grow angry all over again, looking at the bruises on her face caused by her brother yesterday, and I want nothing more than to inflict more pain on the bastard.

I grab my cut, shrug it over my shoulder then walk back toward her. "I'll send Raine or Ember with breakfast." Leaning down, I kiss my woman one more time.

"They don't need to wait on me. I can fend for myself."

"Mouse," I warn in a cautionary but empathetic tone, and she sighs.

"Fine, but I'm not staying in this room or bed all day." Her hand lifts, and she palms my cheek. "You're a bit bossy, you know that?"

"You secretly enjoy it," I say as her fingertip traces the shapes of my lips, smiling when she feels them lift in a grin.

"Debatable." She presses her lips against mine.

"You make it hard as hell to leave," I confess, and my woman lets her lips linger. "Seriously, I've got to go." I force myself to pull away.

"Be careful," Lelani says as I open the door and step into the hallway.

"Always."

LESS THAN AN HOUR LATER, my brothers and I are pulling up to Charley's bar and I spot Pop's truck parked near the backside of the building. "What the hell is that old man doin' here?" I question.

"I invited him," Jake tells me. "Charley stayed as well," he says. I know Prez has his reasons, so I don't question his motives as we walk through the front door. Pop is sitting at the end of the bar talking with Charley, and on the bar top beside him lays his shotgun. I walk up to him, eye the glass his hand is wrapped around, and raise my brow.

"Now, before you go lecturing an old man about drinkin' because of his heart issues, just know this isn't liquor." He takes a swallow. "It's tea."

"How's it goin', Pop?"

"I'm fairin', Son. How's Lelani?" he asks, and I look at him. "Don't give me that look. Small town, remember? I know someone put hands on the sweet girl yesterday," he says.

"She's good, Pop."

Jake walks up. "Warren." He holds out his hand. Twisting in his seat, Pop reaches out to shake it. "Appreciate the support."

"Happy to help," Pop tells him.

Jake looks to Charley. "Charley, again. The club appreciates the use of the bar."

"Anytime," Charley says.

With little more to do, the barroom falls silent, and we wait. Charley sits a cup of black coffee in front of me, and I take it to the table at the back of the bar where my brothers gather to sit. We don't conversate. Like myself, they are probably running scenarios through their heads. Arturo is a marked man walking into a den of rattlesnakes ready to strike, and the club, sure as shit, isn't fooled enough to think we have him at a disadvantage. Anything can happen. Especially when you have nothing left to lose. Arturo's track record speaks for itself. His only concern is for himself. He's run the Mancini empire into the ground, taking millions with him. Arturo requesting a sit-down raises questions for all involved.

Why would he need to speak with us other than to convince the club to hand over Lelani?

No way in hell that's happening.

I listen to the clock on the wall ticking as the minutes pass. The air in the room grows heavy and ominous. The only sound I hear is my heart drumming in my ears.

Through the bar windows, I catch sight of a gray SUV turning into the parking lot and abruptly stand, causing a few others to do the same. Gabriel strides to the front of the bar, peering out the window. "Arturo," he states.

Jake and Logan stay seated at the table as Quinn and Reid join Gabriel. I keep my position, ready to pull my weapon.

Pop spins in his seat near the bar, his rifle at rest on his lap, clearly visible for our guest to notice. Charley steps from behind the counter with his 12-gauge ready to use if necessary.

Gabriel opens the door. The morning sun floods in, casting the shadows of men across the wood floor. Quinn and Reid raise their guns, training them on our guests.

"For your safety, we'll need to confiscate your weapons," Jake speaks. My attention zeroes in on the shorter man standing in front of the other men. With his dark, balding hair and beady eyes, the same face in the picture we have on file. Arturo.

"Our safety?" Arturo scoffs. "Then I ask the same in return. Hardly seems fair, should things go sour today," he says, loaded with arrogance.

"You're in my town, motherfucker, so you play by my fuckin' rules, or I'll shoot you and your men where you stand and throw your corpses to the wolves," Jake threatens, his tone dark.

I lift my hand, reaching beneath my cut, and wrap my hand around the handle of my gun.

Arturo narrows his eyes but heeds the warning. He motions to his goons, and they lift their hands to the ceiling. With Quinn and Reid keeping aim, Gabriel searches each man, confiscating their weapons. With each gun, he detaches the magazines, checks the chambers then tosses them into an empty whiskey crate nearby. Arturo straightens his suit like he's wiping away filth, and I want nothing more than to wipe the floor with his pompous ass.

"Have a seat." Jake points to the chair across the table from his. Arturo moves across the room, his face tight with annoyance. I smirk, and he catches it. The fucker isn't used to taking orders, and it shows. Arturo tears his eyes away from me as his goon pulls out his chair, and he sits.

"Fuckin' pussy," I say, not hiding my disgust.

"What the fuck did you call me?" Arturo makes a move to stand, and I have the barrel end of my gun in his face before his ass leaves the chair. The larger man standing a few feet behind his Arturo, with a shaved head and jagged scar running down the side of his face, steps forward. Charley blocks him, shoving the barrel of his shotgun into the guy's chest.

"Don't be stupid, boy," Charley warns him, and the man raises his hands and takes a step back.

Arturo's jaw tightens. My finger twitches, itching to pull the trigger, but he settles back in his chair and clears his throat. "Now, let's hear what you have to say." Jake leans back in his seat, crossing his arms over his chest.

"Mind having your man here lower his weapon?" Arturo continues shooting daggers at me.

"Austin, stand down," Jake orders, and I hesitate, which seems to be a pattern lately. "Stand down," he repeats, and I reluctantly lower my hand.

The room falls silent for a beat before Arturo opens his mouth again. "I'd like to extend an olive branch. I would like for us to not be enemies." His words feel forced.

"Sounds like you lack confidence with the peace offering you're putting on the table," Jake calls him out.

"I've got enough on my plate, and having The Kings as a thorn in my side is not something I need. You also have my niece. I want her returned to me as well. When I have her, I'll leave. We never need to see each other again," Arturo demands, and his words fan the flame already raging inside of me.

"Lelani isn't goin' anywhere, motherfucker. You'll have to kill me first, but not before you eat my bullet." My words drip with murderous intent. "She deserves better than an uncle who marries her off to save his own ass." His eyes go wide, but he quickly schools himself.

Jake eyes Arturo. "We know all about you, Arturo. You owe a fuck ton of money. There are at least two marks on your head if those debts aren't settled soon." Jake leans forward. "Did De Burca offer to pay off your debt?"

Arturo clears his throat. "Thanks to your club, De Burca isn't in the picture anymore. His marriage arrangement to Lelani, which isn't your concern, was dissolved. This meeting is about keeping your club off my back and out of my affairs." His air of cockiness will cost him more than he is bargaining for if he doesn't check himself.

"If you want reassurance The Kings won't kill you before you board that fancy jet of yours and leave town, you have to bring something with worth to the table," Jake states.

Arturo sighs heavily. "Fine. I'm willing to hand my niece over to your club if we settle our troubles." He dismissively waves his hand.

"My woman isn't your fuckin' property, you spineless bastard. She will never be a pawn to save your worthless life." My body trembles from rage. "Prez." I struggle to keep my composure.

Jake's hand raises, signaling for me to keep myself in check. "I'm inclined to allow my man here to beat the life from your body. Make no mistake, Lelani was never leaving with you today, and she is not a bargaining chip. However, I do have someone who may be of value to you." Jake looks to Logan sitting beside him and nods. Logan pulls out his phone. I drop my eyes to his screen, seeing his brother's name before he taps the call button.

"Bring him in," he tells Gabriel. Within seconds, the front door opens, and Demetri strolls in, wearing his signature black suit, smoking a cigar. Nikolai falls in step with his father, looking more like one of us, and Victor brings up the rear, with Lelani's brother, Derrick, in tow.

"Arturo." Demetri's accent is thick when he speaks. Arturo's eyes widen with recognition. "I thought I smelled shit when I walked through the front door." Demetri's harsh words mock Arturo's presence. Mancini visibly swallows the lump of fear in his throat as both Demetri and Nikolai step to the table. Arturo and his men follow Victor's movement as he shoves a bound Derrick into an empty seat beside his uncle.

Arturo takes in his nephew's appearance, and Derrick refuses to make eye contact with him. Demetri pulls a chair from the table. "Volkov," Arturo sneers.

"What? Not happy to see me?" Demetri goads.

"Only good Volkov is a dead one," Arturo scoffs.

Nikolai laughs, then his eyes narrow to sharp slits. "Words mean nothing. We both know your hands have never sinned. Your men do all your dirty work for you."

Demetri eyes Arturo. "My hands know death, felt it, and even crave it from time to time. Killing you would be nothing." Demetri's statement fires me up with a rush of adrenaline as I watch Arturo shrink to the size of a gnat.

"Now that everyone is here let us continue. This is our offer and your only option. Lelani stays with us. Wipe your niece from memory because I can assure you, she will eventually do the same with you and that piece of shit sitting beside you. You'll also give up any information you have on Cillian De Burca. In return, you get to take your nephew home." Derrick lifts his head, his eyes dart around the room, looking for a way out, then tries to bolt, but

Victor slams him back into the seat. "My family lets you and your men live, and you leave town." Jake lays his terms on the table, and by the look on Arturo's face, he finds Jake's words hard to chew.

Like we knew he would, the weasel sings like a canary. "De Burca searched me out first. He used the knowledge of my unfortunate business failures and the promise of helping me with my debt to force my hand when he proposed a merger through marriage."

"Forced your hand, my ass." I grit my teeth, biting back the remaining words I have to say.

He ignores my outburst. "Once Lelani went missing, and he found out she was given to human traffickers my nephew here owed money to, De Burca washed his hands of us."

"What do you know of his men and the attack on my club?" Jake questions.

Arturo lifts his chin. "Nothing. Last I knew, De Burca left the States. I haven't heard from him in three weeks."

The room fills with silence, the air thick with tension. My eyes bore into Derrick and Arturo while waiting for Jake to make his final judgment. If it were left to me, I would kill them all and leave no chance at them harming my woman ever again. Jake eyes Arturo. "The truth is, you're a dead man walkin'. Whether one of us kills you or not, your time is limited," Jake speaks the truth, and Arturo's lips thin. "If you fuck with Lelani or my club, you'll eat a bullet." Jake's face hardens. "We will be watching you. I'll know every move you make. You better sleep with one eye open. If the club finds out you lied here today, we'll make your death a long one. Now get your trash and get the fuck out of Polson."

Arturo stands. Every muscle in my body twitches. Jake letting him go is a hard pill to swallow, but I know what his endgame is, and trust his judgment even though my heart wants to lead my actions. Arturo and his men move toward the door. One of his men grip Derrick by the collar of his tattered shirt, yanking him from the chair. He struggles to break free but fails as he is dragged out the front door. Gabriel carries the crate filled with their weapons outside and the rest of us file into the bar's parking lot. My brother drops the box to the ground, then walks toward us.

We look on, guns drawn in case they get the bright idea to do something stupid. Pop comes to stand at my side, his hand clasping my shoulder. He says nothing, but him being here means a lot. Arturo and his men rearm themselves and head for the SUV they arrived in. Arturo pauses before getting into the back seat. He speaks to one of his men, then turns, giving his nephew a final look before climbing into the vehicle and closing the door.

His man draws his weapon, aiming at Derrick. Before the poor bastard has a chance to react, Arturo's man puts a bullet in Derrick's head, then he robotically gets into the passenger seat of the SUV, which quickly drives away, leaving his nephew's body behind.

"That's cold," Quinn says, shaking his head.

"Shit." Logan sighs. "Someone clean it up," he orders and Gabriel and Reid take care of it.

"You get the cameras planted?" Jake asks Demetri.

"One in the SUV and several on board his jet," Demetri informs him.

"Think he's still suckin' De Burca's dick?" I ask, hoping this leads us to Cillian's whereabouts.

Jake runs his hand through his beard. "We'll know soon enough."

"Come on, men. I'd say we all deserve a drink," Charley announces, and we follow him back inside.

"Thanks for having our backs today, Pop," I tell him as we walk together.

"No thanks necessary. There is no place I'd rather stand than beside my grandson."

17

LELANI

I wake feeling warm. Like being wrapped in a cocoon, only that cocoon being Austin's arms, which is where I've been since he crawled into bed with me last night. I know what happened the other day with my brother affected him. To be precise, it made him angry. I haven't asked about my brother since the first time I inquired. It wouldn't do any good if I tried anyway. When he finally returned to the clubhouse, I sensed he needed to simply be with me. To be honest, that's what I needed too, so we spent another night embraced in each other's arms.

Now I'm wide awake. Judging by the steel erection currently pressed against my backside, along with the hand between my thighs, Austin is too. And though there is a scrap of material between us, I know he can tell how wet I'm for him. With his fingers working their magic over the top of thin cotton covering the spot, desperate for attention, I begin to squirm. "Austin," I gasp.

With his broad chest planted firmly against my back, Austin snakes his other arm up under my neck and then around to my chest, where his large palm cups my breast. Biting at my neck, he rolls his hips, further digging his cock into me. "Austin, I need more," I moan. He responds by slipping his finger into the side of my panties and runs his finger along my slit before pressing it against my clit, causing a choking noise to leave my mouth. The sensation is almost too much for me, and a moment later, I'm on the verge of exploding when he stops.

"No moving," he orders. "Every time you move, I'm going to stop."

"But..." I go to say, only to have Austin cut me off by running his tongue up the side of my neck. "I want you to lie still for me, Mouse," he rasps into my ear. Taking my leg, he pulls it back, draping it over his own thigh, then pulls my panties aside to give himself the access he is after. "Just feel me, babe," Austin rumbles, barely a whisper. On my next breath, I feel the head of his cock kissing my entrance. After a brief pause, Austin begins pushing forward. Ever so slowly, he enters me inch by glorious inch.

"Good girl," he praises, tilting my head back so that he can take my mouth with his. Then slowly, he begins stroking his cock in and out of me. It takes all the willpower I have to keep from pushing back. Instead, I relax every muscle, surrendering my body to him. I let my back settle against his chest, clear my head of every thought, and focus only on the moment. Right now, nothing exists but him and me. By doing this, I become hyper-aware of the pleasure Austin is giving me. Each sensual stroke of his rigid cock, to the way his nipple piercings scape against my back with each thrust of his hips, to the large hand braced around my throat and the thumb pressing against my pulse, or how Austin's thrusts are now in sync with my heartbeat. "Fuckin' love you," he breathes, his mouth against the shell of my ear.

"I love you too." Reaching back, I thread my fingers through his hair. It doesn't take long for an orgasm to build again.

"I could live in this pussy. So wet and tight. And all mine. Isn't that right? Say it, Lelani," Austin orders.

"Yes," I hiss.

"Yes what?"

"It's yours."

"Come," Austin growls, then pinches my clit. That's all it takes to send me over the edge.

"Austin!" I cry out as my release crashes through my body. With one final jerk, he plants himself deep inside of me and groaning low and sexy as he, too, finds his release.

LATER IN THE MORNING, Austin and I have breakfast with Gabriel and Alba. I go to pour myself a cup of coffee but wince at the sharp pain that radiates from my wrist up through my arm.

"Is your wrist still bothering you, babe?" Austin asks, his voice filled with concern.

"Yes. The pain meds and ice haven't been helping much. I don't know if it's all in my head, but I swear the pain has gotten worse."

"I wonder if it's more than a sprain," Alba interjects.

"I'm going to call Emerson and see if she can see you today," Austin says.

"No. Please don't bother Emerson. I'm sure she will be too busy. I will continue taking meds and put the ice pack on it again. I'm sure it's fine."

"Babe, you're not fine. Alba is right. It might be more than a sprain. Besides, if Emerson was to find out you were hurtin', and I didn't tell her or bring you in, she would have my ass."

"Fine," I grumble. "You can call and see if she will see me."

A second later, Austin is on the phone. "Hey, Em. Do you have time to see Lelani?" There is a pause. "No, it's her wrist. She says the pain has gotten worse." Another pause. "Thanks, Em. We'll be there in thirty." Austin hangs up the phone. "Emerson said to come on down to the clinic, and she'll get an x-ray of your wrist. She said it sounds like you might have fractured it."

"Great," I sigh.

"I'm sorry, baby." Austin puts his arm around me and kisses my temple. "Why don't you go get ready, and I'll fix you some coffee."

"Thanks. I only need to grab my purse from upstairs, and we can go."

WHEN WE ARRIVE at Emerson's clinic, I go to open the door. Austin stops me. "Keep that pretty little ass seated. I'll help you."

"Austin, I can get out of the truck on my own," I huff.

"I'm not going to risk you hurtin' your wrist or your ribs any further. Now do as you're told and sit tight."

I don't get a chance to answer before Austin is out of the truck and at my side, pulling open the door. "You're so dang bossy," I tell him as he grabs me around my waist and hauls me out of the truck.

"Hey, brother. What are you two doin' here?" I hear Quinn ask over Austin's shoulder as my feet hit the ground.

"Brought Lelani to see Em."

"She okay?"

"Yeah, man. Just her wrist. Em thought it was best to get an x-ray done on it."

With Quinn trailing behind us, we make our way inside the clinic, where the receptionist greets us. "Can I help you?"

"I got them, Zara," Emerson calls out as she approaches us. "Lelani, you can come back with me."

When Austin makes a move to follow, I stop him. "I'll be okay on my own. You said you needed to discuss something with Quinn anyway. You can do that while Emerson looks me over," I suggest. There is something I wanted to bring up with Emerson, but I would prefer Austin not be in the room while I do.

"You sure, babe?"

"Of course." I smile.

With a kiss, Austin leaves me with Emerson, and she leads me to the back of the clinic and into a room where she takes a quick x-ray of my wrist then leads me into another room. "Go ahead and have a seat. The bed is to your left. I'll be right back with your x-ray."

Doing as she says, I hop up on the bed and wait for the verdict.

"Well, there does appear to be a fracture," Emerson says, returning to the exam room. "I'm sorry, Lelani. I should have had you come in before."

"It's not your fault, Emerson. It really didn't hurt that bad after my attack. You couldn't have known."

Emerson lets out a heavy sigh. "I can imagine the pain you've been in. The good news is, we can get a cast put on and have you well on the road to recovery. I'll also give you a prescription for the pain. Nothing too heavy, just something a little stronger than the over-the-counter stuff."

"Um...speaking of prescriptions, do you think you can prescribe me some birth control?" I ask awkwardly.

"Is this for a refill? Are you taking anything now?"

I shake my head. "No. I've never taken anything. I uh...never had a reason to before."

"Okay, that's fine. I can definitely write you a prescription for something. I can go over the different options we have as far as contraception and decide which option you think is best for you. I'll also set you an appointment with a good OBGYN. Have you ever been to one?"

Again, I shake my head no.

"That's no problem. I can send you to Doctor Spears. You'll like her. In fact, she's my doctor as well."

"Thank you, Emerson. I appreciate that."

"No problem. Now before I write that prescription, I have to ask if there is a chance you could be pregnant now?"

I take a shuttered breath. "It's a possibility. Austin and I...we haven't been...we haven't been using anything."

"Okay." Emerson's voice goes soft. "Would you like me to give you a quick pregnancy test? I can't prescribe you any kind of birth control until we do."

"Please, I'd like to take the test."

Ten minutes after peeing in a cup, Emerson walks back into the exam room. I sit on the bed with my knee bouncing a mile a minute as I nervously wait for the result.

"Lelani," Emerson says my name in a way that is telling.

"It was positive, wasn't it?"

"Yes, the test came back positive. You, my friend, are pregnant."

At those words, I'm rendered speechless, and my entire body starts to shake. *I told Austin something like this would happen. We're too new. This is happening too fast.* I go from panicking about actually being pregnant to the possibility of something being wrong with the baby and suddenly I can't breathe.

"Lelani." Emerson places her hand on my arm. "It's going to be okay. I need you to calm down." At this point, I start to hyperventilate. Thoughts of my attack start flashing through my head, my brother kicking me while down on the ground. Is the baby okay? "Take a deep breath for me, Lelani. In through your nose and out through your mouth," she instructs.

Doing as Emerson says, I focus on my breathing. It takes me several minutes but finally, I get myself under control. "Sorry," I apologize, my voice shaky. "I didn't mean to freak out like that."

"There is nothing to apologize for. Finding out you're pregnant can be a scary thing."

"It's not really that. I mean, it is scary. Austin and I haven't been together long. This is all happening way too fast."

"Fast doesn't necessarily mean bad, Lelani. All that matters is you love each other."

.   .   .

"You're right." I take several deep cleansing breaths. "I mean, we talked about the fact I could get pregnant and he didn't even seem to mind."

Emerson laughs. "That sounds about right coming from one of those men." On a more serious note, she asks, "Do you have any more concerns?"

"Do you think the baby is okay?" A tear slips down my cheek at the thought of something happening to my unborn baby. "Because of the attack? My brother, he kicked me pretty hard. I have bruising. Do you think...?" I can't even get the words out of my mouth.

"I'm sure your baby is fine. You'd be surprised at how much a woman's body can withstand. To be safe and for peace of mind, how about I perform an ultrasound?"

I nod. "Thank you."

"No problem. Let's get a cast on your wrist before we move forward."

Fifteen minutes later, I'm lying back on the exam bed while Emerson performs the ultrasound. "I can't guarantee I'll be able to pick up a heartbeat." Emerson draws out, then pauses. "Wait one second." Another pause. "Here you go." The sound of Emerson tapping on something is followed by a whooshing sound.

"Is that?"

"Yep. That Lelani is your baby's heartbeat. And as you can hear, it's strong."

"Oh my, god," I breathe out in awe. "And everything looks okay?"

"Everything looks perfect. You're still very early, but from what I can tell, your baby is fine."

Finally, I'm able to breathe easily.

"I'll print out some pictures for you to keep and share with Austin if you choose to do so."

"Thank you. I guess I will find a way to tell him tonight. A lot is going on with the club. You think maybe I should hold off on telling him? Wait until things settle down a bit?"

"I think Austin would want to know. But then again, that's only a decision you can make. Are you worried about how he will take the news? I know you guys are new but I have to say, I think he will be happy. Austin adores you."

"I'm a little nervous. I'm mostly worried about the added stress."

"I think a little good news amongst all the chaos will be welcome. What do you think?" Emerson asks.

"You're right. I don't think I could hold something like this back anyway." I smile. "I'll tell him tonight."

WHEN EMERSON WALKS me back out to the front of the clinic, Austin is there waiting for me. "You were right to bring her in," she tells Austin. "There was a small fracture. She can come back in six weeks to remove the cast."

"Thanks, Em," Austin tells her.

"You're welcome." Emerson then lightly touches my shoulder as she addresses me. "Feel free to come to me with any questions you may have."

"I will. Thanks again."

On the way back to the clubhouse, I can't help but think about the fact I'm carrying Austin's baby. The thought brings a smile to my face, and on instinct, I rest my palm over my flat stomach.

"What ya smilin' about over there, Mouse?"

"I'm just happy. I mean, I know things have been crap lately with my family and all, but being here with you, makes me happy."

The hand Austin has rested on my thigh grips me tighter. "You don't know how fuckin' thrilled I am to hear that, babe."

"You..." I go to say, but the rest of my words are interrupted when Austin curses, "Fuck!" Followed by the truck tires rolling over something in the road, causing a loud pop. I don't have time to ask what happened or react. Suddenly Austin loses control. I let out a shrill scream as the seat belt tightens across my chest, and the truck crashes into something. When the impact happens, my head bounces off the passenger window causing it to break, and shards of glass fly all around me. "Lelani!" Austin shouts, but his voice sounds muffled and distorted over the sound of metal grinding against metal.

By the time the truck comes to a stop, I'm disoriented. I soon realize my body is dangling from the seatbelt as if the truck is not sitting upright. "Austin!" I call out. "Austin!" I try again. Still not getting a response, I panic. With shaky hands, I work at unbuckling my seatbelt. After several attempts, the belt finally releases, and I fall sideways onto the console between the passenger and driver seat. "Austin." I reach out and feel around until my hand touches his face, feeling wetness. When I pull my hand away, I rub my fingertips together. *Blood?* "Austin, please," I plead, running my hands along his chest and torso in search of more blood and breathing a sigh of relief when I don't find any. My next thought is to get help. Think Lelani. Phone! I need my phone. Knowing Austin always has his cell on him, I pull open his cut and search the pocket. I don't find a phone, but I do find something else, his gun. "Where is it?!" I cry, then try searching the front pocket of his jeans. Again, I don't come across his phone. Maybe I can make my way to the road in hopes of flagging someone down. On that thought, I twist my body and maneuver my way out of the passenger window. That's when I hear two male voices approaching.

"You better hope she's still fucking alive. De Burca will slit both our throats if we fuck up."

Terror sweeps down my spine when I hear the men say the

name De Burca. Cillian did this. With my heart feeling like it's about to explode out of my chest, I do the only thing I can think of. I dive back across the center console, reaching into Austin's cut, and pull his gun from the holster. The moment I have a grip around the cold steel, a hand clamps down around my ankle. "Got you."

I start kicking and screaming, my foot coming in contact with something or someone. "Let me go!"

"Shut the fuck up," the guy sneers, giving my leg another hard yank as he pulls me through the busted window of the truck. With the gun still in my hand, I swing my arm in front of me. The man I'm currently struggling with stops tugging on me. "Let me go," I order.

"Or what, bitch. Do you know what you're doing with that thing? You can't even fucking see your target."

"I'll take my chances," I say, pulling the trigger. I brace myself for what may happen, but nothing happens.

"Stupid fucking woman. You're all good for nothing," the guy cackles, dragging me the rest of the way out of the vehicle, not caring that I still have the gun in my hand.

"No, it's stupid fucking men like you who underestimate women," I say through clenched teeth just before I aim and pull the trigger a second time.

"Son of a bitch!" the guy spits, releasing his hold on me. I take the opportunity to try and climb to my feet. "Austin!" I scream. "Somebody help!" I start to run, not knowing what direction I'm going. I don't get far when I'm grabbed from behind, and the gun is knocked from my grasp. "Stop fucking fighting." I stop struggling when I feel something cold and hard against my temple.

"Ricky, get your ass over here and deal with her so I can finish the fucking job."

"The bitch shot at me, Martin."

"Yeah, well, the bullet only grazed you, you fucking pussy. Quit your damn crying, and come get her ass in the car."

"Let's go." I'm passed off to the guy I took a shot at and tossed into a car. This is followed by my wrist being cuffed. "Austin!" I cry out again.

"You're wasting your breath. Your precious boyfriend is done for."

"What are you going to do to him?" The second the question is out a gunshot rings in the distance. Realization dawns on me, and a blood-curdling scream rips from my mouth. "No!"

I REFUSE to believe it's true. Austin can't be dead. He's going to be a father. We are going to be a family. We are meant to be together and happy. God would not give me Austin only to rip him away.

I don't know how long we've been on the road or where we are going, but by the time we come to a stop, I'm a shattered mess. Sobs have taken over my body, and the despair I feel is soul-shattering.

"Let's go." Ricky, the man I shot at, removes the cuff from the handle and not so gently forces me from the vehicle. I'm then led up a set of steps and through a door where a blast of cool air hits my heated and tear-streaked face.

"What the hell happened to her?" A new voice asks, not sounding pleased.

"Martin used the strips. The fucker's truck rolled. It's not a big deal."

"Not a big deal." The new guy's tone turns murderous.

"Chill the fuck out. She's alive, isn't she? Can't say the same for her boyfriend, though," Ricky laughs.

"Go see if Martin needs any help out back," the new guy grits out. "I'll handle shit from here."

"Suit yourself. The bitch is a fucking headache anyway. Don't know why the boss is going through so much damn trouble for her."

"Just do as you're fucking told, Ricky."

A moment later, a door opens and slams shut, leaving me alone with the new guy. I swallow past the limp in my throat and wait for what's to come next. Nothing would have prepared me for what does. The guy moves in closer to me, and I flinch.

"I'm not going to hurt you, Lelani. Neither will anyone else. You have my word. This will be over soon, and you'll be back home with The Kings in no time."

18

AUSTIN

I slowly become aware of something wet passing across my cheek, followed by a soft whimper. My eyes feel heavy while attempting to pry them open. "Fuck." I groan. I feel like a Mack hit me. I continue to open my eyes while struggling to move. Pain radiates over every inch of my body. I take a few ragged breaths before the fog lifts from my brain, and the reason I'm here rushes back. My truck rolling down the embankment, then feeling disoriented. I recall Lelani's screams as I scrambled from the wreckage, searching for her—the fear in her voice as she yelled my name and the cracking sound of gunfire bleed together. My head feels fuzzy as I fight to remain conscious. I struggle to hold on to the memory of the accident. Wait. It wasn't an accident. I blink a few times. Someone ran us off the road. They took Lelani and shot at me.

My eyes open to darkness before adjusting to the lack of light around me. King barks the moment my eyes connect with his as he stands over me. "Hey boy," I croak, my throat feeling like I swallowed rocks.

Not being able to pinpoint the cause of pain, I breathe through it. "Shit. Focus," I tell myself. Jagged edges dig at my back as I stare up at the starry sky above. The feeling of cold settles over me, and my body begins trembling uncontrollably. I make a second attempt to move. When I do, water sloshes. It's then I become aware of being near water. I kick my feet feeling the water move around the lower half of my legs.

This isn't good. Fuck. Nothing about this situation is good. I need to move.

Channeling every ounce of energy I have, I roll my body onto my stomach. The sharp stabbing pain that rips at my shoulder and side as I haul the weight of my body from the lake almost does me in. "Fuck!" I roar so hard my lungs burn.

I only manage to drag myself a few yards into some thick grass, but I'm out of the water and the rocky bank for now. I spot a large tree log to my right, slowly work my way over, then prop my back against it. I raise my right hand to my left shoulder. As I pull my hand away, I find it coated with blood.

Two shots. I remember someone shooting twice before feeling the ground slip from beneath my feet.

I assess the rest of my body, noticing scraps and cuts over my forearms and my pants ripped along my right knee, all the way down to my boot, revealing a deep gash in my calf—blood trails down the side of my leg from the open wound.

Kings sit at my side and whimpers again. "I know. We need to get out of this mess and get our girl back." I tell him. In the distance, I can see my truck lying upside down at the water's edge at the bottom of the bridge. Even if someone manages to drive by and notice anything, they wouldn't know I was this far down from the accident site. "King. Listen, boy. I need you to get help." He lays his head on my shoulder, and I scratch his ear before kissing his head. "Go home, King." His head lifts, and those ears perk up. "Get help. Go Home." I give him the command, and he hesitates before taking off toward the highway.

If anything, someone might see him wandering the roadside, and he can lead them back to me because I don't have the strength to get that far right now.

Time slows as I wait. Every second that passes, I struggle to stay awake. The minutes are ticking by, feeling more like hours while fighting against the cold gripping my body. Every time I take a breath, it feels like someone is kicking at my ribcage, leading me to believe I fracture a few bones.

I try again to remember the details of the crash. I try putting the pieces together and figure out who is behind the ambush. Only one name comes to mind—De Burca. It has to be.

Those bugs Demetri planted in Arturo's SUV and plane proved valuable in obtaining more intel on Cillian's whereabouts. Arturo wasn't lying when he said De Burca washed his hands of him. We heard every sordid detail from inside his private jet shortly after he landed back in his city as we watched some men board the plane. They were there to deliver a message from De Burca. Unfortunately for Arturo, his sins finally caught up to him, and Cillian didn't take kindly to his loose lips speaking shit about him. My brothers and I had a front-row seat, sipping whiskey as we watched the massacre unfold. By the end of the brief encounter, De Burca's men shot Arturo and his four men dead before they ever stepped foot on Vegas soil.

I move, and another ripple of pain courses through my body. Needing a distraction, I focus all my thoughts on Lelani. She's out there somewhere frightened with no way of knowing where she is. The idea of something happening to her rips at my insides.

The night finally blankets the sky. I sit listening to the broken sound of water slapping against the bank a few yards away and frogs croaking in the trees. The sounds of nature surrounding me begin slipping away and my mind drifts to an empty place, void of thoughts. My pain fades into the background, and I feel myself nodding to sleep. I fight at first, but within seconds lose the battle. At the moment, just before the shadows close in on me, my thoughts clear. I hear Lelani call out my name. As if her voice is carried away by a breeze, she softly whispers, *don't give up.*

19

JAKE

After a long-ass day, there's nothing better than enjoying a cold beer surrounded by family. Sitting back, I chuckle and watch Grace chase after Ellie, who decided to snatch a handful of cookies from the table when her mom wasn't looking. My daughter runs toward me, but Grace scoops Ellie into her arms. "Daddy," my little munchkin says in a fit of giggles.

"Grace, babe." I attempt to help the little ·spitfire, but my woman isn't having it.

"Oh no, you don't." Grace manages to snatch one cookie from her flailing hands before our daughter tries smashing the other two into her open mouth. At this point, I step in, grabbing the cookies before she devours them.

"Ellie, did momma say you could have a cookie?" I ask, and she shakes her head. "Tell momma you're sorry." I try my best to keep a straight face, but it's hard when her sweet face looks so much like her beautiful momma.

Ellie Kate looks at her momma. "Sorry," her little voice causes me to crack, and I smile.

I clear my throat. "Next time, wait until momma gives you the cookie." I bop her nose, and she swishes in her little sundress. The kid has me wrapped around her finger. I look at my woman, and she sighs.

"Go ahead," she tells me, and I hand our baby girl a cookie. "Go play," I tell her, and she toddles away, the cookie devoured before she makes it to the other side of the room where the other kids are watching TV.

"You're impossible," Grace claims as I pull her onto my lap. I rest my hand between her knees.

"Give me those lips," I tell her and grip the back of her neck, pulling her lips close to mine.

"Are you trying to shut me up?" Grace smiles.

"Possibly," I admit.

"Then shut me up already."

"Fuck, you're perfect." I kiss her.

A moment later, the clubhouse door opens, and Quinn walks in with Emerson and their daughter, Lydia. I look around the room, counting heads now that night has fallen, and everyone should be settling in. "Anyone seen Austin and Lelani?"

Emerson tosses her bag onto the bar. "I saw them earlier when they swung by the clinic so I could take a look at Lelani's wrist. Turns out it was fractured, so we put a cast on it." She places a hand on her hip. "But that was a few hours ago."

"Maybe Austin decided to stop in at his grandad's. You know he checks in on the old man regularly," Quinn mentions, so I pull out my phone and give Warren a call to check.

"Warren."

"Jake."

"We're lookin' for Austin," I say, and the line is quiet for a beat.

"Haven't seen my grandson since the day at the bar," Warren states. The hairs on the back of my neck stand on end. Warren picks up on my silence. "Jake, where's my boy?" he asks, his tone serious.

"Warren, I don't know, but we're going to find out. He and Lelani haven't returned. My gut is tellin' me somethin' isn't right." I don't hold back my worry.

"I'm heading out the door now. You call me the moment you have eyes on them." Warren's words are sharp and demanding.

"You know I will." I disconnect the call, shoving the phone in my pocket. It's only when I stand that I realize the entire room is void of noise. Even the kiddos are quiet. The whole family has their faces turned to me.

"Jake?" The uncertainty of what's going on is prominent in my woman's voice.

"Warren hasn't seen them." I look around the room, setting eyes on my men. "Let's hit the road. Somethin' isn't right. Grey, Blake, Reid, Sam, you four hang back to keep watch over our families and in case our brother and his woman turn up." I grab my woman, giving her a rushed kiss.

"Jake. Please stay safe. I don't like this." Grace frowns.

"Take care of the kids. I'll be back soon." I brush her cheek with the back of my knuckles, then file outside with the men and mount my bike.

I throw my hand in the air, taking off toward the gate, and my men fall in behind me. Once our tires hit the blacktop, we gun it, keeping our eyes open and alert to our surroundings. The roads are dark this far out, making it hard to see. All we have are the motorcycle's headlights and the moonlight from above. The wind feels cool against my skin tonight, and a chill runs down my spine. As soon as our bikes break around the bend in the road, my headlight catches movement. *King?*

I slow, causing my men behind me to do the same. Limping toward us is Austin's big-ass dog. I bring my bike to a dead stop. I whistle, then call out, "King!" The dog continues making his way toward us up the opposite side of the road. Throwing my leg over my ride, I cross the road, jogging the few extra yards left between

King and me. Wet, muddy, and exhausted, he wags his tail slightly as I squat down. Surprisingly enough, he plops his head against my body, which is not like him. This isn't good.

Boots crunching against the loose gravel along the roadside turn my head, and Logan is coming up behind me holding a flashlight. He shines the light on King. "Somethin' happened. That dog would never leave Austin or his woman's side."

"Agreed. He looks like shit." I say, then King whimpers and pulls away. He walks a few feet in the direction he was coming from, then stops and stares. "What is it, boy?" I ask the dog, and he gives a sharp bark, then moves a few more feet before looking back at us again.

"I think he wants us to follow him," Logan states.

"It sure as shit seems like it," I stand. "We'll soon find out," Logan and I jog back to our bikes. "Follow the dog!" I shout over the other engines, then take off in the direction King is traveling. We ride slow until the dog disappears near the bridge. We pull our bikes further off the roadside, shining our headlights down the embankment.

"Shit," I'm off my fucking bike so fast I don't have time to fully process the scene. I'm running toward Austin's truck that is overturned, a portion of the front end in shallow water. Glass is shattered all over the rocks as I navigate through the dark. The men aren't far behind, most of them with flashlights. Logan rushes toward the mangled wreckage, shining the beam through the driver's window.

"Empty, but there's blood." Logan states then he canvases the area around us. The dog barks and Logan swings the light to his left, spotting King several yards off near the water's edge. He barks again. "He brought us this far," Logan says and heads in that direction.

After maybe twenty minutes of trekking along the lakeside, Quinn shouts, "Over there!" shining his light to his left. There propped against a large log, half slumped over is Austin. *How the fuck did he get so far from the wreckage?*

King lumbers to Austin's side, and I rush toward my brother, feeling my heart thudding against my chest, praying like hell he is still alive. I hit my knees and press my fingers against the side of his neck, feeling for a pulse. "He's alive," I call out and trail my eyes over his banged-up body. "Gunshot to the shoulder." I take in the rest of him and notice the large open wound on his leg, which is swollen, still oozing with a small amount of blood—my phone rings.

"Shit." I grab it from my pocket, and Austin's grandfather's name lights up the scream. "Warren, we found him." I waste no time with my words.

"Is my grandson alive?" I hear the desperation in his voice.

"He's alive. We need transportation back to the clubhouse," I tell him.

"I'm on the side of the road where your bikes are located. I'll be waiting." He hangs up, and I move.

"Let's get him back to the clubhouse," I tell the men, and Gabriel is the one to hoist his limp body off the ground and carefully throws him over his shoulder. Austin moans from the movement. "We've got you, son," I tell him.

"Lelani," he manages to grind out as his arms swing freely across Gabriel's broad back.

"We'll figure it all out as soon as we get you out of here." My breath is heavy from the fast pace walking.

"They took her," he groans.

"Who?" I ask, but Austin doesn't respond. Peering up the embankment, I see Warren standing outside his truck, with the engine running.

"Someone ran us off the road," Austin replies, then lets out a pained, "Fuck," when Gabriel has to adjust his hold to keep Austin from slipping.

Logan and Quinn look at me. Their expressions are dismal, and my gut tightens. Someone deliberately ran one of my men off the road. Anger fills my inside like an out-of-control inferno. Whoever it was left my brother for dead and took his woman.

King barks and makes it to Warren's truck before we do, and Warren has to help the exhausted dog into the cab of the vehicle by lifting his back end. "Where's Lelani?" his grandad questions as Gabriel places Austin into the passenger seat.

"Don't know. Austin mentioned someone taking her," I tell him. "We'll sort it all out soon. For now, we focus on getting Austin to Doc." Warren nods at me and rounds the front of his truck, climbing behind the wheel. Not waiting, he puts the truck in drive and takes off toward the clubhouse.

It's not long before we're pulling onto the compound, rushing Austin inside the building, and placing him on one of the couches. I look around, thankful the women have already cleared the children from the room. "Move back. Let me get a look at him!" Doc shouts. Austin is half-ass alert as Doc assesses his injuries. "He needs fluids, I need to flush his wounds before infection sets in, and antibiotics."

"On it!" Grey shouts and rushes from the room.

Austin's eyes shoot open the moment Doc presses hands against his ribcage. "Motherfucker." He swings, narrowly missing Doc's chin.

"Settle down, son. You're at the clubhouse," Doc says as Austin finds a sudden burst of strength. "Quinn!" Doc calls out. "I could use your woman's assistance."

"You got it." Quinn jogs up the stairs.

"Austin, what more can you tell us?" I ask, knowing time is all we have, and the more we know, the sooner we get to finding an answer on who took Lelani.

Austin clenches his teeth as Doc pricks his skin with a needle. "We were ambushed." Austin breathes heavily while Doc begins flushing the debris from his leg wound. "All I remember is two men in an SUV, the truck leaving the road, my woman screaming my name, and staring down the barrel of a gun. I have no idea how long I was out. When I came to, I was partially in the water a good distance from the accident site."

Quinn returns with Emerson a beat later, and Grace is following behind them.

"Oh my God," Emerson approaches the couch Austin is laid out on, taking in his appearance. She scans the room. "Austin, where's Lelani?" her voice shudders.

Austin lifts his bloodshot eyes to Emerson. He doesn't say anything. His expression says it for him, but to clarify, I say, "Someone took her."

Emerson sinks to her knees. "Austin." she looks him in the eyes. "It's not my place to say this, but given the circumstance, I think you should know."

"Know what?" Austin tries to sit up, but Doc prevents him from doing so.

"Lelani's pregnant," Emerson tells him and what color Austin had drained from his face.

Austin looks at me, then his eyes land on Warren, who stands beside me. I see him teetering on the edge of losing it. Austin swallows hard. "Pop," is all he manages to say before his voice breaks, and he can't say no more. My chest tightens, and I have to keep my shit together. I know what he's feeling at this moment. I glance at the faces of my brothers standing around, bearing witness to the newfound news of a new family member on the way. We all know what he's going through because we've been in a similar situation that put our women and children in harm's way.

"We'll get your family back," Warren says with conviction. "Or I'll die trying," he tells his grandson.

"Truer words were never spoken," I speak for everyone in the room.

My phone vibrates in my pocket with an incoming call, and I wonder who the fuck it could be. The screen flashes *unknown caller*, but something tells me not to ignore this one, so I answer. "Jake speaking."

"Delane."

I instantly recognize the gravelly voice. "O' Rourke?" I'm thrown off guard for a second, and Grace's attention shifts from Austin to me.

"I need to make this fast," he states, and the urgency in his voice puts me on alert. Without dismissing my woman or Emerson, I put the phone on speaker for my men to hear.

"I'm listening," I tell him.

"I'm with Lelani."

"The fuck!" I boom, my words vibrating through my chest. "You'd better get to explaining why the hell you have my brother's woman," I growl as anger grips my insides.

"First, Lelani is fine. Banged up, but okay. I've been working undercover, and have been for several months." O' Rourke keeps his voice low, almost a whisper. "De Burca's men are behind the kidnapping. They have Lelani held up in a cabin in the mountains."

"You'd better not have played a part in any shit that's taken place over the past few weeks. My family, women, and children were fired at. I have a man here busted all to hell, left for dead from a fuckin' ambush, and his pregnant woman is missing. I don't care who the fuck you are, I'll put a bullet in your ass," I threaten.

"I don't have time for detail, Delane. Just know, I had no part in what has transpired. De Burca is my objective, that and getting Lelani the fuck out of here." O' Rourke falls silent for a beat, and I hear muffled voices in the background before he rushes his words. "I've got to go. I'll be in touch." Then the call is disconnected.

My hand falls to my side, my grip tightening around the phone as I process everything. De Burca has Lelani, and for now, all we can do is sit on our ass and wait for O' Rourke to contact us, hopefully providing the club with their location.

"Jake," Grace breaks through my wall of thoughts, and I pull her to my chest. "If Finn's with her, he'll do whatever it takes to keep her safe, even if that means blowing his cover."

The energy in the room feels heavy.

The silence is broken when Austin speaks. "Prez." Austin struggles to move. "Fix me the fuck up. I'm gettin' my woman back."

20

LELANI

Detective O' Rourke put me in a room alone for what seems like forever ago, but in reality, it has only been minutes. I haven't heard a peep from him or the other two men since. When I first arrived, the detective told me who he is before leading me to a room without much explanation before disappearing, leaving me nothing but my thoughts. All I think about is Austin.

The sound of a door slamming followed by heavy footfalls has me holding my breath. A moment later, the entrance to the room I'm in opens. "It's just me, Lelani," Detective O' Rourke announces himself. "I got a first aid kit. Will you sit over here so I can clean you up?"

"I want to know what's going on."

"I can't say much." He keeps his voice low.

"Are you really a cop?"

"Yes. I'm going to get you out of here. You just have to trust me."

"Trust you?" I cry. "I was just abducted and brought here against my will while my boyfriend is probably on the side of the road hurt or..." I clamp my hand over my mouth to stop a sob from escaping.

"Lelani, I need you to calm down." Detective O' Rourke helps me over to a chair, and I sit. "Austin is okay. Jake and his men found him. He's going to be fine."

"What?!" I snap my head up.

"Shh. I need you to be quiet."

"They found him." Relief washed through me. "Wait. You know The Kings?" I ask.

"I do, but that's a story for a different day. Right now, we don't have time to go into all that. Just know Austin is okay, and this whole ordeal will be over soon."

"Why can't you take me home now?" My voice trembles.

"If I blow my cover now, it will get both of us killed. Cillian landed in Polson twenty minutes ago and is on his way here."

"Oh, God." I clamp my hand down on O'Rourke's forearm.

"I'm not going to let anything happen to you, Lelani. You have my word," he states, and I swallow past the lump in my throat and nod.

"Now, this is how things are going to go down. Cillian will be here any minute. I need you to keep your cool and not let on knowing anything about what I have told you. Jake and his men are on their way."

"I can do that."

21

AUSTIN

I'm going to be a father.

I've repeated the same thought in my head too many times to count as I stare at the same discolored spot on the ceiling I've been looking at for the past hour.

It's been nearly five hours since we last heard from O' Rourke. I'm also fed up with laying in this bed, knowing my woman needs me. Knowing someone on our side is with her does nothing to rid me of the guilt eating at my insides. It's my fault she's not here. My body protests as I toss the sheet to the side, sit up, and put my bare feet against the cold floor. My ribcage tightens like it's caught in a vice, and I take a few deep breaths. Doc says I cracked at least three ribs in the rollover. I also have a few stitches from the gunshot wound to my shoulder, which isn't far from the injury I received a few weeks ago from the attack on the clubhouse. I look down at the gauze wrapped around my calf. It throbs with the beat of my heart and is swollen. Doc left that wound open to prevent any infection setting because it was exposed to bacteria in the dirt and water.

Doc told me to rest, but I can't, and I won't until Lelani is home and De Burca and his men are dead. I stand—too fast, and the room spins. My palm smacks against the wall to hold myself upright as a wave of dizziness hits. My vision blurs for a second before my eyes return to focus. On unsteady legs, I stroll across the bedroom to the bathroom, flick the light switch, and stare at my reflection in the mirror. My skin looks pale, and my eyes bloodshot. I turn the faucet on, splash cold water against my fevered skin, then pick up the brush lying on the counter and run it through my matted hair. I pull it all back, securing it at the base of my head with one of my woman's hair ties.

Walking to the dresser, I pull out some clean clothes. Everything I had before was either cut off my body or stripped, between Doc and Emerson cleaning my injuries. I painfully pull my shirt down over my head, slip on a pair of pants, then step into a different pair of boots, leaving them unlaced. My weapon lays on the top of the dresser. Not wanting to lift my arms again to slip the holster on, I tuck my gun in the waistband of my jeans. My cut hangs on the wall near the bedroom door where Grey placed it. I snatch it on my way out the door, shrugging it on as I slowly make my way down the hallway. The clubhouse is quiet, but I see my brothers gathered in the common area. All of them eye me as I maneuver down the stairs, grinding my teeth from the sharp pains that radiate up my leg.

"Any word?" I ask, pulling a chair across the floor to sit at one of the tables. I prop my leg on another in an attempt to keep some swelling down.

"Nothin', brother," Jake says, sitting a cup of coffee in front of me. "The rest of us are fueling up, waitin' for word. As soon as O' Rourke calls again, I want us ready."

"I'm going," I inform him.

"Wouldn't have it any other way." He sits, and we wait.

Several pots of coffee later, Jake's phone rings, and we're all on the edge of our seats as he puts O' Rourke on speaker. "Delane."

"Give me somethin'." Jake grips the edge of the table.

"We're out in an area known as Pine Ridge. The road leading to the abandoned cabin is overgrown, with no address visible and no neighbors nearby."

"Lelani?" I speak.

"She's unharmed," O' Rourke states.

"And De Burca?" Jake questions.

"He's here." My gut tightens, and I'm on my feet, fighting through the pain of moving too fast again. "Jake. I just learned he's turned his attention on the club. This just turned into an act of revenge for his brother."

"Can you get Lelani and yourself out?" Jake asks.

"Negative. Even if I blow my cover, giving her time to make a run for it, she won't get far. If by chance she did, we are on a mountain surrounded by thick forest on all sides. Lelani would never find her way out. If we attempt to leave together, we're both dead. I won't risk Lelani's life. If you get here and can get close enough, she'll have a better shot of running without getting lost." O' Rourke falls silent for a beat, but it feels longer before he speaks again. "He brought more men with him."

"How many?" Jake's jaw clenches.

"Twelve total." There's a beat of silence. "Travel fast and stay alive. I'll keep my eyes open. Cillian is desperate and out for blood. He wants a war."

"He wants war; we'll give it to him." Jake snatches his phone from the table. "Arm up, and let's ride."

We hear movement and notice all the women on the staircase above. Jake speaks directly to them. "We need every brother on this one. The moment we walk out that door, you women lock this place down like Fort Knox. There are extra weapons and ammo down in the basement. If you have to, use them." He doesn't mince his words, and the urgency in his voice is felt throughout the room.

"Pine Ridge is, if we travel fast, a twenty-minute drive west of here. Most of that area is undeveloped and largely used by logging companies," Reid informs us, then jogs up the stairs and kisses Mila. My other brothers quickly do the same with their women before we walk out the front door. Being early morning hours, it's still dark outside. We may have three hours until the sun rises.

Ignoring the pain, I swing my leg over my bike and quickly fall in behind Quinn, who follows Gabriel. Once on the open road, our eight engines sound like thunder rolling in ahead of a storm. The heavy smell of exhaust fumes invades my senses as we gain speed. The vibration of my bike as the tires turn against the blacktop has the same effect on me as it always does, and the noise in my head clears. I'm able to focus. The pain my body is in becomes nothing. I'm one with my Harley and the road.

My thoughts shift to our child growing in her belly. I'm fighting for more than just her or us. I'm fighting for our child. I'm fighting for my family's future.

Sometime later, Jake and the ones ahead of me slow. We've made it to Pine Ridge, where there are no streetlights. It's dark on this side of the mountain. "We leave our bikes here and travel on foot in search of this cabin," Jake says. Turning off our engines, we walk our bikes just off the narrow road, into a thicket. The darkness surrounding us feels heavy and oppressive as we keep off the road. It's quiet, only hearing our breaths and footsteps as twigs and dry leaves crunch beneath our feet. After some time, my eyes play tricks on me, seeing shadows amongst the tree branches, giving off supernatural vibes.

Before long, we happen along an overgrown road with fresh tire marks. "Let's see where this leads," Jake whispers, and we're on the move again, still keeping to the trees, staying vigilant.

"Shh," Logan whispers, stopping. "You hear that?"

"Generators," Reid states, and we move in closer to the sound until a dimly lit, maybe five hundred square feet cabin comes into view.

We crouch down to the ground. Several yards away, I take note of the three SUVs parked out front.

"Shut the fuck up, I'm taken a piss, okay." We hear the disembodied voice of a man through the darkness.

"Listen up," Jake speaks low. "Men are probably scattered everywhere. Our best bet is to separate. Take them down quietly, one at a time, working our way to the house."

All I care about is getting to Lelani. Staining my hands with another man's blood means nothing to me. Without responding, we all go our separate ways. I move along the north side of the perimeter, approaching the backside of the cabin, where I spot movement near the side of a small, dilapidated shed. I pause, focusing my eyes. The man's back is turned, taking a piss. I pull my knife. Just as I get within two feet of him, before he even puts his dick away, I cover his mouth and drive my blade into his jugular, then rip it from his flesh. His thrashing body wreaks havoc against my broken ribs as I struggle to maintain control and stifle his dying breaths from being heard. The fight soon leaves his body, and he's nothing more than dead weight in my arms. I lower him to the ground and take some deep breaths before pressing forward, closing in on the cabin itself.

Movement catches my attention, and I duck back behind the shed. Chancing a look, I notice Quinn near the back corner of the cabin, the dim light coming from the small window gives just enough visibility to make out my brother taking down a man.

The back door slings open, and Quinn is quick to pull the guy around the corner. "What the fuck, Conall?" A large guy, the size of the door opening, steps outside. "Get your ass in here." He looks around. "You little shit." He starts walking toward my direction, and my eyes drop briefly to the dead guy on the ground at my feet.

This must be Conall. "Conall, you dumb fuck. De Burca wants to leave in twenty."

I step back, making sure I'm in the shadows enough where he can't see me. When I do, a twig cracks beneath my boot. *Fuck.* The guy pauses, puts his hand at his side, and slowly draws his weapon, then aims in my direction. "Conall." He waits for a beat. "Whoever you are, show your fucking self." He keeps his aim, and I know my only option, which will also blow our cover. It's him or me.

I pull my gun. Aim, and pull the trigger, which sets off a chain reaction. Gunfire explodes all around the property. I rush toward the cabin, not knowing if I'll make it or what I might find once gaining access to the inside.

I press my back up against the side of the home. Suddenly everything stills, and gunfire ceases.

"I know you and your men are out there, Delane," a harsh voice speaks from the inside. I make my way to the back door, still open. Quinn rounds the corner, gives me a nod, and we cautiously step inside. It's not long before we happen across a man lying on the floor, fresh blood pooling beneath his body. I kick at him, checking if he's dead. A stray bullet must have hit him.

"De Burca. Your men are dead!" Jake shouts.

"I'm calling your bluff. If they were dead, you'd be in here by now. Nevertheless, I have something you want," De Burca calls out. "She's a sweet little thing. It would be such a waste to kill her now."

My stomach drops. Cillian has my woman. Before Quinn stops me, I rush toward the direction of De Burca's voice. Two men stand between me, De Burca, and my woman when I enter the front of the cabin. Quinn is quickly at my side. We find ourselves in a standoff with the three men, and one of them is O' Rourke.

"Take one more step, and she eats a bullet for breakfast," De Burca uses my woman to shield his body.

I look from O' Rourke to De Burca, then to Lelani. "Lelani," I speak, letting my woman know I'm here with her.

"Austin." She tries to pull from her captor's grasp, but his hand shoots up to around her neck.

"So, you're the dirty biker who took my future wife." De Burca cuts his eyes at me.

"I'm not your anything." Lelani struggles, and he applies pressure to her neck, causing her to cough.

"Get your ass in here, Delane," De Burca says aggressively, jerking Lelani back against his body. In seconds, Jake, along with the rest of my brothers, step through the front door with their guns ready.

"Like I said. Your men are dead," Jake states.

De Burca smirks. "The mighty Jake Delane and his Kings." Jake moves. "Don't" De Burca digs the barrel of his gun into Lelani's temple.

"Austin, please." The fear in her voice is like a knife to my chest.

"Shut up," De Burca shakes Lelani, and her fingertips grip at his forearms, trying to break free. "You and that slut, Grace, killed my brother."

"Speak my woman's name again, and I'll cut out your tongue," Jake growls.

De Burca looks at Jake with disgust. "You and your pathetic club are nothing to me." He pauses a beat, and my attention shifts to O' Rourke, who's staring at me, his gun aimed at my chest. I can tell his wheel is turning. Like me, he's trying to figure a way out of this mess without risking Lelani's life. All I need is one second. One clear shot, and it's over. I shift my eyes to De Burca's other man, whose weapon is aimed at Quinn. Any one of us makes a move, my woman is sure to die, and quite possibly Quinn.

"The De Burca and Mancini merger will still happen. I'll wed this defiled woman and take over Vegas. Like a phoenix rises from the ashes, the De Burca empire will rule again."

"You're delusional to think I'll let you walk out of here with my woman," I warn him.

De Burca's hands slip down Lelani's chest. Bile rises up my throat as he gropes her. "I don't do sloppy seconds. Once she carries my name, and I have control of her money, I'll have no use for her." His lips turn up in an evil grin. "Perhaps I should make an exception. Just this once." De Burca keeps his eyes locked with mine as he buries his nose in Lelani's hair. "She is tempting."

Every fiber of my being wants to get my hands around his neck. I want to kill the motherfucker with my bare hands. "Over my dead body," I grind out.

"That can be arranged," De Burca counters, then shifts his attention to Jake. "You see. My pretty redhead here found herself the pawn in a little family coup. A brother desperate for power, an uncle desperate to live. Like the fucking saint I am, I swoop in to make all their troubles disappear. Marry the Mancini princess and become king of two kingdoms," he sneers.

"Too bad for you her brother fucked you in the ass when he tried to get rid of his sister. Now here you are, and desperate," Logan speaks, and De Burca's lip twitches.

"Yes, and now Derrick and Arturo are dead," De Burca announces, and Lelani gasps, hearing the news for the first time. "It was going to end the same either way," he says casually. "Then the opportunity to come to Polson presented itself. I can take my meal ticket home and ruin the man who destroyed my family. Brilliant if you ask me."

"You don't have enough men or bullets," Jake states.

"Don't underestimate me, Delane. I have more men on their way as we speak. You and your men are sitting ducks."

My eyes dart from my woman to O' Rourke. I see it in his eyes, and the way he slightly shifts his body, our ally is preparing himself to do something drastic. My heart thuds heavily against my ribcage. If De Burca has extra men on the way, my brothers and I are screwed. I look back at De Burca, who's still fixated on Jake. I make sure my aim is steady and exact—just one clean shot.

The next moments play out in slow motion. Times slows as O' Rourke takes his weapon off of me to the man who aims at Quinn, and puts a bullet in his head. De Burca shoots O' Rourke, and Lelani breaks free, dropping to the floor. Just as De Burca points his gun at my woman's head, I pull the fucking trigger. What felt like minutes lasted only seconds.

O' Rourke is on the ground, and De Burca stumbles back against the wall, holding his neck in one hand and his gun dangling loosely in the other. I advance on De Burca, grabbing his wrist as he tries to lift his weapon. "Someone get Lelani out of here!" I shout, my voice harder than steel. Gabriel lifts her off the floor. Cradling her, he totes her toward the front door. I look back at De Burca, crimson soaking his expensive suit caused by the bullet hole in the side of his neck. My father's face flashes before my eyes as De Burca begins to choke on his own blood. I smirk at him knowing he will soon die. "You lose, motherfucker."

With a strangled gargle, De Burca manages to speak. "Fuck you."

I tuck my gun away and lift his limp hand, using mine to help him hold his own weapon. My trigger finger rests on top of his as I press the barrel end of his own gun into his mouth. De Burca coughs and gags. "Go to hell." I pull the trigger.

I breathe heavily and watch his lifeless body slump to the floor. It's not until that moment I begin to notice my own pain again. Ignoring it, I walk out of the cabin to get Lelani. She's standing between Gabriel and Reid when I step outside. "Lelani." My steps quicken on my way to her.

"Austin." Her hands search to find me, and I grab her the moment I'm within reach. She buries her face in my chest, and that's when she loses it. Her tears soak my shirt as I continue to hold her tight.

"I've got you," I console her.

"Don't let go." Her voice trembles with emotion.

"Never." I kiss the top of her head, then look at Reid and ask, "O' Rourke?"

"He'll be alright. The clever bastard was wearing Kevlar under his suit," Reid tells me.

A couple of SUVs come barreling up the overgrown road, causing all of us to take aim. They stop, their headlights lighting up the vicinity. Demetri and Nikolai step out of one of them. "Looks like we missed the party," Nikolai says, and we all lower our weapons.

"Demetri," Jake acknowledges him. "How'd you know where to find us?"

Demetri tries hiding back a grin. "A little birdie told me." And Jake shakes his head.

"I'm going to put that woman over my knee." Jake chuckles.

"Lucky for you she did. We ran into more of De Burca's men at the turnoff to Pine Ridge."

"Thanks, brother," Jake tells Demetri, then shouts, "Find all the bodies, and throw them in the cabin!"

"Then what?" Quinn yells back.

"Light it up, then let's get the fuck out of here!" Jake walks over to where I stand with Lelani.

"Prez." I look at him.

"Son." He nods, then looks at Lelani. "You okay, sweetheart?"

"I am now." Her hold on me tightens, and I clench my teeth from the strain against my ribs, and my discomfort doesn't go unnoticed. "Demetri!" Jake shouts. "Get Austin and his woman off this mountain."

I give Jake a nod before walking toward Demetri's SUV with

Lelani tucked at my side. I pull my keys from my pocket and toss them at Nikolai. "Mind takin' my ride?"

"You got it," he tells me.

Demetri's man opens the back door, and I guide Lelani into the backseat then climb in beside her. Demetri settles in the front passenger seat as Victor climbs behind the wheel.

"Austin, I need to tell you something," Lelani lays her head on my shoulder. "I'm pregnant."

I smile. "I know."

"What—how?"

"Emerson," I tell her.

"And you're okay with that?" I hear the concern in her voice.

"You're it for me, baby. I will risk anything to have a future with you. A child that our love created grows inside you." I press my palm against her still flat belly. "I'm more than okay, Mouse." I turn to take Lelani's face in my hands and look at her. "If I had taken my last breath today, it would have been worth it knowing I've experienced a once-in-a-lifetime love worth dying for." I kiss her, stealing every breath she gives, making it my own.

A throat clears. I'd forgotten we are not alone. "I fuckin' love you, Mouse."

"And I will always love you," Lelani whispers before my mouth is on hers again.

In the background, I hear Demetri say, "Victor take us home."

EPILOGUE
LELANI

I n the months that followed being kidnaped, life only became better. Cillian De Burca is dead, and though Austin never gave details, nor did I ask, I knew Uncle Arturo and my brother were also destroyed at the hands of evil. I don't know what it says about me, but my brother and my uncle's deaths had no effect on me whatsoever. Not in the way you would expect. I guess you could say the only thing I felt was relief. There is no more looking over my shoulder. No more of the constant worry if my life is in danger. I'm simply free. I also found out my parents left me an inheritance. That is something my uncle failed to tell me. Once the dust had settled, Austin had Reid look into things for me, and let's just say I'll never have to worry about being financially stable.

"So, what do you guys think?" I'm pulled out of my wandering thoughts at Nikolai's question.

"It's perfect," I breathe, taking in the rich scent of cedar as I run my hand along the sleek wood mantle above the fireplace. Seven months ago, Austin's grandfather gave us a piece of land down the road from his place as an engagement present. A week after the kidnapping ordeal, Austin put me on the back of his bike and took me to his favorite spot. The same place he took me swimming after I first moved to Polson. We spent a perfect day together. Just as the sun was starting to set, I sat between his legs with my back to his chest. Then, I felt him slip something on my finger, a ring. The ring once belonged to his grandmother. I, of course, said yes.

From that day on, the two of us began planning our future together. After Austin's grandfather presented us with the land, Austin and I went down to Kings Construction to talk to Nikolai about building a house. Ever since moving to Polson, I dreamed of one day living in a log cabin. I had a particular vision too. I want this house to be a home that Austin and I will raise our family in for years to come. Nikolai listened intently and assured us he would make my vision a reality. He even called in an extra crew from out of town to help build to ensure it would be ready before the baby is born.

Well, Nikolai came through, and today, Austin and I are doing our last walkthrough. The cabin has two levels with four bedrooms and three bathrooms. The living room has floor-to-ceiling windows that face west. I wanted the sunrise to shine through every morning, giving me a little piece of my mom.

"You did a hell of a job, brother," Austin tells Nikolai. "You gave my woman everything she asked for. It's fuckin' perfect, man."

"I'm happy you like it. It was my pleasure. Here are your keys." There is a light touch on my shoulder, and I hold out my hand. Nikolai drops them into my palm.

"Thank you, Nikolai," I say, beaming.

"You're welcome."

Nikolai addresses Austin, "I'm going to head back to the office. You can stop by whenever to pick up and sign the final paperwork."

"Will do, brother. Thanks again."

A pair of arms snag me around my waist, just above my

massive baby bump. Austin kisses my neck, his beard tickling my skin as he rubs my belly. "You happy, Mouse?"

I smile and place my hand over the top of his where our son or daughter grows. "As long as we're together, I'll always be happy."

"Forever, baby."

"Forever, Austin."

THE MOOD as I stand in the middle of the bedroom while in my wedding gown is bittersweet. As a little girl, I imagined sharing this moment with my mother. Though I know she is here in spirit, I can't help but feel her absence. I felt the loss while shopping for my dress. The ladies helped make the day extra special, knowing how deeply I wished my mom was with me. I know they could tell I was a little sad, and their efforts to keep me happy were heartwarming. Plus, they made finding the perfect dress easy. I remember looking at pictures of my mom in her wedding dress when I was young and knew I wanted mine to be just like hers. After describing what I could remember to the boutique's sales lady, I walked out with exactly what I was searching for.

My dress is a vintage ivory lace, v-style fit flare with a lovely long lace sleeve and is backless. The seamstress was able to alter the gown to fit across my belly comfortably. Bella worked her magic with my hair by styling in a half updo with a touch of bouffant height on top, along with some curls cascading down my back. My makeup was kept light and classic with a red lip.

"What are you thinking about?" Lisa asks as she fusses over placing the veil on my head. The chatter in the room halts, and the room is silent. Another thing that has changed in recent months is the relationship between Lisa and me. She has become more like a mother figure, much like she is with the other women. Bella, Alba,

Mila, Grace, Emerson, Sofia, Leah, and Glory are like my sisters, whose eyes I feel are right now trained on me.

"I'm thinking about how beautiful I feel and about my mom."

"Oh, sweetheart." Lisa takes me into her arms. "She's here with you. She's watching you right now."

"I know she is." I touch my hand to my chest over my heart. "I feel her here." I take a deep breath feeling a little shy about what I'm about to say. "I want all of you to know how thankful I am to have you in my life. My mother is not here to celebrate this day with me, but each of you has helped to make it special. I didn't have sisters growing up, but I think there is something to be said about choosing who you want as your family. I'm blessed that you chose me, and I chose you. Even though I'm saddened by the physical absence of my parents, I don't feel like my day is missing anything. It's all thanks to you guys. I feel in my heart of hearts you all were sent to me by my mom and dad. This is the kind of life they wished for me." When I finish speaking, the room is still silent, aside from the sounds of sniffles.

"That was..." Glory chokes out. "Awe hell. Group hug, bitches."

The room suddenly fills with laughter as everyone forms a circle around me, where we hug the crap out of each other. A moment later, we're interrupted by a knock at the door.

"Come in!" Lisa calls out.

"You ladies about ready?" Jake asks.

"What do you say, Lelani?" Lisa fluffs my veil. "You ready?"

"More than ready."

"I'll go let the guys know."

"Jake!" I call out and stop him as he goes to leave. "Can I ask you a favor?" When planning the wedding, I told Austin I didn't mind walking down the aisle by myself. His grandfather had offered, but there was no way I could make him choose between walking me down the aisle or standing with Austin. But now that the time has come, I know the person I want to give me away. He's not only like a father to Austin and the rest of the men, but a man who has done nothing but treat me like a daughter since I moved to Montana.

"What ya need, darlin?" Jake comes to stand in front of me.

"Would you..." I stop and take a moment to get my nerves under control. "I wanted to ask if you would walk me down the aisle?" When Jake doesn't respond right away, I try to backtrack. "You don't have to, I just..."

Jake cuts me off, his voice sounding gruff. "It would be an honor to walk you down the aisle and give you away to my brother, Lelani."

IN THE BACKYARD of the clubhouse, soft music plays, I link my arm with Jake's, and make my way toward my future. Before stepping out of the house, I asked Bella to describe in detail what Austin is wearing. I told her I wanted to ingrain every detail of my future husband and this day into memory. As I walk toward my soon-to-be husband, I envision him standing tall in a pair of black denim jeans and a navy button-down shirt paired with his cut. I love when Austin wears his long hair down, and I was pleased when Bella told me Austin chose to wear it like that today.

"You ready, sweetheart?" Jake asks.

I smile at him. "Yes."

"Let's get you hitched then."

AUSTIN

MY LEGS DAMN NEAR GIVE out at the sight of my woman walking toward me. I take in every inch of my bride and the way she is glowing. I love seeing Lelani round with my baby. So much so that I have plans to keep her that way.

"You're a lucky man, Austin," my grandfather says.

"That I am, Pop," I agree, not taking my eyes off of Lelani. When Jake steps in front of me, holding onto the woman I'm about to marry, I take her hand and pull her to me. "Thanks, Prez."

"My pleasure, brother." Jake turns toward Lelani and kisses the top of her head before retreating to the crowd of family and friends, taking a seat beside Grace. Before Quinn begins officiating, I take Lelani in my arm and kiss the fuck out of her.

"We haven't gotten to that part yet, brother," Quinn remarks, and our guests erupt with laughter.

The reception carries on well into the night. Most of our guests have gone home, leaving just my brothers and their women except Pop, who is sitting by a bonfire while enjoying a beer and good conversation with my brothers and me. Peering down at my watch, I note Lelani has been MIA for almost twenty minutes. She disappeared into the clubhouse with Bella to change out of her dress and into something more comfortable.

"Where you off too?" Reid asks when I stand.

"I'm goin' to check on my wife."

"Yeah, right. You're goin' to check on your wife." Quinn uses air quotes. "Is code for..."

Quinn doesn't get a chance to finish; he is cut off by Gabriel punching him in the shoulder. "Cállate, *shut up.*"

"Damn, brother. I was jokin'. Why you gotta be so hostile?" Quinn rubs at his arm.

I shake my head at their antics. As I turn to make my way toward the clubhouse, Bella rushes out the door. "Austin!" she yells, and the urgency in her voice has me on alert. "Lelani's water broke!"

I'm across the yard in a flash, bursting through the clubhouse, only to find Lelani calmly standing by the bar with King at her side and a smile on her face, cupping her belly. "It's time," she announces when she hears my approach.

Without much thought, I stride right up to her and scoop her up into my arms.

"Austin!" she shrieks. "I can walk."

Instead of listening, I hustle out the front door with my brothers and the women hot on my heels. Making it to the truck, I fling open the door. King jumps in first, then hops into the back seat as I set Lelani inside. I do all of this without saying a word. I'm running on nothing but pure adrenaline and excitement.

"Austin, you can slow down?" Lelani giggles when I go to buckle her seatbelt. Finally, it's her hand on my cheek that stops me. When I look at her face, she's glowing. "I love you."

Cupping her face between the palms of my hands, I kiss the top of her nose and then her lips. "I love you too, Mouse."

"Let's go!" Jake whistles and throws his hand in the air, signaling for his men to fall in behind him. I watch each of my brothers mount their bikes and their women climb behind them one by one. Seven strong, they peel out of the clubhouse parking lot, leading the way to the hospital. Behind me in a black SUV is Victor, who is driving Demetri and Glory.

Seven hours and fifty-six minutes later, my son finally makes his appearance, weighing in at eight pounds and two ounces. "Congratulations, you two." The doctor passes my son to Lelani, where she immediately clutches him to her chest and starts to cry. Even after nearly eight hours of labor, her red hair soaked with sweat and stuck to her face, my woman is still the most beautiful creature I have ever laid eyes on. There are no words to describe the overwhelming emotion I get as I watch my wife run her fingers over his tiny face, eyes, nose, mouth, and chubby little cheeks, soaking in his features.

Leaning down, I kiss the top of her head. "I'm so proud of you, baby. He's beautiful."

Still crying, she asks, "What color is his hair?"

I grin at her question. "It's red. Not as red as yours. It has a little brown, but mostly, it's red."

Lelani turns her face toward mine. "I love you."

I rest my forehead against hers. "I fuckin' love you too, baby."

After the doctor and nurses are gone, it doesn't take long for our family, who have waited patiently in the waiting room, to finally get their chance at meeting the newest member of the family. "Can we come in now?" Addilynn, my sister, pokes her head in the door.

"Come on in," I call out.

Addilynn opens the hospital room door wide and motions for everyone to join us. One by one, my brothers file in. The women go straight to Lelani's bedside to gush over the baby, whereas the men offer me handshakes. "Congrats, son." Jake pulls me in for a hug and pats me on the back.

Next is Gabriel. "Felicidades, *congratulations*, brother."

"Thanks, man."

"Well, brother, what's the little dude's name?" Quinn asks.

I walk over to the bed where Lelani passes my son over to me. "Everyone, I'd like you to meet Massimo Austin Blackstone. We named him after Lelani's father."

"I love that name," Sofia swoons.

"I think this calls for a toast," Quinn announces as he reaches back and pulls a bottle of Jack from the waistband of his jeans. Each of the men follows suit by retrieving shot glasses that were tucked away inside their cuts.

"Only you would sneak a bottle of liquor into the labor and delivery ward of a hospital." Emerson rolls her eyes at her husband, making us all laugh.

Jake offers me a shot glass, and one by one, Quinn fills them.

"You'll never find anything in life that gives you greater joy or purpose than the love of a good woman and the moment your child is born." Jake raises his shot glass, and my brothers and I do the same. "Welcome to the family Massimo Austin Blackstone. Congratulations, brother."

An hour later, the hospital room has cleared, Lelani is sleeping soundly in the bed behind me, and I'm standing at the window looking out at the Montana sunrise with my son in my arms. Closing my eyes, I take in the warmth of the new day as it shines bright through the window—an unexplainable sense of calm washes over me. I open my eyes to a sky that has turned a shade of pink I have never seen before. I peer down at Massimo then back out at the sunrise. "No more worries Nalani and Massimo. I'm going to spend every day making sure your daughter and grandson are happy. You have my word."